THE
WAR
ZONE

THE WAR ZONE

ALEXANDER STUART

A
BANTAM
TRADE
PAPERBACK

BANTAM BOOKS
NEW YORK · TORONTO · LONDON · SYDNEY · AUCKLAND

All of the characters in this book are fictitious,
and any resemblance to actual persons, living or
dead, is purely coincidental.

This edition contains the complete text
of the original hardcover edition.
NOT ONE WORD HAS BEEN OMITTED.

THE WAR ZONE

A Bantam Book / published by arrangement with
Doubleday

PRINTING HISTORY
Doubleday edition published April 1989
Bantam Trade edition / June 1990

ISBN 0-553-34878-7

Published simultaneously in the United States and Canada

Bantam Books are published by Bantam Books, a division of Bantam
Doubleday Dell Publishing Group, Inc. Its trademark, consisting of the
words "Bantam Books" and the portrayal of a rooster, is Registered in
U.S. Patent and Trademark Office and in other countries. Marca
Registrada. Bantam Books, 666 Fifth Avenue, New York, New York 10103.

PRINTED IN THE UNITED STATES OF AMERICA

OPM   0 9 8 7 6 5 4 3 2 1

FOR

ANN AND JOE BUFFALO

WHOSE LOVE

IS EVERYTHING

1

A lie: the three of us together on the water, me and two people I'm tied to for life.

It's a perfect day, if you trust perfection. We're on the river, me, Dad and Jessica, piled into a canoe. We've had no sleep. Our new brother has been born this morning and it's jolted me, it's no small thing, it has taken me where I breathe and chucked me onto the rails of some thundering, life-fucking train I knew nothing about. Or maybe I did. Maybe it's just confirmed that so much of what we're told is important all the time is crap. We're afraid of what's real, what's there, just under the surface. I know I am.

■

So we're celebrating. We are having a good time. At least, I think that's what we're doing. I, for one, am so wired by the night and the incredible sunshine we're having and by what happened to the car that the details tend to be a little blurry. Of course, it could be the wine. Dad brought a bottle of wine, so he had no option but to share it with us.

What did happen with the car? When we left it wherever we left it, its nose was all punched in, like a prizefighter down on his luck. Did that happen before the baby was born or after? I'm not sure. The last twenty-four hours seem to have got all twisted, so that today still feels like yesterday and the soccer match I watched on the video last night when we were all so restless might have been this morning after the birth but before this drunken cavort on the river.

Actually, I've had very little of the wine. Dad and Jessie polished off most of the bottle. It always tastes like petrol to me, but I love the burn in the stomach, the buzz in the head.

■

We are drifting under a bridge now, using the paddle to avoid scraping against the moldy brickwork on one side. The air down here is dark and dank and cooler than in the sun. This is it, the English countryside, green and untouched—well, maybe just fingered a little by the bastards whose chemical plants pump out crap right into this water, or the other sort, the really desperate buggers who wait here in the gloom with the bats and water rats, hungry for a friend, waiting to pump something else out, hungry for their brief taste of life on the TV news or in the tabloids. At least Devon has some balls. It's a little bit wild, not all afternoon tea and morons who actually believe what they hear on BBC radio. But it's not the city.

As we emerge back into the light, a hail of small pebbles hits the water around the canoe, thrown by three kids, a little older than me, a little younger than Jessie. They whistle and shout at her, not bothered by Dad's presence, asking if she isn't too hot in her bikini. They seem very keen to draw her attention to something floating on the water, one of them curving a cigarette packet through the air to splash down close to the object in question. I stare at it, puzzled at first by what looks like an old surgical glove—or a monkey's bulbous arse at the zoo. Then I realize the truth: it's a Durex, swollen with water (and milk or something, I don't want to know) and tied like a balloon. Jessica smiles darkly and looks back at the boys, insects all, waving and jeering. They haven't a clue. They haven't a clue what they would be tangling with if they tangled with my sister.

■

This isn't my life, my life was something else. Days ago, that's all, but already out of my reach.

North London. The Harrow Road. I've cycled up here from the poncey foreign calm of Bayswater. Two black kids have just tossed a woman's shopping bag off a moving bus, then jumped after it. They don't want what's in it, they just don't want anything to stand still.

A plastic carton of eggs hits the pavement near the relics of a second-hand furniture shop. Squeeze-wrapped sausages vanish under a car tire. My bike scrunches across a box of cornflakes and one of the kids chucks a loaf of bread at my face. It's amazing, the punch sliced white can carry.

"Fuck off!" I shout.

"Fuck you, Maurice!" the other one yells, making the name sound French and faggoty. A ketchup bottle buzzes past my ear and smashes in the road.

"Maurice?" I wonder. I pedal harder as both of them come after me, one on the pavement, the other dodging the traffic to try and catch hold of my rear mudguard. I turn two corners and wheel down a street pitted with ruts and potholes, then slide through a piss-smelling alley between dark houses and come out on waste ground. The boys will find me if they want to, but I don't think they're that motivated.

I take a breather and stare out over the view, my pulse racing. Through a wire fence and down an embankment, railway tracks stretch into the distance. A single line curls off at one point into a shed half buried by the shadow of the road bridge. Nearby, the gravel under the sleepers is stained with rust, a color you don't see much of in Bayswater.

I'm on high ground and the land dips away from me across the tracks, toward the poky back gardens of terraced houses. Their scraggly lawns and washing lines edge onto a dumping ground littered with rotting mattresses, a wrecked pushchair, black rubbish sacks, the scarred remains of a fire.

Above all this hangs a big expanse of sky, blood red where it touches the backbone of the houses, spilling out overhead into a great, glowing fish tank of orange and blue. London is wonderful, I love it. It's alive, spreading out before me, old and new, humming like the railway track, telling me everything's great, I can do anything here—if only we weren't moving next week.

■

This is my sentence, then, for a crime I'm guilty as hell of but can't put my finger on just now, there are so many. Devon, tranquil Devon, the Devon we have moved to, maybe not as tranquil as it used to be, but too bloody tranquil for me. Rubbers in the river are nothing—I want the scum of London, turds in the doorways, the stench of telephone boxes, the heat from a burning car. London looks beautiful with all that stuff. Everything's falling apart, but still the city has splendor. The country, well, the country doesn't know what to do with itself anymore. It doesn't have a hope, it doesn't know how to be healthy: the water we're paddling through must be thick with invisible pollution, acid rain, radioactive fallout, and yet . . .

And yet Jessica has just slipped out of the canoe to swim in that muck. It's clear enough, even the green and slimy weed three feet down is visible, but it feels too warm to me. English water is never warm, not outside, not without the help of some factory somewhere, pissing out hot waste—or a minor cock-up at the nearest reactor. But there's no time to think such thoughts. Something else is happening, something I'm a part of but can't quite understand. Perhaps I'm just tired, confused, heat hazed?

We have turned a bend in the river and are well out of sight of the boys on the bridge. The trees here grow right by the water, their branches almost meeting overhead so that the sun shoots a web of light across us all. Jessie is swimming close to the canoe, her back flashing in the triangles of sun, her skin browner than I ever manage to get. She kicks hard, reaching awkwardly behind her to untie her bikini top. . . .

But wait a minute. None of this is going to mean anything unless I can make you understand how weird we all felt that afternoon, how watching a fresh little bastard come sliming into the world from the collective pool of your family blood makes you think about things you might otherwise not choose to consider. We felt close, all right, but it was a closeness that cut through the bullshit of family life and suspended the rules. I'm talking about honesty. And, you know, when you get down to it, honesty—life without the lies, the protective film of accepted behavior—is bloody dangerous.

■

2

Three o'clock in the morning and the family is on the road, Jessie wearing sunglasses, tight black jeans and a T-shirt that doesn't quite fit. She's developed well, Jessie has. If she wasn't my sister, I could take a lot of interest in equipment like that. But the sunglasses? I think it's the hospital—she doesn't want to be seen there looking like someone's daughter. Maybe she's out to score one of the doctors, I don't know. I'm scared of those places, too. Scared of the power they have over you, the way they stomp all over you with their jackboot-administration mentality, leveling everyone to cases, to broken arms, drug overdoses, pregnant bellies. They know it. They revel in it, the control, the right to tell you they don't give a fuck who you are, what unique traits of character you may possess; you need them, and they know it, so don't come the smart dick around here, sonny.

But we're not there yet, far from it. We have only just left the village, and that was a struggle. The car doesn't like those hills by daylight. By night, it has a whole different vocabulary of bollock-breaking, metal-wrenching, exhaust-farting outbursts with which to remind us that living in a valley is a dumb thing to do. And this is a Bentley. Not a new one, admittedly; it has seen finer days, it was proud once—just not during our tenure.

It has an excuse, of sorts: parked in the front passenger seat, right in front of me, is the unnatural load of Mother's weight, itself enough to sink many a worthy ship. I see them as two separate things, Mum and the cargo she carries. My mother is the same as she always was—warm, pretty, a lot tougher than she looks. She has impressive reserves of temper, my mother, most of them reserved specifically for me. She can match me, foul language for foul language, if she chooses. But I have the trump card: I can make her cry. And when I do it makes me feel like crying, so then we're both happy. She has that occasionally mournful quality anyway, that sense of being somewhere else, of drifting to some far-off memory (she's part Polish; I think it comes with the territory), and it's a quality I've noticed I already find attractive in the girls I want to boff.

But this belly of hers is something else. I've seen pregnant women before, of course, and they've always worried me. They patrol the streets and supermarkets like God's Chosen Few, innocent of every crime, swinging those great protruding whales of flesh before them like the perfect weapon. They look so fucking self-righteous! And now my mother's joined their ranks, I look at her and think: "It's a pod, it's an alien, it's a foreign thing growing inside her, poking at her flesh, stirring the soup of her insides." It smells already of milk and shit-smeared nappies. And when I consider its connection with me, the fact that I set up tent under her skin once, I don't want to know. I don't want to think about wobbling bent double in her jar—it makes me feel less individual, less me.

"Well, this is fun," Jessie says in that wonderful, Chelsea schoolgirl voice of hers—a schoolgirl on the make. (I have never fathomed how, given the obvious bond between us, we can sound so different. She's all gym-slip deb, while I'm one of Nature's born-again yobs; at least, that's what I've worked for.) The car has just hit a rut in the road and shot us all about six inches into the air. "You should have babies more often. Of course, this one may come out wearing splints and a crash helmet, but think how boring London would have been, only five minutes from the hospital on well-paved streets."

"Well-lit streets," I add, just to exercise my mouth, as the Bentley's full headlights sweep across another turn in the endless wall of hedgerow lining the road.

"How far are we?" Mum asks.

"One more bend," says Dad, taking it too fast, "and we hit the main road. Then we'll sail through—fifteen minutes, maybe twenty to the door."

"That might not be soon enough."

"Are you all right?"

He looks at her. She's sucking in breath like a Rasta taking a toke. The sweat is pouring off her, but it's hot, it's a hot night for rattling through Devon back roads with a baby bursting to get out (though it was her choice to have it in the first place, you've got to admit).

"I'm fine," she says. She doesn't look it. She holds her stomach, as though she'd like to disown it, as though she'd be more than happy to watch, just watch, but why does she have to go through this pain? "I'm great," she says. "Just get us there."

I feel for her. I feel for us all in this heat, sticky arms and sticky arses niggling the seat leather, the air in here—even with sunroof and windows open—too close to breathe. It's not what you expect of an English summer night, not at this time in the morning, but if the heat can surprise you, can inconvenience you at all, it will. It's OK, though, this heat. It makes tonight more of an adventure, so long as it doesn't actually lay Mum out or anything. I like it, I like my crotch itching and my armpits smelling, the fact that no one can disguise their own distinctive whiff, even if Jessie's lively musk odor is largely hidden by the powerful and predictable memory of her sun oil.

There's something wild in the air tonight, on top of this heat. The heat has laid its fat palm over the countryside, smothering us all, making us struggle to break through, to get at the oxygen we know is up there somewhere, but it's not. Behind the heat, riding its back, is a threat, a rawness, a great maw of savage breath and glinting teeth. There's a monster out here tonight, and it's us. It's Mother, with her dam ready to burst. It's Jessie, wanting to be in on the woman-secrets of childbirth without for a moment having to lower her guard of eighties-girl cool. It's Dad, the thirst for a beer raging in his throat, sleep in his eyes, driving like the filth, all concern and uprightness, adrenalin masking his conviction (come on, Dad, I can read you, I see it) that, basically, he's done his bit on this one, now he's just putting in time. It's me, happy to chuck a petrol bomb on any blaze, hungry, always hungry, for the details of my life to burn more brightly, alive to the crackle and fizz and pop on the wires tonight as we tear through Devon on a mission from God. Who gives a fuck what anyone else is doing? We're the action now, we're hooked into life's bubbling hotpot, we're going to let rip with a new scream just as some old sucker cops it elsewhere. Listen to those jungle drums.

"God, he thinks he's bloody Jesus Christ again!" Jessie's voice calls up to me as she elbows my ribs. I am standing, arms outstretched, my head sticking up through the sunroof as I fly into the night. It's beautiful up here, the wind burns my skin, tears drag over my eyes, smearing stars into wet ribbons in the sky.

"Good, is it?" Jessica asks, pulling herself up into the gap beside me and scratching my arm with her nails in the process.

"I can't see a bloody thing behind me," Dad says, his voice below us, far away. We must be blocking his rear vision. "But that's all right, I'll find a low bridge somewhere, that'll sort you two out."

"Slow down," Mum says, holding her stomach. "They're getting closer." What are? Oh, yes. "And Jessica, Tom—sit down!"

"In a minute," Jessie answers for both of us. "This is brilliant. Don't worry. Nothing's going to happen."

I wish she hadn't said that.

It's like a replay goal, perfect slow motion, every movement already determined, impossible to escape. Jessie is standing beside me, cropped hair erect in the warm rush of wind, wraparound shades still hiding her eyes. Our feet jostle for position on the Bentley's back seat. We balance precariously, leaning forward, a twin-headed creature riding through the night, our necks wide open to a guillotine slice from the lip of the sunroof.

The road is clear, climbing steadily through low-rise woodland to a hill, nothing dramatic, no real peril to compensate for the lack of red traffic lights to beat, no drunken arseholes gunning at you from hidden side streets or negotiating one-way circuits the wrong way. At Mum's request Dad has momentarily slowed the car but can stand the gut-grinding distress of the Bentley at low speed no longer and is already letting his foot edge back down on the accelerator. My mother, beside him, has slumped in the seat, her knees crammed up in front of her, both hands resting on the mountainous belly where her seat belt (I know what is coming) should be.

We are almost over the hill. The trees on either side bend over backward to give themselves—and us—some space, some air. Stoned by the heat, Jessie and I let out jungle cries, bird shrieks, monkey calls which Mum and Dad can't hear. "EEEEIIIIRRK!" we scream, competing to split each other's eardrums. "AAAARRCH!" Then, in unison, as the car reaches the top and we see what lies ahead, only a few yards away: "SHHIIITT!"

There is a tree across the road, a big one, big enough to block both sides. Dad hits the brakes, but to those of us poking vulnerably out of the sunroof, it's clear he hasn't a hope in hell of stopping. We drop,

Jessie and I, but we are not fast enough. We miss the worst option—decapitation—but as we dive back into the inner space of the decelerating car it punches into the fallen tree, throwing my head against Jessica's shoulder in a spasm of pain and light.

■

Not my first thought, but almost my first, is to wonder how Mum is. My head feels mushy, like battered fruit, but only on the inside. I could throw up if it wasn't for the effort it would take. Jessie is leaning forward, clutching her shoulder, trying to reach between the seats to Mum. Dad, I see in lurid nausea colors as I pick myself up, is conscious but holding his neck at a weird angle and working his jaw as if trying to click something back into place. My own bones all seem to have taken a trip independently of the others.

"Mum—" Jessie says, before I can.

"Sonia," Dad says. "Christ . . ."

Her eyes are open. There is a trickle of blood from one corner of her mouth. She is crying through clenched teeth, sobbing hard and long, leaving the tears to run with the blood and sweat.

"Help me," she says, heaving on the seat to raise herself a little.

"Mum—" I say.

Then she lunges forward, letting out a scream that scares me shitless. Dad reaches across, but he looks as panicked as I feel.

"No, leave me," she says, as he tries to move her. She is panting, whimpering, doglike. "Leave me!" She looks back at Jessie and me. "I'm OK." She tries to crack a smile, but her face looks swollen and bruised. "It's started. Just give me a minute."

It takes two hours. Two hours of stuff I know nothing about. Two hours of what sounds like hell. I never knew it was such hard work. Those films they show you, of the hump-bellied woman, legs apart, beaching a gunk-smeared nipper, then smiling into camera, don't show the half of it. It hurts, I see that now. It hurts bad. Coming into this world is clearly on a par with bursting the sound barrier—and if you're the mother, you are the sound barrier! And there was I thinking it was going to be like *Bambi*.

It's complicated by our situation. We are stuck on the road, in the middle of nowhere, in the middle of the night, a huge great bloody tree blocking our path, the car knocked about a bit, all of us badly shaken, probably suffering from shock (I know I am), with a woman who is now in the throes of giving birth. It could be worse. It could be raining. Instead, the sun has decided to stir, the birds are screaming blue murder at one another, and already it is so hot that I've stowed my damp and fragrant T-shirt in the back of the car.

Jessie and I hang around outside for most of the time. Her shoulder isn't too bad, though she has some things to say about the rocky consistency of my skull. More seriously, her sunglasses are broken and there is nothing she can do about it. If we ever get to the hospital, she's going to be in trouble.

Dad has already inspected the tree and given up on it. I'm not surprised. It's an oak and about the size of two London buses laid end to end. What's astounding is what it took to tear this bugger from the earth. A network of cracks extends from the crater where its roots used to be, as if the ground suddenly retched and shook and spewed this thing up. It's the heat, this country can't take it. Even the land is cracking up.

Mum is grunting powerfully from the car as I stand staring at the roots, watching fleshy, leggy things crawl over the parched fibers, out of their element. My mother's pain worries me, but what can I do? I'm thinking about football, maybe it's a reaction, a defense mechanism. There's been no traffic, not a car on the road as yet. Jessie has gone back to ours to speak to Dad, and I'm thinking about football. I was watching a tape of the last World Cup before I went to bed this evening—earlier this evening, tonight, whatever, before I got up again for this gig. Not the final, but the crucial England-Argentina match which we fucked up as always. What wankers! We never pull out the stops until it's too late, no wonder luck and the refs never shine on us. On the tape you can watch and watch a handball goal like Maradona's and, fuck it, you just know that if one of our boys had scored that way he would have owned up. We're strong on appearances, we Brits, I think we use it to mask something else—a lack of passion maybe, a deep-seated sneakiness that's always liked putting the boot in where the bruises won't show. We should have kicked the Argies anyway.

Jessie comes over. "Dad wants us to find a phone and call for an ambulance."

"Is Mum all right? Has it happened yet?"

"Moron. We would have told you." Would they? "But we ought to get someone here, a doctor or something."

"It's going to be dead easy, finding one of those around here."

"Well, let's try."

"We'll probably meet some nutter who'll rape us both and bury us in a ditch. Devon's full of wonderful people."

But as we turn to go we hear the first sign of civilization in ages—a lorry straining up the hill behind us, out of sight. Terrified that it's going to come rolling over the top and straight into our family group, we run to flag it down. It's moving on overdrive, a massive articulated Eurolorry which makes even the fallen oak look small. We stand in front of it, forcing the driver to stop, almost blown off our feet by the hiss of hydraulic brakes.

The driver gets out, jabbering. He is young, tanned, French, wearing the kind of vest they just don't sell over here. His companion follows, heavier set, another Gauloises-smoking-beach-bum-muscle-prick. They both have arms like weight lifters. I can feel Jessie's hormones humming beside me as she appraises them; I bet the boys are loving the shot of her navel they're getting where her T-shirt doesn't meet her jeans.

Jessie's French is a lot better than mine—I don't have any—so she takes the lead. Predictably, it's her they want to speak to anyway. They follow us, prattling and watching her arse quite blatantly in front of me, as we go over the hill back to Mum and Dad.

The one word I recognize as we all come face to face with the tree and the battered Bentley is "Merde!" The lads are clearly impressed. Either they haven't been listening to Jessie or she's got something wrong, because when they see Mum lying across the front seats of the car, her bare feet jammed against the doorframe, her sweat-soaked maternity dress barely covering the rain forest between her legs, they actually look embarrassed. Of course, I am too—a bit—and not just because they are here. Mouths which moments before had smirked with Gallic lust suddenly hang open, unsure of the ground rules for this sort of thing in Protestant Britain.

"I don't know what the fuck I'm doing," says my father, who is attending to Mum in much the same manic way he does to the car's engine when it gives out—without a clue. "Any chance you could help?"

Jessie has cooled noticeably with the French boys in front of Mum's sprawled helplessness (or does she just feel they've had enough encouragement? I don't think Jessie turns off ever), but Dad takes over, babbling fluently in the way that always makes me feel out of it. God, I hate French at school—not just the language, but their whole prissy *Paris Match* culture. They'd let a dog fuck their country if they could carry on looking chic.

Mum seems to go into a new gear as the French prats concentrate their attention on the tree. They even give it a shove with those well-packed arms of theirs, but they have to be joking. Next, they want to try and lift the car off, but suddenly it's fireworks time, it's all happening, Mum is screaming and moaning and moving her head around as if she wants to be in ten different places at once.

I don't know where to look. Her dress is pushed back now and between her hot, spreadeagled thighs is the kind of vivid detailing of wet cunt that even the magazines I buy never manage to provide.

"Does it hurt?" Jessie asks, a little girl again, gripping Dad's arms as we all look on.

"Yes," Mum gasps. "Yes, it does."

She yelps, and I think we all move forward into the haze of sweat, motor oil and birth smells that hangs over the open door. Dad takes Mum's hand as something foreign pushes its way past her hole, and slowly a wrinkled curve of skin and bone becomes a head. My face burns, with what I'm not sure, either it's the thought of those two French bozos being here to witness this, or the waves of realization that hit me concerning my own humble beginnings. It's one thing to know that we were all born once, quite another actually to see a straggly ape take its place in the world as your brother (so this is the idea, is it, Mum, of having us kids along for the ride?), especially with all this nature around—collapsing trees, symphonic birds, the sun's heat. It's a shock to the system: my cells seem to recoil from the reminder of where they came from—and where they're going to. For standing here, watching a new life take shape, watching the blood, the pain, watching my mother on her back like an animal, I understand for the first time in my life that I am going to die one day—we all are, Mum, Dad,

Jessie, me, even the baby. It's so obvious that it hits home like a hammer and yet it doesn't depress me, fuck it, I can take it, I can live up to it, when it comes I'll go fighting. I'll take some life with me!

The kid is out now, squirming in the light, eyes peeling apart through layers of blood and muck, its mouth opening and closing but making no sound so that my mother urges Dad, "Quick, slap it, make sure it's breathing. . . ."

It is. "God, what a sound!" I say. Its wail seems filled with such rage and indignation that, I swear, already it's blaming us for something.

Mum is laughing and crying at once. "What is it?" she asks.

"An alien," Dad says, wiping some of the gunk from the creature's face. "A boy, I think. . . . Right, it's a boy." He stands back from it, turning to us, grinning like a witch doctor, his hair and eyes alive in the morning light. "This is just the start," he says, staring at his offspring. His face contorts as he looks at it, getting ugly for a moment, almost scaring me, then brightening, grinning again. "It's too late, skip," he tells it. "You've got your papers. You're stuck here with the rest of us now."

"What the hell do we do with this?" Jessie asks, touching the limp cord of flesh that connects our brother's belly to a disgusting lump of liver and blood. (Funny to think that her navel had one of those once. And mine. Of course, Jessie's is still on display, what's left of it—a neatly curled little bump, protruding slightly from her soft, tanned belly, beaming satellite messages at those French bastards.) "We can't just leave it like that."

"That's the beauty of hospitals," my father says. "They do all that shit for you."

"Tie it," my mother says, lying back exhausted.

"With what?"

"Find something," Mum says. "A shoelace . . ."

But we're all wearing sandals or slip-ons. Then one of the French dickheads obliges with some kind of canvas cord from the back of their giant. They have been standing about through all this, unable to go but not able to do much either except cry when the fucking baby appears as if it's one of theirs. Now they take the lead. After checking that Mum can withstand a bit of movement, they trot round to the wrecked nose of the Bentley and start hefting it off the tree. Dad stands by at the open driver's window and steers as he helps push it back to the verge of the road. It rolls onto the rough grass with a gliding, uncontrollable scrunch, then sits there, dead, useless, an expensive junk heap.

And the boys aren't finished yet. Having cleared a path to the tree, they get the life roaring in that great shitpile of theirs, haul it up over the brow of the hill and aim its huge metal bumper at the heart of the oak. A belch of diesel, the rumble of literally man-sized wheels, then branches splinter and the metal bar takes whole chunks out of the timber, but nothing budges. The muscle-bound dick at the wheel spits past his vast side mirror, kicks the machine into lower gear and lets the engine burn itself into a frenzy of deafening, air-blackening meanness. Choking on the fumes, my father tries to stop the contest, aware that the last thing Mum needs now is this. He's pissing in the wind. Even if they could hear him, these boys are determined. No tree is going to fuck with them and get away with it. The French choose their battles well.

It ends predictably. The tree doesn't want to win, that's its problem. It just lies there, taking a beating, letting the artic pound away at its bark. The driver is smart. Having failed to get it rolling head on, he maneuvers the lorry perilously close to the dipped verge and pushes from the side. There is a glorious moment of doubt, when it looks as if the truck is going to tip over, rather than the tree move, but then something snaps in the tree's resolve and it goes. With a sound like splintering beer crates, the trunk is shunted free of the road.

The rest is anticlimax. A timeless journey in the elevated cabin of that lumbering Euro-lout. These truckers don't have it bad. Behind the driving cab, their sleeping space is like a budget hotel room: curtains, a washstand, a portable TV, a fridge full of plonk. And the art on the walls makes it interesting. If those girls are French—if those girls are my age, which they look—maybe I've been wrong about the race, maybe another trip is overdue.

Mum lies on the bed with her newborn. For a while there, she was glowing; now she just looks washed out, eager to hit the hospital sack. Dad plays with the baby, teasing its tiny fingers and staring at it, trying to read its mind, trying, from the look of him, to leap inside its skull and get some answers. The kid just frowns, mistrustful of everyone for the moment, as well he should be. Jessie plants herself firmly next to

Dad and the baby, giving the French boys nothing now, staring straight at them when they glance back with ugly scowls. And me? I'm all over the place. I'm knackered, my bones ache, but I'm flying. The morning feels great, sleep seems like a drug I'm not ready for, and I'm even getting to like the idea of having a kid brother.

"Fuck me," I think. "This could get awfully boring."

3

So we're back in the canoe. Mum is in hospital, and we're lazing on the water, trying not to think, which isn't difficult. That slightly sick feeling you get in your stomach with lack of sleep goes well with the heat and the wine.

Dad and I are paddling. Jessie's between us, doing a Cleopatra number, radiant in the sun on her barge while her minions sweat.

I dip my wood in the water, test its weight. I feel like everything's fine, this is one of those times that is preordained. Nothing can cock this up, we're all too powerful.

"I could take more afternoons like this," I say generously.

"God, he's actually enjoying himself." Jessica's voice is like a cool breeze behind me.

"Don't pressure him. Can't you see he's suffering withdrawal symptoms?"

I glance back at Dad, who is scratching his leg beneath his ridiculous Hawaiian shorts. "I'm not giving any ground," I warn him. "The country still feels like bullshit to me. It's not real."

Jessie prods me in the back. "You mean you get confused because you can't tell the difference between a flower and a tree."

"Nothing's real," Dad says, "that's part of the problem. I heard some Ministry of Defence wanker the other night, talking about how defense contractors had to learn what it was like in the real world. Everyone thinks that some other part of life is more real than their own, or that theirs is the only real world. They're both equally dangerous points of view."

"What's real to you?" I ask him.

He thinks about that. This is an afternoon that makes you challenge ideas of reality. School's out, everybody's holidaying. Is anyone working today? Well, those hospital Nazis looking after Mother—all crisp linen and fluorescent faces. But they enjoy their work, stoking the boilers with anesthetized patients.

Dad answers me. He sounds like a chum, not my father. I think we could get on well, if we could ever get rid of these family ties between us.

"The fact that life goes on," he says. "It doesn't stop going on—well, it might, but I wouldn't want it to. And you two. No escaping you two."

"You wouldn't last a minute without us," Jessica tells him. "And Mum."

"Oh, yeah?"

I can hear him smile.

■

We pass through a village, marvelously deserted on this weekday afternoon—but not in a cozy way, more as if the entire population has been wiped out and the buildings left standing. Radio One drifts hollowly from open windows and open doors of cream-gray Devon cottages and ugly new houses, full of themselves, full of premeditated, parceled country charm. A Ford estate car stands silent outside the confectioners-and-sub-post-office. A new bike is upturned against a wall, awaiting a puncture repair. The sun beats down, accentuating any cracks in the road visible from the river.

Then someone appears to spoil the illusion: an old woman, older than we allow them to live in London, wearing a cardigan—in this weather—over her faded summer dress. She calls across the street.

"There's fluoride in that water. They put it in for the teeth, none of us want it, but they put it in anyway."

"Not in the river, surely?" Dad shouts.

She makes no move toward us, just stands in front of the shop next to the sub-post office, its windows empty save for a small yellow notice taped up inside.

"The sheep drink it," she says. "They make sure we get it, one way or another. The sheep drink it, or we do."

We stop paddling as we approach the village ford, where the water is barely deep enough to let us pass. The canoe scrapes the concreted bottom, but we push it on with our hands and float under a road bridge and away from the center of town.

"Why'd you only bring one bottle of wine?" Jessie asks Dad as we pass a dingy white shed, its paint peeling, a pile of abandoned oil drums outside. "I feel like getting smashed."

"That's why."

"It's not enough."

She shifts her weight behind me, rocking the canoe. I turn to make a face. She is holding the empty wine bottle in the river, enjoying the push of the water against it.

"You could," I point out, half complaining, "always try paddling." But she shakes her head, studying the bottle's neck in her hand. She looks far away, like Mum does sometimes.

Then she looks round at Dad. Neither of us is paddling now. He is sitting, head back, cocked toward the sky, eyes closed.

"Do you feel older . . ." She pauses, trying to pin down a thought in her mind.

"He looks it," I offer, to help wake him up. He does and he doesn't. He hasn't shaved, so the slight sag of his jaw is usefully hidden by stubble. His hair is as wiry and uncontrollable as ever, but the skin round his eyes looks tired, dark and folded like a wary old lizard.

" . . . or different?" Jessie goes on. "Having a new son? I mean, it's been awhile."

Opening his eyes to an impending collision, Dad quickly cuts water with his paddle to curve us away from the bank. He shoots me a look. "One of us ought to watch where we're going." Then, to Jessie: "I feel—I feel like it's time to let loose. You know what I mean?"

"Was it like that with us?"

"Was it? I don't know. I was a different person then. You gave me my balls. I'd got one in! I felt on fire. I felt, 'Piss on anyone who doesn't think my daughter is the best thing in the world!' "

"And me?" I ask, thinking: "Let's see how he handles this one." But I have to look away, because we're about to hit a sapling growing right in the water. Trees seem to have it in for us today.

"You I was just worried about. You were a forceps delivery, you came out with this great strawberry mark all over your face. . . . I thought: 'It doesn't matter, he's healthy, that's what counts,' but already I could see you having a hard time. By that evening you were fine, it had gone, it was just the forceps that had done it, but you looked like a little bruiser."

"Still does," says Jessie.

We are approaching another road bridge. The banks here are steep and grassy, and there's a smell of cow shit from somewhere. Or horse shit—I wouldn't know the difference, right? Jessie has taken the bottle out of the water and is rolling the wet glass over her skin. I know, because she tried it on mine. It's not cold enough, that's the problem. It's not even cool—there is definitely something strange about this water.

"I sort of wish Mum hadn't wanted us there, last night," I say. "It's going to make it harder being rotten to him."

"Dad . . . ?" Jessie asks. "Have you and Mum ever really had problems over us? Do we make it more difficult, if one of you wanted to leave?"

We've thought a lot about this, Jessie and I. Whenever serious bother has hit our household, we've nearly always been able to pin its cause down to one of us. Those nights when voices have been raised after we've gone to bed, when silence has seemed more threatening than a row, we've wondered: "How does this measure on the scale of things?" Most of our friends' families are divorced or remarried or something; we've always felt like the odd ones. But you never know what's coming. This move to Devon was long talked about, but no tempers were lost —except over me.

"You want an honest answer?" Dad says. We're under the bridge now. There's a smell of mold.

"Yes."

Dad pushes us off the brickwork with his paddle. "It depends on the time of day. It depends on how selfish you're feeling."

∎

Then we're out into the light, and pebbles are raining down on all sides. There's a Durex in the water and some boys are taunting Jessie. I'm sure she enjoys it. A little farther on, she slides out of the canoe and swims alongside, her turquoise bikini dazzling against the dull green fur of the riverbed.

The trees form a sort of cathedral around us. Sunlight plays on her skin, on her bruised shoulder (and my bruised head), as she unties her bikini top, then turns onto her back to let her tanned breasts bob out of the water. Her feet kick and she glides away, struggling to remove the other half of her bikini without touching the weed under her feet. Then she rolls over again and swims back toward us, evil intent in her eyes. She grabs hold of the canoe with one hand, hesitating only a moment before putting her full weight on it to tip us in.

"You stupid bitch!" I think, without malice, as I go under. I was just getting comfortable. But really it's OK, the water feels good even if it is giving me cancer.

The canoe floats upside down. Jessie pisses herself laughing as Dad thrashes about, trying to locate the car keys (our other heap, not the Bentley, that's definitely out of commission for a while) before remembering that they're in the buttoned-down pocket of his shorts.

But then he's laughing, too. And suddenly we've all got our shorts off, swimming bare-arsed in the middle of Devon on a Thursday afternoon, and it's only me who's feeling weird, who's feeling as if there's a party going on and I'm not invited.

■

4

Jessie and me are close. We talk a lot. We talk about everything. She's a major source of information for me when it comes to the inner rumblings and eruptions that go through girls' heads, and I want to know that stuff, especially the darker side, the really funky, creamy, fuck-the-feminists-and-fuck-all-men-this-is-really-what-I'm-about sort of thinking. I'm already developing my own style. I've found I don't just want to fuck girls' bodies—I want to get inside their minds. Because unless you get that mental bang, unless you listen and you probe and you challenge and you push (to the edge, if need be), sex is like pissing about with a chemistry set without reading the instructions. You're missing the potential for real danger.

And it seems to work. I'm doing OK. I'll be honest—I haven't actually get there yet, not all the way. But it's getting closer. And even the dumbest girls I've met have a kind of poetry about them, if you can get past all the teen magazine and cosmetic counter bullshit they get brainwashed with.

But how do you ask your sister, "Is something happening with you and Dad?"

It's not easy.

■

Jump ahead a week, maybe two. I'm not sure when, but there's more water, it's raining—the kind of warm, hard, summer rain that gets you properly drenched, like standing under a shower with your clothes on.

It's one of those summer holiday days that makes you wonder if the rest of your life's going to be like this: always waiting for something to happen while the world turns somewhere else. I remember when the ships sailed for the Falklands, when the Yanks were in deep shit in Iran, these were weird, distant, shapeless events that seemed like a bad dream but terrified the hell out of me because they were happening, in fact they seemed to be rolling toward disaster all too fast, and no one had asked me! I remember, with the Falklands, the words "National

Service" or "conscription" or something being used, and I thought, "Fuck, if this thing develops, if this thing goes on for long enough, it could drag me down with it." But nothing lasts for long anymore, thank God. The Falklands was a video-age gig. I don't think there's ever going to be a major Western war like the Second World War again. Not now. Not with a population whose maximum attention span is three minutes.

Anyway, it's one of those days. My life feels like it's stuck away from the action, which is hardly surprising in Devon. Clutching at straws, I've actually been shopping with my mother. The compulsion suddenly hit me that I had to have a particular album and have it now, so I struck a deal with Mum: I'd go with her and carry the food if she'd get me the tape. Of course, I'd forgotten we were in the wilderness. Not only did the shop in Sidmouth not have the cassette I wanted, but it was a real struggle finding something worth buying. I'm starting to dream of those megastores in London, I can almost taste them, the Clingwrap round every release, the splashy record company displays. It's all bullshit, but I'm getting to the point down here where I'd love to be exploited, I want them to take my money (or Mum's) and fuck my mind.

We drive through the village and up to our cottage, which looks oddly deserted in the rain—or vulnerable, like a house in a horror movie, waiting for the maniac to call. What I like about the house is its oldness: there's lichen and stuff in the cracks between the stones, tree roots poking up right outside the front door, which itself is so hard to open and close that it might be easier to climb in through a window, and the garden is overgrown with the sort of lushness you see in old country graveyards (what's under that soil?). What I hate about the house is its oldness: I bang my head on a beam every time I go upstairs, those tree roots outside work hard at breaking your legs and at night the timber and plaster that just about hold the cottage together sound as if they're wanking in unison.

"Tom, you carry the bags in, will you? I thought I heard Jack." This is one of the first times Mum's left the baby with Dad and Jessie. I've noticed that although Bratto is already clearly an independent being, she still has some kind of radar link with him. It must be hard for her, I suppose, letting go of something that's your flesh, though Jake (he looks like a Jake to me, none of this Jack shit)—Jake, I've watched him, just regards her as dependable room service.

I grab the thin white plastic carrier bags, all set to split, and leave Mum to run through the rain to the front of the cottage while I perversely walk round the back, slipping and sliding along the grassy bank on which I've already twisted my ankle once since we've been here. This route takes me past the bathroom—and the bathroom takes me some-where else.

It's occupied. I know this even before I'm close, because I can hear water (more water, there's enough out here) swilling about. No voices, just water. Something makes me stop and approach more warily, so that even though the windowpanes are frosted and rain-streaked, who-ever's in there won't be able to see the shape of me and the white bags outside. I'm a natural spy, not just a nosy bastard but someone who prides himself on being able to enter a room, give it a thorough search and get out again without leaving a trace of my being there. This time I'm outside, but I'm totally frozen, silent, wet, looking in.

From where I'm standing, body pressed against the wall in best guer-rilla fashion, legs angled against the treacherous bank, I can just see past the small top window, which is open. The bank gives me some height—the cottage windows are low to start with—and by straining I have a clear view of part of the bathroom mirror, opposite. This in turn lets me see who's there.

I hear Mum shouldering open the front door, the scrape as it jams open on the hall floor and the double grind as she struggles to close it (I should have done it for her). The effect of these sounds on the steamy figures in the mirror (unless I'm misinterpreting, and I don't think so) is powerful.

Jessie is in the bath, her face dripping, her short hair clinging wetly to her scalp as if she's just ducked under the water, her tits like a burn in my brain, closer than the image in the mirror, so that I can feel the pulse beating beneath them, even while my own has stopped.

Dad is kneeling, facing her. His knees (I register this in a flash, like part of a puzzle) must be between hers. In the instant I witness, as the first scrape of the front door takes effect, Jessie's hands are scooping water to pour over the part of him that bobs above the surface of the bath—a string-operated thing, his tackle, a horse's prick, uglier and more fascinating and more threatening than I've ever seen it.

Maybe I'm wrong. Maybe my mind has just run off through the rain and what I'm seeing is a waking blast from a weird dream. But the bags are at my feet, crammed with cereal boxes, salad stuff, baked beans. The cheap white plastic stretched around these lumps and corners has rivulets of water running off it onto the tangle of dead and living grass on the bank. This much is real, sharp, hyper-real if you like. And in the mirror, my sister's eyes lock with my dad's as he lurches forward, struggling to support his hands as he clambers out of the bath, suddenly too big for it.

I'm frozen for a moment longer as Dad, grabbing a towel, vacates the bathroom with a guilty speed. Jessie is left alone, left with a backward glance from him that in one shot is so much the father I know and a person I don't that I want to stick my fist through the glass to let him know I'm here.

Mum is with Jack, I can hear him crying now. I can imagine Dad walking into the bedroom, having toweled himself furiously, playing it cool: "Sorry, Jack was so quiet we left him. I needed a bath, it's so fucking sticky. Jessie's just gone in now."

And there she is, flushed with the heat or something, soaping herself like some prim tart in a TV commercial. God, I'd like to know what goes through that head of hers, what makes her radiate rightness and ripeness. She's so like me, so much my sister, my flesh, that the truth dangles in front of me, a carrot I can't quite touch.

"Fuck them both!" my mind cries, as rain snakes unpleasantly down my back. I kick the carrier bags, which is a stupid thing to do, since it only makes me lose my footing and land hard on the unyielding rim of a tin. "I don't want to know," I try to kid myself. "I don't even care."

■

5

There is a moment which is so beautiful it makes everything else worthwhile. You stand on the cliff above the village, early in the morning or late in the evening, and you gaze out at the sea—a huge, changing wash of light and movement, bigger than any of us, a joker with a patience longer than any one life and an inconceivable strength that can snap your back against the rocks as easily as you might flick a fly off your nose.

I can feel how cold it is, even when it's warm. Even when the water's not skimmed with a purple film of oil, and the pebbles and seaweed are stewed in the sun, I can sense the ocean's cold heart further out, out by the skyline. Jessie's tried to paint it, but she can't get close. Either the beauty is there or the darkness, but not both. Most of the time, I couldn't give a shit about art, but I've noticed that in British paintings the sea always looks sort of murky or angry or drab or just somehow different from the way it really is. Jessie's pictures are nothing like that: she sees with a foreigner's eyes. If my sister's a reincarnation, I'd say she was African, via the slave route to Barbados, then on to Nicaragua or the like (and she probably fucked herself into some luxury and some whiteness along the way). But even she can't get to the heart of the water, not with her powder blues and her baked-earth red.

It's not just the color, it's the color of light, it's the mood of the sky and your own cross-wired soul. Down on the beach, it's the druggy thunder-hiss of the surf dragging at thousands of pebbles, as if the sea's in training for the greatest glue-sniffing contest on earth. Up here, with a view of the sheep and the cottages and the coastline, there's just the image, no sound, and a faint tang of brine in the air, like a taunt or a memory.

It's more than a moment. It's repeatable, though it's never the same twice. It's where I go to stay sane down here, it's where I go when I miss London, when I want to work out what the fuck I'm doing with my life.

■

I'd be there now, getting soaked, if I wasn't so determined to speak to Jessica. If I can get her alone, there are a good few questions I'm going to ask, but it's as if she senses this. She's playing for time, Miss Florence Nightingale, helping Mum change the baby and scrub the vegetables for dinner. I'm in the doghouse, meanwhile, for dumping all the shopping in the rain.

I watch Dad. I watch everyone. Suddenly I feel like a spy. I'm the one who's different, I'm the one with the knowledge—I wouldn't trust me, if I was them.

What's changed? My mind is working overtime, reassessing everything. But Dad seems the same, snapping open a beer as he dumps himself into one of the cottage's chintzy armchairs to sort through a pile of unopened office mail.

"How far would we have to go, do you think," he ponders aloud, screwing his face up into a mask of weariness and disgust, "to get away from all this crap?"

"Not much further," Mum offers from the kitchen. "Another phone call like yesterday's and they'll probably take you at your word."

There's a long pause in which Dad seems to be replaying yesterday's phone call, enjoying the recollection of what was obviously a choice exchange.

"They love it," he says. "Panics the accountants. They won't know what they've got unless they're made to sweat blood for it."

When it comes to work, Dad likes a bit of passion to enter into things. I don't think he's happy unless emotions are aroused, and certainly where his current scam is concerned—a bloody great steel and glass pyramid for a Texan bank in Docklands—he's played devil's advocate from day one. Bad enough that he has to work for these cowboys, he says—no reason to make it easy for them. But I think it's a bluff. I think his work is what drives him, and coming down here to Devon has nothing to do with getting away from it all, it's just another way of giving them the finger.

Dad peers in the direction of the kitchen, stuffing the torn envelopes he's been opening into one of the big manila ones. "Why?" he asks

Mum. I stare at his eyes, his mouth, my dad, my chum, and see him pointing his dick at Jessie. "Does it bother you?"

"What?" Mum is slicing carrots or something, chop, chop, on the wooden board. Jessie darts through the room and goes upstairs, trying to avoid my eye but not quite succeeding.

"The phone call. Would you care if I just said forget it?"

Mum appears in the kitchen doorway, knife in hand, and lets him have her shrewdest gaze. "The only way you'd forget it would be if you could take it away from them and even then you'd want to twist the knife an extra turn. We could be in Peru and you'd still find a way to fight them long distance."

This seems to satisfy Dad, which is no doubt what it's designed to do. Mum's great strength is that she's a master bullshit-detector; she keeps us all on course, and how do we repay her?

"You're right," Dad says, suddenly restless in his chair. What's he thinking now, is it the way Mum's holding the knife? A thought knocks through my mind—it's chaos in there. "Peru wouldn't solve a thing."

■

Jessie is upstairs, doing whatever it is sisters do in their rooms by themselves. I burst in. She's got one shoe off, one bare ankle on the bed, the other decorating the floor, her back to me, her leg twisted sideways out from under her, an incredibly awkward position which seems to have her deep in thought rather than involved in any change of footwear.

She turns as I come in, guilty, lost, absolutely aware of the power she has over me.

"Are you happy?" she asks.

"Why, don't I look happy?"

"Don't know." She brings her foot down to the floor, kicks the other shoe off. "How do you look when you're happy?"

"I'll let you know. Jessie, I want to talk."

"Right." She's marvelous. Her guilt—if that's what it is—is instantly banished. "I'm looking for something. You can help or keep out of my way."

She dives into a large cardboard box crammed with the stuff she wouldn't let the removal men touch when we came down here. I don't know how to start. I stand staring at a postcard tucked into her mirror, a Rodin sketch of a woman contorted into a far more uncomfortable position than Jessie's when I entered, her muscles all pushing against her penciled flesh like life trying to get out.

"If you hide your real feelings all your life," I ask her, trying to edge into this and wondering why I don't just go on the attack—"Fuck it, I saw you! What were you doing?" But I don't. Instead, brother-sister conundrum number four thousand and forty-eight: "If you hide your real feelings all your life," I ask, "which are your real feelings—the ones you use as cover or the ones you never use?"

She turns, looks up over the seat of her jeans which faces me. "You've been reading comics again, haven't you?"

"Well?"

"I'm trying to find something."

"Jessie . . ." I'm not feeling patient.

She bobs back inside the box, retrieves a tattered brown envelope which rips as she picks it up, scattering scraps of paper, letters, drawings, what looks like an old napkin smudged with crayon. "Shit!" She straightens up, arches her back, shoots me a bottomless glance. "How do you use a feeling? Tell me."

I sit on the bed. Somehow or other, I'm going to get through this.

"OK." Jessie moves to the mirror, touches the Rodin postcard, as if I had willed her to do it. She picks up a scent spray, feels its weight, pulls the front of the black camisole thing she is wearing above her jeans and belts a jet of lighter fuel down her tits. Well, it smells like lighter fuel and it's designed to have much the same effect. She knows I hate that stuff.

"OK," she says, "you don't like it down here, do you? You don't like Devon. But there's not much you can do about it, is there, except complain? But the more you complain, the worse you feel—unless you get a buzz off complaining, which you probably do. What don't you like? It's all instinct or emotion or something. If you wanted to like it, if you wanted to find things to like, you could. At least you could make it better than it is. . . ." I'm barely listening. This is not what I've come here for. "What's real about any of that? Is there something wrong with Devon or with you? Of course, if you ask me—"

"Jessie," I blurt, "I didn't drop the shopping in the rain."

"It got wet."

And I'm off and running again, a mad, tangential babble: "Do you remember that time I was meant to be marking them in as they came back from the cross-country run? I was pissing about with Steve down by the stream and I fell in? I got soaked, everything. I had to say I fell in a puddle."

She knows what it is now. I can see it in her eyes.

"What's this about?"

"You."

And I start to cry. I can't believe this, but I'm sitting on the bed blabbing. Her arm goes round me. "Christ, Tom, shush, what is it?" I feel her warmth, her closeness as she hugs me. This is why I love her—she's my sister. But she's also someone I don't know nearly as well as I think, she's a body—a very pliant body—into which all kinds of men I'll never meet will be sticking more than just a casual finger. And then there's my dad.

"I saw you." I stop sobbing, feeling sick, heaving for air. I pull away, my face burning. I get up and swing the bedroom door shut, this is private; whatever happened, this is between Jessie and me. "In the bath. With Dad." I'm still gulping air, the fear wrapped tight round my throat.

"Yes?"

"What does it mean?"

Any hint of knowledge in her eyes has been banished. I am faced with such young, clear-faced honesty that I doubt myself. I want to doubt myself.

"It doesn't mean anything."

It's not enough. I want more. I'm up on that cliff above the village. The truth is bigger than anything else, it doesn't care about the rules. You make the rules, then you find yourself in the middle of that cold ocean anyway.

She goes on: "We had a bath. I got in, he got out."

"That's not what I saw."

"Well, that's all there was." She draws back. A certain petulant set to her mouth makes me doubt her now, not me. "Christ, where were you? What do you think you saw?"

"Don't give me a hard time! I don't want to talk about this, it's scaring the shit out of me, it makes me feel like throwing up. I feel sick, Jessie. I'm not being melodramatic, but I feel like I want to die. This is real."

I break through for a moment, then it's gone.

"Do you know what you're saying?"

"Yeah, now I've thought about it. And I have thought about it."

"You're wrong."

"Don't lie to me."

"I'm just telling you you're wrong."

I want to grab her, shake her, hurt her in some way, but I just take hold of her wrist. "Please don't lie to me." I grip tight. "I'd rather know. We don't bullshit each other—we don't, do we?"

Jessie lets me hold her, as if this gives her the edge. I've lost and she knows it. I know what I believe, but I'm going to let her tell it her way because I don't want to be shut out.

"Look," she says, "you saw me in the bath with Dad, right? I don't know what you saw, but you know what I'm like, I like physicality. God, we touch each other enough"—she looks at my hand, grasping her wrist—"but it doesn't mean anything earth-shattering. I tell you everything. I'd tell you."

"No, you wouldn't." I feel my fingers dig in, pressing hard on to the bone. I want to bruise her, I want her to remember this. Then I let go. "You couldn't."

"What is it? Are you all right?" Her expression has changed. She looks at me, concerned, as a thought strikes me like a wave of pain, washing over me, blanking everything else out.

She touches my face. Contact. She needs contact, constantly. "Look," she says, "I haven't screamed and told you to fuck off or anything, which I probably should have." Yes. Why not? "It's a pretty weird thing you're suggesting. I'm not saying I'm not pretty weird, but really it's something on a level I've never thought about." She stares at me, trying to measure whether she's getting through. "Not seriously."

But I'm falling, groundless. It has only just occurred to me that I never for a moment thought that Dad might be the instigator here. His prick looms large in my skull like some kind of medieval puppet, but I don't see Jessie at threat. Somehow I felt she must be in control, she always seems in control to me—would I even know if she was in trouble? So much for the protective brother.

She touches my arm, smiles encouragingly. "Are you all right now?"

I don't know. Am I?

■

6

I did a deal with Dad for coming down here—before, when he was just my dad. Now I don't know what he is. I look around me and I see other selves warring with the ones we thought we knew, the ones we felt safe with.

I got a video camera out of it, but I also got Devon. I was wrong. This is the Dead Zone. Devon may have some balls, but the people down here don't know they're alive. They don't know what's happening. They think everything's still the same, they think we're OK, it'll work out, Radio Four will still broadcast shipping forecasts and agricultural reports. They don't know what's going on. They haven't seen the politicians pissing in doorways, the football thugs jumping up and down on the roofs and bonnets of cars until they crease like cardboard, the snouts of police dogs slobbering over the surfaces of restaurant kitchens.

It's all right for Jessie, she's got art college to go to, this is just a break for her before she aims herself back at London, back to all that. There's no addiction to chaos here, no love of the fire. Maybe I can't read them, maybe they go home at night, switch off the TVs and radios and tear at each other, mentally and physically. I stand in the pub with Mum and Dad sometimes and wonder: there's an open-faced bluster, a beer-bolstered glow, that you don't see in London, that maybe is what good health used to look like. Mum's healthy, she looks fresh and happy and shiny, like an apple, firm, somehow recharged by having a baby —but she works out, my mother, she's a leotard childbearer, city-fit.

Anyway, I did a deal. I saw it coming, I saw the inevitability of it, this was no whim, this was going to happen. I could sense a new will in the air, as if my little embryonic brother was dictating his terms from the darkness of the womb. They were already committed to Devon, Mum and Dad, even while they were going through the motions of discussing it with us. Jessie was no problem, she could shack up in London with her friend Kate (and who knows who else?) under the supposedly watchful eye of Kate's parents. Which makes me think— when did it start? If Dad and Jessie are really going at one another, .

when did it start? Dad wanted to move down here, yet he knew Jessie would be going back to London to art school. Was that a factor? Did he want her alone up there, or did he even think about that? Is this Jessie's madness? I don't know anything anymore. Nothing is simple, nothing is ever what it seems. It's like the level of life we all think we live on only scratches the surface. We're blind to the rest, except when violence or anguish or some other kind of pain or beauty makes us break through, forces us to glimpse a larger world. The nightmare is that I can't see any connection between that larger world and our little one that isn't a lie.

I could fight Devon, I realized when it all started, the talk of the move, but I'd already blown my best argument—my education—by battling through three schools in two years. I don't hate school, it's not worth the effort, it just seems such a sham, so very far away from anything to do with real life, that the only sensible response is to pit your will against theirs and see who breaks first. In the first two cases, they did—and I left. The jury's still out on the last one. I had a maths teacher there who saw that I got a sort of buzz off the patterns numbers make and who not only pushed me but protected me when I fucked up elsewhere. I got into trouble and he got me out of it—mostly—I think because he respected my spirit, he thought the system was shit himself. It taught me something useful, really useful, not just how to fake effort or skim successfully. It taught me that natural allegiances come in handy, don't waste them, they can buy you a lot of space.

Anyway, it came down to schooling, my love of London and my friends. Those were my three arguments against Devon, and I'd as good as blown the first one because, even while my maths teacher was calming the waters, I was pissing in them again. My complaints about school were like a religious dirge over the breakfast table at home each morning, so that when the prospect of Devon was raised, my father would offer various alternatives:

"We could move further, to Cornwall. They've still got tin mines down there. Perhaps you could leave school altogether and they could reinstitute child labor?"

"Couldn't be worse."

"There must be religious seminaries in the area. Maybe you'd like to be beaten by monks, daily?"

"Jessie would go for that." A kick under the table from her. So then I'd come back: "Why don't I just board somewhere up here? It's London I'm going to miss."

"I'd give him three days," Mum would remark.

"I'd give him three hours," from Dad.

"I wouldn't give him anything." Jessie.

And my mother would look at me, knowing my answer as well as I did: "Do you want to?"

"What?"

"Board."

"Not a chance. Forget it." So I'd wail on. "I'm going to lose all my friends. I'm never going to see them."

"These are the kids you referred to as 'mindless scum' only a few days ago?" A sharp look from Dad.

"Yeah, well, they are. But at least they're the mindless scum I know. The kids in Devon all have giant foreheads and fingers sprouting from their shoulders. They're all thalidomide kids down there. They lack social graces."

"That's a sick remark." Mum.

"It's a sick world. Why do we have to move?"

So Dad would come down to my level. "I don't know why you're so hooked on London. You want medical allusions? Well, London is brain-dead, it's on drips—it's got aggression pumping in one arm and money in the other, and neither can make it work. It's a lousy place for a baby. Anyway, it's depressing as hell all winter."

"You think Devon will be better? The people in Devon probably forget how to speak English between the time the last tourist leaves and the first of the year arrives."

And on like that.

So I set fire to the art department stockroom. I went into school one morning and my mate Luke and I torched the stacks of paper, each vertically arranged in neat compartments. It's a bastard of a job, getting a good blaze going, but we managed it just as the rest of the school was going through the attendance registers. Couldn't have been me, could it? I wasn't there.

It wasn't a real fire, I mean the school didn't burn down or anything, but the art department didn't look the same again. There's something beautiful about what a lick of flame can do to wood, the charring effect, little bits of black carbon spiraling up to touch the ceiling—makes a place look lived in. And oil paints have their own excitement when they blaze. This was performance art on a grand scale, but Luke and I didn't get any points for it. In fact, we chickened out. I wanted everyone to know we'd done it deliberately, but maybe that would have been a bit heavy duty, so we opted for the having-a-quick-smoke-oh-dear-look-what-happened line. We got a bollocking, suspension and all that, the threat of expulsion, but it could have been worse. I mean that. Someone could have been hurt.

That did it for Dad, though. As far as Devon went, that took me out of the contest. I think he knew it was no accident. Schools don't really know you, but parents have a good idea.

I knew he was angry, because his face changed, as if the tension was wrestling through a forest of muscles and veins in his forehead in an attempt to get out.

"There's a school nine miles from the village with a good record in maths," he told me. "There's a school bus. It takes about forty-five minutes each way. You just gave up your right to choose."

I wanted to ask, "How far is the nearest fire station?" but it was too easy.

■

7

The deal came later. I knew I'd get something. Dad suffers terrible guilt when he loses his temper, and he must already have been feeling bad about this one, because he did everything to make the move bearable for me. It was Mum I had to watch. The little incident over the fire had severely dampened her faith in me, and while I could cope with Dad's brief outburst of anger, Mum's disappointment was harder to live with.

■

"This is probably a big mistake." Dad's voice comes to me with an undisguisable edge of love and concern, despite his determination still to sound pissed off as he hands me the camera. A moment accompanies the giving of a gift like this, it happens outside considerations of value or acquisition, beyond the emotional range of the TV commercial. I know how much he must have paid for it, he knows it's going to turn me on, for all the right reasons. There's magic attached, we both know that: it can do things, this camera, it can steal little bits of life. This is a key father-son experience (he wants it as much as I do, that's part of it—and Mum, with the baby due, home-video time), but it comes with a lecture.

"This is no reward, buster, OK? Tell me something. When you started that fire, couldn't you see how it would end up? Couldn't you see the kind of trouble it would get you into?"

Nothing from me. What can I say? It's our second day in Devon, and I'm playing it cool. Even with all the doors open, the cottage smells foreign, like someone else's bed. Outside, the sun is blazing. Time for a spot of cricket and some fighting in the streets. But I'm not looking for aggravation, not today.

"Well?"

"I suppose. . . ."

"I hope so. You're not stupid, Tom, don't try and pretend you are. You're very full of yourself and you like flirting with danger. But think long-term for a moment. If you can't persuade yourself out of such ideas now, what's going to change? Are you going to be pissing about setting things on fire in ten years' time?"

"You're going to be an older brother soon," Mum says, watching me, working on my conscience, convinced that I have one. "You may not want it, but that gives you a certain responsibility. I think you're bright enough to know what you were doing. But I don't know which is worse—the thought of you doing it with a degree of premeditation, or being so out of control that you couldn't stop yourself."

"I wasn't out of control," I say quietly.

"Right," says Dad. "And we're not unaware of the way that the move's tangled up in this. Maybe it's a very selfish decision on our part, but it's just for one year and sometimes . . ." He searches for an acceptable argument.

Mum finds it for him. "Sometimes," she says, "either way you choose, someone loses."

"I know," I say. I feel awkward now, I want this to be over. "I like change," I say. Which is true.

"What I want you to remember," Dad says, looking at the Japanese-packaged box in my hands, still unopened, "is that you'd better think long and hard about the kind of decisions you make in the future. Colorful is one thing, but stupid is just plain stupid, do you understand me?"

■

So I use the camera. It's great. This really is the video age. Things look better on TV. I point the camera at the family and they look more real, just like actors. They try and smile a bit at first, then they forget about that and try to pretend I'm not there, which doesn't work, of course—then, when they realize that I'm not going to go away, they start to look irritated, you catch a moment in their eyes that says, "I want to get on with things, I've got things to do, but I don't want you watching." Why are they so secretive? Why is it even the smallest acts seem to expose us to ridicule? On video, everything's the same. Watching someone drink a glass of water is as private as watching someone pee. It makes you realize we don't see each other most of the time. We look, but we shut out the important stuff.

I know why I got this camera, and the baby knows too. I think he knows everything. He doesn't care about any of this shit, he's watched all the time anyway, nothing is private for him and he hasn't learned to care yet. But already he understands a gift. He understands transactions, that's what it's all about. Jessie and I haven't been raised to respond to tips and bribes, and he won't be either—we know all the moral complications inherent in gifts (you don't thank someone for saving your life, you hate the bastard for making you owe him so much). I got this camera not to buy my future good behavior—Mum and Dad wouldn't do that, they know I wouldn't go for a deal like that. No, I got this camera because, by burning the stockroom, I eased the pain of a decision they wanted to make but knew I'd never agree to willingly.

■

8

Nothing much happens. We're in the garden, Mum, Jack and me. Dad and Jessie are somewhere else, in the car. This is before the bathroom window, when I still thought I was the weirdest thing in my life. It's another staggeringly hot day, this summer is sick, lurching between nuclear fission and bullet-hard rain. The weather is getting aggressive. I hate all that crap about scientists messing around with the weather, but there have been one or two fallout clouds floating over Europe this year and it snowed in Italy in July. The Italians probably love it; gives them a chance to get on with a bit of off-season football practice.

Mum is in the garden in her bikini. She looks different, now that Jake's out here and not in her. Thinner, for a start, but also sharper, hipper if you like—more attuned to what's going on, less of a heavy-weight smiler.

She's lying on the grass, drinking Pimm's and lemonade or something equally ridiculous, and reading an incredibly boring-looking book about social welfare. She takes all that stuff fairly seriously, being a solicitor, certainly a lot more seriously than Dad does. He's a total cynic—but an optimist, too. Mum has her cynical side, she's worked with too many hard-core villains and thugs not to, but she still holds on to a vain belief that the system is worth fighting. I'd certainly want her on my side if I was stuck in a courtroom, but I'd like a couple of hand grenades in my pockets as well. It's all so fucking middle class—I'm so fucking middle class. There's a conspiracy in this country. We all play our roles, even the yobbos in the streets just fulfill some middle-class night-mare, they don't have any real ideas of their own. It takes an outsider to inspire genuine fear—someone whose skin is a slightly different color from ours, someone who doesn't know the rules, even if he's lived here a couple of generations. Then watch us. We're wary as hell. I mean, these guys don't know when to take their hats off. They could get serious, they might forget that some ponce in a wig referees the match, they might just go and wack him with a machete.

Mum's on the lawn, lying prone on a huge beach towel which follows the bumps and pockmarks in the ground. She's covered in sun oil, I can smell her from here, and listening to some opera or other on her headset. Jake is lying murmuring in his sleep like a drunk on a binge, his lightweight wicker carrycot placed just inside the shade of the kitchen door. Every now and then, Mum looks up from her book, lifts an earphone from one ear and checks that he's OK. He looks OK to me, he looks like he's having wet dreams or maybe planning the baby-aspirin dealership that's going to set him up. Jake looks like a survivor, but you never can tell. There are times when he looks small and helpless like any other baby, but I think he's only faking.

Me, I'm so desperate for entertainment that I'm taping the little bugger. I could be down at the beach, getting tossed around by the waves they have down here. The beach is brilliant, I'll say that for it —a great ridge of pebbles that drops like a shock down to the sea, throwing you off balance if you're not ready for it, deliberately angled to send you careering into the water, unable to stop. Instead, I'm hanging around, hot as hell in my shorts, a little buzzy-headed from a glass of whatever Mum's drinking, trying to kill time and look interested as I range my camera over sleeping Jake, the ants massing by the cracks in the step outside the kitchen door, the tangled grass beyond that, like ropy fruit-and-veg-stall matting, and Mum's eyes scanning her book, darting up to look my way, then ignoring me, her tits cupped in her untied bikini top, a trail of sweat running from the small of her back down a slight fold of her waist to the shadow between her stomach and the towel.

The truth is I'm waiting, and the righteous are rewarded, for, as I scan the camera over the wooden trestle table by the far wall of the garden, I hear a sound behind me. There is movement in the heavy air, the waft of a body cutting through the stillness of the kitchen, a local voice cooling my neck.

"Aren't you bored, Tom, taking films of the baby? I didn't think to find you here on a day like this."

She can make me blush, Lucy can. It's stupid, but everything she says to me makes me prickle with embarrassment. Does she know this? Am I ahead of her, London boy to Devon girl? Not a chance.

"You look hot." I don't know what else to say. Her face is shining, her hair damp at the edges with sweat. She's not exactly beautiful—certainly not as pretty as Jessie—but she has a sense about her that's quite unmissable. Whereas Jessie is totally aware of what she can do with her whole body, the power it gives her, Lucy looks as if she might fuck on the stairs while cleaning house for us without missing a beat. They'd each have their own importance for her, the screwing and the cleaning, she'd take them in the same matter-of-fact way she seems to take everything. But what do I know? I just wish she would.

"I am hot," she says, as I lay the camera on the kitchen table, next to a pile of Jessie's junk. Lucy has the fridge door open, kneeling as she drops ice cubes into the lime cordial she's made. "I think I stepped on a wasp on the way over, but it was too tired in this heat to sting much." Her feet are bare. She turns and looks at me, straightening up. She lifts a foot to show me; the sole is black, but I can just make out a small red welt.

"You should clean that," my mother shouts from the garden, all-seeing when it comes to injuries and health.

Lucy goes outside. I follow her, wishing she were six or seven years younger, my age.

Mum puts aside the headset and the book and looks up. She has a smoothness, Mum, a healthy and refined sheen which makes Lucy look coarse. I think it's the coarseness I like.

"I'll wash my feet in your bath, if that's all right," Lucy says. She crouches for a moment, next to Mum, glass in hand, the light bleaching her off-white dress and shadowing the outline of her legs. I don't know what to do with myself. I just want to stare, but I think Lucy suspects this, so I take myself off to the broken stone wall which edges two sides of our scraggly lawn and sit on it, arching my back to throw my face and chest up to the sun.

Jack stirs and Lucy says, "I'll get him," her voice sounding further away than it is, swimming with the sunspots inside my head.

"What's your problem?" she says a moment later. "Too hot—or hungry?" Then, to Mum: "How is he?"

"He's fine. He's in charge, why shouldn't he be? But at least he sleeps at night. Apart from feeding, he doesn't wake."

"He looks like you."

"I think he looks like himself. He's his own person." I open my eyes as Mum slips a tit in his mouth. Lucy is standing over them, watching Jake suck furiously. Sensing the moment, I make a move for the house.

"Already he's got a strong will," Mum says, trying to shift Jack into a more comfortable position in the shade.

I walk past, unnoticed, and dart into the house.

"And a strong mouth," Lucy says, still with Mum. "Does that hurt?"

I hear Mum laugh. "He doesn't care if it does."

■

When Lucy comes in, I have the camera in my hand again, trying to look as if I'm doing something when all I want is to be inside while Lucy's inside. She starts vacuuming and I tape her, hoping she won't know there's barely enough light to see anything. I follow her as she pulls the lead out of the cleaner and finds a socket, then lugs the machine to the top of the stairs and starts working her way down. She always does the stairs before anything else, maybe because she wants to get them out of the way first, because they're the most boring part of cleaning the house —although, in terms of vacuuming, I can't imagine that one thing is more boring than another. Lucy is too bright to be a cleaner, and yet somehow I don't think it matters much to her. God knows what she thinks life is about, but I don't think cleaning enters into it. Then again, she has a curious respect for the oddest things. Maybe she knows something I don't.

I position myself at the bottom of the stairs, pointing the camera up at her.

"You're wasting your film on me," she says, not irritated but not really interested in the camera either, the way some people are.

"It's tape."

She pauses a moment and runs a hand across her face, wiping it dry. "How come you're always around the house when I'm cleaning?" She knows. She must do. "Do you like to get in my way?"

I want to say yes. I want to say, "Lucy, I think you're amazing. Please come up to my room and let me touch you." I stare up at her, forgetting about the camera. As she leans forward over the cleaner on the stairs, her dress hangs from her. I feel hot, flushed, almost paralyzed with fear or something as I see a nipple brush against the fabric inside and disappear back into the darkness.

I force myself to speak. "It's better watching you work than doing anything myself," I say, desperate for her not to see what an absolute moron I am.

She twists her mouth, frowning at me as the vacuum head sucks noisily at the worn stair carpet. "Lazy little sod." She looks away, dismissing me from her thoughts. "Do you think you could get me another drink, or would that be too much effort?"

I get it, my mind only on the image of ice cubes sliding down against that small dark nipple. I run a cube over my forehead and chest, feeling its cold edge draw a sharp line across my skin, then watch it bob in the glass, believing that by this feeble, not entirely hygienic magic I might communicate to Lucy what I seem totally unable to say.

I must spend ages over all this, because by the time I get back to her, Lucy has finished the stairs, gone back up to the top and has vacuumed the better part of my room.

My room doesn't look like my room—I have so far refused to admit to any permanence in terms of being here—but there is one magazine picture stuck on the wall by my bed, a two-page spread of some kids in Beirut, ripped down the middle and taped together.

"You're a strange boy, aren't you?" Lucy remarks, looking at this as I come in. She takes her drink, turns off the cleaner for a moment. "What do you want a picture like that for on your wall?"

I glance at it, the barbed wire, the burned-out car and the doubt on the children's faces seeming both a lot like I feel and like an anti-dote to the blandness of my life. "I thought it might annoy Mum and Dad," I say, feeling strangely guilty all of a sudden. Lucy makes me feel as if I'm using the picture, using their suffering, which I suppose in a way I am. "It didn't work," I add. "They don't seem to mind."

I watch Lucy drink, unsure what to do next. She's here in my room and there seems to be some point of contact between us, but I feel ridiculously young. I turn to go.

"You've caught the sun, haven't you?" she says, before I can leave. "Your shoulders are all red. You should get your mum to put something on them."

"She's got Jake to look after."

"Jack. Jake doesn't suit him."

I look at her, standing rolling the ice cubes—my ice cube—around in her glass. "Are they really red?" I ask. "Maybe you could help? I'd do it myself, but it's difficult reaching behind . . ."

She watches me curiously. I catch my breath, not quite believing this is going to get me anywhere.

"OK," she says. "Let me finish my drink first. You're just lazy, Tom, aren't you? You think anyone's going to put up with this when you're older?"

I don't care, not now, not at the moment. I run down to the bathroom to get some cream, noticing the smudgy black footprint Lucy has left in the bath. I glance out the kitchen doorway at Mum. Jack has gone back to sleep and she is reading again, headset on. Then I race back upstairs, back to Lucy, who has the cleaner going again and is just finishing my bedroom. She switches it off.

We sit on the bed and she uncaps the tube. Suddenly I know nothing is going to happen, nothing more than her massaging after-sun muck into my back. I don't know what I expected, but I feel disappointed.

"God, you're going to peel," she tells me as she rubs my shoulders. It feels wonderful, cool and burning at the same time. "How did you let yourself get like this?"

"I don't know. Do you sunbathe much?" It's a stupid question, in keeping with my mood now.

"I don't get the time."

I twist my head round at her. "You must, sometimes. Weekends?"

"I work in a pub, weekends. I'm trying to save enough to go and live with my aunt in France for a year."

I don't want to know this—not because it means she might leave at some point, but because it reduces everything to normalcy, to the quiet pattern of everyday life.

"Why don't you work in London? Wouldn't you get more money there?"

"London's full of people like you," she says, squeezing my shoulders hard, sending a bolt of pain through them that stuns me. "Out to make trouble." I look round again. She stares at me—a look which makes me feel as if I've just leaped through about ten years.

"I've got to get on," she says, getting up, leaving me sitting on the bed with the most incredible erection I've ever had, aching to do something yet literally in shock, unable to move. She taps my belly with the knuckles of one hand, just above my hard-on, just where my stomach is wrinkled over my tightened shorts. "You're getting fat." She smiles, recapping the after-sun cream. "Too much sitting around. You don't want a paunch, do you?"

She walks out and two rival waves of emotion slap into me. The first sends the details of my Devon room—the few I'm aware of to start with —spiraling into outer space. I might as well be in Beirut, the small-paned windows seem so foreign. My bed could be an old mattress in a shelled doorway; the razor wire begins just over there, right by that bombed shopfront and that gloomy old chest of drawers. I'd rather be in a Lebanon street right now, watched by a sniper, waiting for the bullet or the bomb blast, the flying glass, nothing. Sitting here, sitting in safety, in the bizarre heat of an English summer day, that seems much clearer, the choices mean something—even if it isn't you who make them.

The second wave is my normal response, my hearty "Fuck this!" attitude that I know I can rely on. I bounce off the bed and go to the door. Lucy is in Jessie's room, the lead of her vacuum snaking round Jessie's door from the point on the landing. My door is half closed. I take a chance. Hidden behind it, I toss off—awkwardly, hurriedly, energetically—into a paper handkerchief. Halfway through, I freeze when I hear Lucy pulling the plug out. I look round the door, debating whether to cram my hard-on back inside my shorts. I don't. I want her to see me, but she doesn't and my hand just works harder with her in sight, retreating down the stairs.

I finish and shove the balled tissue under my bed, reminding myself that I must remember it later. Dad's voice downstairs makes me jump—I didn't know he was back. He is talking to Lucy when I go down, showing her the bag of barbecue charcoal he has bought, as if she could possibly be interested. Jessie is carrying in a box of food topped with sausages and steaks. For the briefest moment, she looks like a teenage housewife—one of the saddest sights known to man. It's only the gaping square hole cut out of the seat of her jeans, revealing pale blue boxer shorts underneath, that gives the lie to this vision of Jessie and Dad as an oddly matched but small-horizoned provincial couple. I don't give it a second thought. Maybe I should.

■

9

A nuclear summer's evening and we are in a foreign land—well, it's familiar enough to us by now, but we're the foreigners, Jessie and me, we don't fit in, we're not entirely trusted yet and why should we be?

Voices swim in the hazy golden air, laughter mixing with car exhaust and cigarette smoke and the richer, sicklier smells of dried sweat, worn leather and the grasping flowering plants which snake up and around the old stone walls of the alcove we're crammed into. We're with the hard boys, the local yobbos, Jessie's crowd, admirers all, working their nuts off to make sure she notices them. There's a couple of village girls with us, too, drinking and joking, somehow recognizing that they can't fight Jessica, she's got to win, so they might as well learn from her.

Half the populace seems gathered here outside the local watering hole, beer-bellied phantoms flitting past my range of vision, alcohol slopping from overfilled glasses, dark blurs moving at their feet like dogs from hell.

I'm pissed, I realize that, it's one of the perks of having Jessie as an older sister. I get a bit of stick from the bunch we're with now, but they're all a good few years older than me and basically they treat me OK. Better to be crushed between four drunken bikers and their girlfriends than standing with Mum and Dad at the side of the road where the overspill is, talking to some of the local dead about church fetes, income tax and point-to-points. Mum and Dad don't fit in, either. I can see from here the strain involved in talking to these people, the occasional wild-eyed glances in our direction. But that's their problem; they wanted to come down here.

At least the mob we're with have some life in them, a few years of madness left before they buckle down. Only a couple of them have jobs, because there's nothing much to do locally except work for the grocks, the tourists—us (except Jessie and I are just about beginning to lose this taint)—and they'd rather die first. Caz, the heavy, punky girl across the table from me, did it for a while and hated it. She actually prefers working on a till in the supermarket in Sidmouth. John, the hard-looking, big-nosed, cocky bastard next to me who keeps deliberately shoving his elbow in my ribs, is a trained mechanic, but lost his job a month ago for telling his boss to fuck off when the boss kept on about him coming in late. Nick, the one who's winning where Jessie's concerned, is the quietest and also the youngest, yet he's somehow acknowledged as in control, the one the others listen to and follow. He's on some government training scheme which pays for his lodging (he's from North Devon) while he works as an apprentice at the local forge. I didn't even know what farriers did until I met him, and I'm still not sure, but Jessie goes for that quiet, individual determination, and obviously so does everyone else.

"Did you hear about Potter?" The greasy-haired toe-rag on my right, the other side of me from John, is trying to get everybody's attention. My mind is sharp for a moment, but as he speaks it all begins to swim again. I try to fix on Caz, concentrating on her mouth and the spiky black makeup around her eyes in an effort to stop my head from sliding under the table. They think Jessie's a punk, this lot. Even though she doesn't go for the obvious trappings like Caz, that's the only way they can work her out. They think that's still pretty dangerous.

"Potter and Martin," Toe-rag continues (I've forgotten his name—I think I've forgotten mine), "only go and break into Dr. Arnold's surgery the other night, didn't they? Totally rat-arsed, they were, drunk about a gallon of Guinness each, and Martin's dad's been in to see the doctor the day before. So they thought they'd have a bit of fun, mix his urine sample up with someone else's or something. Anyway, they're in there about twenty minutes, nobody bothers them, so they're pissing about when the fucking bill arrive. Really heavy, they were. Thought they'd gone in there to score drugs—Potter! He'd shit himself if he took two aspirin. Anyway, Martin's got about two weeks' dole money on him, because he's been painting and decorating a bit, so the bill think he's taken that too. Questioned them both for hours, they did, in separate rooms and everything. Bastards!"

"Who was it?" the girl next to Caz asks. "Sergeant Collis?"

"No. No one they knew, that was the problem. Took them to Colyton. Kept them there half the fucking night."

"Potter's a walking disaster," says John, draining his glass and knocking me in the ribs again. Drunk as I am, I bring my shoulder up quickly and make contact with John's arm, cracking the glass against his teeth. His head spins round as he checks his teeth with his tongue. "Fucking little—"

"Want another one, John?" Nick dives in, convincing John that I'm not worth bothering about while sending Jessie all the right signals. "I'm going to have one more, then let's go. Let's do something."

Nick gets up and I try to do the same, sensing an urgent need somewhere between my stomach and my mouth.

"Here, Jessica," a weasel face—or is it a weasel voice?—says somewhere behind me, beneath me, whatever. "Your brother reckons he used to drink in London. Is that right?"

Caz smiles across at me. "He doesn't look too brilliant." I manage to inch my way round the alcove toward her. "You look like you've swallowed a bucket of worms."

"I think I have." I steady myself on the shoulder of Colin, I think it is—a fat-faced wanker who's the hanger-on of the group. "I'll be back," I manage through a clogged mouth.

The next few moments are a dreamlike journey, weaving through the tiny pub garden, banging into everything there is to bang into and doing about three unnecessary circuits as I try to keep out of range of Mum and Dad. I get a vivid, whirling picture of the whole village falling down three hills toward this focal point, where an uneven mass of increasingly noisy drunks straddles the road, lit sporadically by the sick white or slow red of cars' reverse and brake lights scarring the growing darkness as they move in and out of the car park round the back.

It's here that I'm headed too, stepping right in front of an oncoming Jap jeep in my struggle to reach the toilets in time. I almost don't make it, feeling my mouth fill with something vile and fluid as I stagger up the step, into the welcoming stench and silence of the gents. My gut pushes upward, like a drum hit from the wrong side, my mouth falls open and I throw myself over the urinal as a torrent of vomit comes out, nearly choking me as I gasp for air.

There is a quiet which follows throwing up, a sense of peace and achievement matched by an incredible lightness of the stomach. Only your mouth tastes like shit. The rest of you is elated, alive to the freshness of a world unsullied by waves of nausea. Every detail is pure, from the echoing drip of the cistern overhead to the graffiti by the condom machine, like a torch shone on someone else's mind: "Helen—we want to screw you. MM. NH. TF. Clelia can swallow it whole."

I'm feeling great by the time I get back outside, ready for anything —even Jessie's friends. The trouble is, I'm with them, they're not really with me, and as I walk back round from the car park, I have a momentary doubt as to whether I should call it quits now and leave them to it. They're still there, jammed into the stone alcove by the entrance to the pub, glasses on the table, stoned expressions all round. Jessie and Nick are at one end of the group, a little apart from the rest, deep in some intensely private conversation, their eyes locked in some middle zone where nothing else exists. For a moment, she looks like any other older sister. For a moment, I wish I could be where they are. Then, as I skirt round the serious drinkers, crunching over the crisps and shit their dogs are eating off the ground, I glimpse Dad, hard to spot at first in the dark but half lit by the curtained glow of a cottage across the street.

He is talking to a woman who has The Mouth some of the locals have: like a chicken's arse, drawn tight with string. I am close enough now to see him as he looks away, glancing at Mum—who is laughing at something someone else has just said—then moving quickly in Jessie's direction, his head making minute adjustments as he fixes on her and Nick. I want to read something into it, but the thought of them together, her washing his dong and doing what else, seems far away, not possible at this moment, yet I know it's there. What is it to me? Why should I care if it's Dad's prick or Nick's prick she's interested in?

He looks away, drinking his pint and nodding at the woman with The Mouth as if to say, "Just disappear back into the stonework, why don't you?" I feel for him. I feel for both my parents. There are very few interesting people around, most of them just give up or never had it, never had the edge, the urge. When I think about it, maybe Mum and Dad are seriously fucked up—but at least they're still conscious.

"Has anyone got any chewing gum?"

No one hears me. Caz and the other girl are talking. Toe-rag is wiping the beer scum off his glass with a finger. John is nodding his head to the blows of some inner battle. My mouth is a toilet, a graveyard. I want to spit, but I swallow instead.

"What are we going to do then?" asks Colin, bulbous cheeks wobbling in the dim light from the pub. He's more of an outsider than me, I think. He's stuck there, practically doubled over in the most cramped part of the alcove, the resident butt of jokes, the jester figure, any group has one. He's the one who'd be a future captain of industry in the stories, but somehow I don't think it's going to happen to Colin.

"I want some danger," Caz says. The other girl laughs.

"Sit next to Colin then," John tells her. "He's been farting all night."

"Piss off!" Colin can risk this. Nobody takes him seriously.

"Let's just go," Jessie says. She is standing with one hand on Nick's shoulder, totally in control, not threatening Nick's position as leader but rather enhancing it, reinforcing it.

"Let's take a ride." Nick's voice is softer than the others, a slightly different accent. He seems to know something they don't—nothing tangible, maybe just something about himself. "Let's go," he says. "Tonight's too beautiful to miss."

And they all get up. Caz turns and looks at me, standing behind her. She frowns. I think she half likes me, though I'm hardly a serious proposition for her. It's only when all of them start working their way out of the alcove and through the tight-knit boozers in the garden that I fully realize just how much a part of the picture they are. Everyone knows their names! If they were a threat—some really ugly fuckers from out of town, say, some dyed-in-the-wool Hell's Angels—the local constabulary would be down on them like a ton of bricks. And no polite questioning, either—they'd be stuffed in the back of a police van, driven around for a few hours over some remarkably bumpy country roads, then dumped across the county line where their bikes would be found in a tangled heap. But Jessie's friends are just playing, and she's just playing with them. She wants the real fire.

"Is there a good beach we could go to now?" she asks Nick as we head round the back to the bikes. "I'd love to swim in the dark."

"Fucking tourist!" Toe-rag says. "I need a slash." And he disappears into the ladies, singing out and banging on all the doors, but there's no one in there.

"OK," Nick says. "Yeah . . ."

"OK, yeah," Jessie mimics, giving him a hard time. The bikes are in front of us, a mixed bunch, none of those monster machines that weigh more than a house and hit 60 mph before your bum's even on the seat. Jessie stops by Nick's Honda. She looks right for this, she looks more dangerous than the bike—I don't know what it is about her, she's only wearing jeans and some sort of half-amputated shirt.

"Pauline's party is tonight, isn't it?" Caz says, coming up behind me, accidentally kicking a can or something that rattles across the stones of the car park.

"Boring."

Caz's friend tilts her head mockingly at John, who is checking something on the rear axle of his bike, an old but powerful Yamaha. "Been there, done that one, have you, John?"

"Fucking right."

"I heard she's got AIDS," fat Colin says, toughing it out with the rest of the boys. "Got it off a marine."

"Probably got it off me," John says, lighting a cigarette and sitting on his bike.

"Shut up," Caz's friend tells him.

Toe-rag comes out of the ladies, startling a middle-aged matron on her way in, and saunters across the car park like a bovver boy looking for trouble. It's all an act. I'm not saying he couldn't handle himself, but he's not really a bastard. I've known a few.

"Well, then . . . ?" Jessie says to Nick, perching on his bike with her feet up on the seat in front of her, blocking his place.

Nick takes his bike off its stand, throwing her off balance, but Jessie's hands grab the seat under her and she stays where she is, feet still in front.

"Anyone got any money?" Nick asks, sitting on her feet so that Jessie has to struggle to slide them out from under him. "We can pick up some beer in Sidmouth."

He starts the bike, a loud, farting rumble that stirs up the heavy air of the car park. Caz climbs on behind John and he starts his, Toe-rag following next, with Caz's friend on the back, so that now there's a rich, belting roar filling the night, compromised only by the stuttering ph-ph-phut of Colin's machine, half motorbike, half wimp.

"What about Tom?" Jessie asks Nick, and I think, "All right!" She proves herself, Jessie does, in moments like this.

"Oh, he's coming," John states firmly above the noise of the bikes.

I'm not sure for a moment what he means by this, but he edges Caz off the back of his bike, staring at me steadily with what could be menace left over from earlier in the evening.

"I'll take him," Nick offers quickly. He's bright, Nick, he sees the moves. "Jess, John'll give you a ride, won't you, John?"

So everyone moves round, Colin being the real winner, since he gets to take Caz whereas before he had no passenger.

"You've got to ask Mum," Jessie tells me as she shifts from Nick's bike to John's, more than slightly pissed off at this upheaval.

"Fuck that!"

"You've got to." She looks at me seriously. "You disappear with us and they'll have the police out. Go on."

So, feeling like a twerp, with the bikes razzing me noisily as I jog across the car park, I hurry to find Mum and Dad, but they're not where they were and I'm worried that the others might leave without me. The pub garden is thinning out now, only the committed bores and soaks left. The lights are going out in the village—this town does not live after dark. Maybe Mum and Dad have gone home, but I doubt it; they would have checked on us first. I push open the old door of the pub, the one that leads to the hotel reception desk as well, and turn into the bar, which stinks even before you enter it of cigarette smoke, stale breath and dog smells, not necessarily in that order.

"I've been looking for you," Dad tells me, approaching from the other door, ducking to miss a low beam. The pub is a haze of last-order drinkers, ears pricked to anything prejudicial we might say, but mouths still moving, the conversation slowly winding down.

"Where's Mum?"

"She went home. She was worried about Jack—we told Lucy we'd be back half an hour ago."

A flash of Lucy. A tightening of my balls. Perhaps I should go back home with Dad and see her? But she might already have gone. Dad moves past me, toward the door. I hold back, not wanting Jessie's crew to see me asking for permission.

"Jessie's boyfriend has offered me a ride on his motorcycle. Can I go? It's such a beautiful night."

Dad turns, looks at me, interested. Is any of this real? I don't know

THE WAR ZONE   53

what's going on. Fuck it, it's a simple question. I don't want to think about this all the time.

"Which one is he?" Dad smiles. He looks like a dad at this moment, a good one, the kind you'd want, the kind who hasn't screwed down his attitudes any more than you have. "I thought you hated hippies," he taunts. "They all look as if they've come through a time warp."

"I know."

"Is Jessie all right?" The revving of motorcycles outside.

"Sure. Can I go?"

"It's late."

"It's the holidays." They're going to go without me, I know it.

"These roads aren't safe. I don't know."

I stare at him, man to man, son to father, urgently. "Have you heard that thing? No one's not going to know it's coming. Anyway, the world's asleep down here."

He frowns. I've won—if they're still there. "Does he have a helmet for you?"

"Yeah."

"How long are you going to be?"

"It's just a ride," I lie. "Just up the hill for a while, it's such a beautiful night." We move to the door, me eager to finish this before we get outside—establish my independence and go.

"Don't go mad," he says. "And tell Jessica she's got to come home too."

"I'll tell her."

We step outside. Nick's out there, but John and Jessie have gone. And Toe-rag. But Colin's there, with Caz stuck behind him.

"Tom . . ." Dad asks, looking at me differently as I turn to go. "Are you all right? You look a little the worse for wear."

"It's my stomach." I hold it, or hold where it used to be. "I think it's some crisps I ate."

"I wish—" He breaks off, looks from me to the bikes and back. I want to say something to him, I want to touch him, it's one of those weird pauses that feel like last-chance situations, except I don't believe in last chances. He grins. Standing there, my dad looks like trouble— even in his white yachting trousers and summer shirt he looks like trouble, but the best kind of trouble, not some sick bastard who's fucking my sister.

Caz calls to me. The bikes rev. Dad nods his head to indicate that I should go. "I wish you weren't bound to repeat my mistakes," he says. I don't know specifically what he means by this, but it's depressing advice. It's like one of those double-think mind-benders: once said, you can't escape it.

"See you," I say and run and jump on Nick's bike. Then, for a beautiful while, I stop thinking.

■

10

On the beach I take Jessie aside and say something very strange to her.

"It happened, didn't it?" I ask, because my mind isn't working right anymore, I don't trust it, I can't. "What I saw—in the bathroom. You and Dad. Just tell me, just let me know I'm not going crazy, because I don't want to be imagining this." I should be asking her to deny it, I know, but I want her admission of guilt. I know what I saw, but I want to hear it from her mouth, then maybe I can shut it out of my mind. "And then—"

She looks at me impatiently, water breaking at our feet, a rushing sound, a dragging back. This is the last thing she wants now. "And then?"

"Then please make me believe it was only once, it was a mistake, it's never going to happen again." I feel feeble asking this—I should be able to handle it—but I can't. Can I trust her? Her eyes seem disappointed with me, glazed suddenly, distant. "Please!"

■

But before that there's the bike ride, fast, cooling in the heat, the speed wrenching away thoughts before they can form, like being part of your own dream, watching yourself move but with no way of getting off or out.

Nick's bike seems suddenly wider, heavier, taking the hills like a breeze, eating up gradients which have Dad's Bentley wheezing. I've never done this: ride pillion on a motorbike through flashing hedgerows, dark and blurry, a wall of nothingness hurtling by on either side, like a mind-blasting trip through a maze. The light beam ahead is a gunsight, a border patrol night light. We're flying, feeling the bumps and falling into the curves, the machine noise and the speed drilling me hard, pumping my adrenalin. I'm in the helicopter napalming the geeks. There goes the village! There goes the whole of fucking Devon!

Then it's different. We're in the trees, spiraling down toward Sidmouth, dropping onto a shadowy blanket of lights that cuts off where the sea starts. This can't be England. This can't be my life. Why can't it just go on like this, why does the speed have to stop?

Something alive darts across the road right in front of the bike and Nick almost jerks us off the road, but he steadies us, our necks craning back to see what it was. We continue our descent into town, the lights taking form, becoming houses and shops the way they do in music videos when a blur becomes a set. We're moving through a network of one-way streets all leading to the sea and it's party night, a bunch of eighteen-year-olds are crisscrossing in and out of parked cars, gesturing back at us, moving hunkered down like terrorists, sliding past pub doorways in pursuit of some prey. We glide over the battlefield, glimpse a couple kissing or struggling by a bow-windowed shop, then Nick drives us straight at a curb, up onto the pavement, down a pedestrian alley and out on the sea front where the others are waiting for us, John launching a beer bottle to smash in our path as we approach.

"Don't damage anything you can't fix," Nick says quietly as we draw up alongside them, his voice still carrying above the sound of his bike. He looks at Jessie, angled back behind John on John's bike, and even in my ravaged state of mind I see that there's something clear about Nick, something powerful in his intentions, which gives him the edge over John or anybody else. But I also get a flash that Jessie's playing around, more than I thought. She's teasing Nick, very quietly she's flirting with John, and I'm not sure that I like that.

"Where the fuck were you?" Toe-rag quizzes Nick. He looks at me, the obvious cause of the holdup. "You must have crawled here backward."

But Nick isn't listening. There's some unspoken communication going on between him and Jessica, whereby he seems quite deliberately to shut her out of his mind. Picking up on this, but at her own pace, with no evident submission, she gets off John's bike, comes over and stands by me, looking as if she might have something to say but might just as easily walk away. I am expected to move, there's no doubt about that, and for a moment I'm tempted not to, but there doesn't seem much option so I slide off and stand faced with the prospect of a ride on John's bike or no ride at all.

John is turning in tight circles in the middle of the road, waiting to go, waiting to move, frustrated by being here on the front and looking more out of place than usual with a backdrop of fake-elegant hotels, rats' nests with Riviera pretensions, all palm fronds and colored lights, ready to be requisitioned by the government as proof that normal family holidays still take place. Couples walk along the sea front, robots, their kiddies in bed, their brains dead but perhaps troubled by basic motor responses to John's manic circling, Toe-rag's yodels and the general unease our little gathering seems to create.

I'm ready for John's bike and whatever ugly surprises he wants to spring on me now. Jessie is draped around Nick and everyone seems ready to go, so I walk right in front of John and force him to stop, which he does, not interested in me anymore, watching two panda-faced policemen staring at us from the safety of their car, as they wonder, "Shall we have a bit of fun with those boyos? Is it worth the hassle? Are they going to give us a real run for our money?"

I hop on behind John fast, hoping they haven't had a chance to clock my young face, and as if by remote control the whole circus rolls out, Caz and Colin taking up the rear with what I presume to be the supplies of beer in an awkwardly clutched cardboard box.

Then it's twice down the front just for good measure, cranking the noise level up, racing the bikes, thrilling the little teenyboppers waiting on the sea wall for their lives to change. John's Yamaha feels different from Nick's Honda, or maybe it's John—unpredictable, a bit dangerous because he's really quite stupid. The second time, he does a wheelie right across one of the mini roundabouts and nearly kills us as we scoot across the front of an oncoming car. We touch down without me falling off and I feel dizzy with fear or relief as he punches the throttle and takes off after Nick and Jessie up a hill, past a looming five-star Victorian hotel surrounded by a maximum-security wall, into darkness.

■

The water is cold, like it should be, and even though it freezes my balls off I don't care because I've got a bottle of beer in my hand, the sight of Jessie's and Caz's and Caz's friend's tits ahead of me and anyway the night is close—warm and still—not like a night at all.

The bikes are parked at the edge of the beach, not one of the Wild Bunch being prepared to risk his tires on the rocks and pebbles, and we've all stripped down to our underpants, Caz's friend making the biggest deal about getting into the water before she'd unhook her bra and then shrieking with the cold and chickening out until Toe-rag appeared suddenly behind her and offered a helping hand. Jessie, of course, leads the way, striking out into the water ahead of any of the boys, not even playful for a moment but throwing herself into it, cutting through the darkness with an urgency. As the beer hits my stomach I realize there's no way I'm going to be able to drink any more tonight, so I discreetly bring the bottle down to waist level, under the water, and let the beer merge with the sea. I bob into the waves the way I've seen John do it—headfirst, no arms, nutting the water—and, shivering with cold, feel their pull, stronger than it ever seems in daylight. I can understand now the kick of a nighttime suicide from the beach—a swim right back into the hungry hole of your maker.

"Come on, girls!" Toe-rag calls to those of us close to the shore—me and fat Colin included. "Watch your feet—the crabs bite at night!"

"Fuck the crabs!" John calls from farther out, his head coming in and out of view between moonlit waves. "Just no one piss in the water—" He disappears briefly. "It attracts the sharks." Back into view, then gone again, his disembodied voice carrying over the swell. "Big bastards, hang around all summer looking for virgin meat."

"You should be all right then, Caz!" Toe-rag calls, struggling to keep his head above water as he twists about close to me. A hand comes up clutching what I take at first to be seaweed, but then as he tosses the soggy mass in Caz's direction I see that it's his pants. "Here, wash these for me, would you? John won't mind."

Nick and Jessie aren't a part of this, they're off swimming together, out past John. I wish I could do what Jessie does wherever she goes—create this feeling that she is what's happening, that she is cool and everything else hangs or falls on her reckoning. But this isn't bad, this whole thing, being here at night in the water even if you can't see what you're swimming through and there are jellyfish or plastic bags or blobs of scum moving in the moonlight.

■

Back on the beach everyone hangs around in T-shirts and under-wear, drinking beer while Nick and John wreck a stretch of fence and start a fire with the wooden stakes, just adding to the heat. I feel stickier now than before the swim and there's something on the pebbles, oil or tar, which rubs off on my hands and feet and feels like it's there for life.

The air smells great, though, salty and hot, junk food without the food. I can see where Jessica and Nick are headed, it's obvious, and for some totally confused reason this just aggravates what's been building in me for days, since I saw her in the bathroom, since I spoke to her in her room.

"It happened, didn't it?" I ask her, taking her away from Nick and the others, cornering her between the sea and a great fist of water draining in five or six black fingers over the beach into the waves. "Not just what I saw—the whole thing, you did it together, didn't you, you and Dad?"

She shakes her head, almost sad. But not friendly, she's scared, I've scared her a bit. "You're unbelievable."

I hold my ground. I feel like we're somewhere else, we're not on a beach. Nick and the rest don't exist. "Tell me I'm not going crazy." I can hear the wash, that sucking sound, the hiss—evil, faceless. "It happened, but say it's not going to happen again." I'm looking at her, she seems far away, I'm the one who's strange, I'm making her think about this. "Please!"

Then suddenly I'm back on safe ground. No more weird hissing. She's got to talk. I'm in control here. I've got my running shoes on and I can feel my feet sticking to them with the tar from the beach. I can hear the others pissing about. Smell the bonfire, feel the heat, though I'm cold now. Jessie looks at me, guardedly. "I can't understand you," she says. "Why do you keep on about this, it just makes it more difficult, don't you realize that?"

"Because it's important."

"I don't want to hurt you. I don't want any of us to be hurt." She might even mean this, but it sounds like bullshit.

I feel sad. She looks sad, but I feel it. I know she's going to tell me, she wants to, she tells me everything. I don't think I can take it. I thought I could, but I want to turn and walk away, let her go and do whatever she wants to do with Nick.

She looks back at him. I watch her, wondering if he thinks we're talking about him. "It's all right," Jessie says. "We did do it, but it's all all right."

"What is?" I'm stupid. I don't want to think.

Now she's cruel. "Look, any minute now I'm going to walk over there, have a drink, talk to Nick and go off in search of a nice spot where he can fuck me." That Chelsea voice again; she makes "fuck" sound like a long drink. "If you were a little bit more sure of yourself and perhaps didn't have me around and weren't afraid of what John might do to you, you'd try the same thing with Caz—"

"You think?" I try to sound tough, throw it back at her. Anyway, she's wrong. No, she's not.

"It's not much different with Dad." A cool statement. "It's the same act."

"Oh, Jessie—" I want to hear. I want to hit her.

"I wanted to know what it would feel like. The walls didn't come tumbling down."

I can't speak. The waves break, the black water behind her moves, keeps on moving. I don't feel anything. I can't feel, I can just see my father's face, unreachable somewhere in the depths of my mind, but I can't find how I'm supposed to feel now.

Jessie flicks her head as some insect buzzes her ear. Who is she? She's not my sister. "It's no different than me screwing Nick," she says. There's something about her teeth when she talks, very precise, perfect, her tongue loves to find them, touch them. She's a total bitch. Indescribable. She doesn't give a shit about anyone. "It's all all right, OK? I mean there's nothing wrong. I don't want there to be anything I wouldn't do."

I'm trying to take this in. "What? Like murder, torture?" I'm getting angry. "Do you hate Mum? What about me? Do you hate me too?"

"Calm down, will you?" There's a lull in the others' voices. "This isn't the place." We're attracting attention. So what? But they're talking again, John's narky laugh dominant.

"Why—" I'm struggling. "Why did Dad do it?" This is it. This is the worst for me. "Why did you let him?"

Jessie laughs. She actually laughs. Not a funny laugh, she's not that sure of herself, but a laugh. "I didn't let him. I told you, I want to go further than all the way. Nothing's enough, you know that, we've had this conversation. Incest is brilliant. It's scarier than shagging some Adam in a pub car park or stroking another girl's thigh in some Fulham cafe." She stares at the waves, pleased with herself, scared, thrilled. "Dad didn't want to—but he did. It's a pull, it's like the water there. One foot in and you're not sure. A little more and it's got you, it's alive, you want it." A black heart, that's what Jessie wants. She likes the idea, she'd like the Devil to come knocking. Banging, in her case. "Dad wanted to."

I'm not hearing half of this. I'm watching her, I'm taking it in somehow, but not the words, I don't need to hear them—I've already heard them. I look at her. Her mouth is a foreign object momentarily static in space. "You're making this up," is the best I can manage.

"You asked me. You wanted to know."

I turn. Nick is calling her, but Jessie waves him off, she'll be over in a minute.

She touches me. "Look, I'm sorry, OK?"

This is too much. This is the ultimate sick joke. She has to be joking. I punch her, not nearly hard enough, but suddenly, in the gut. "No, it's not bloody OK!" I want to fight her, I want to push her in the sea. "How can it be OK?" Suddenly I'm grappling with her, our feet are wet, I'm shoving her backward, tearing at her face, forcing her down into the spray; but just as suddenly there are hands on me, locking tight round my arms, and Nick is with Jessie.

■

I feel like a wally. I don't care, but I feel utterly useless. I don't really care about anything, but the others all think I had some petty brothersister row with Jessica and I feel about four years old, but more miserable than it's possible to be at four. The beach seems like the end of the world: no daylight, just a yellow moon and a bonfire and I'm stuck with a gang of morons who don't really want to know me, who feel embarrassed by my presence now, I'm spoiling their fun, they want to drink and party and there's this kid here who still fights with his sister. Even Caz has been treating me differently, as if maybe she misjudged me before, I'm younger than she thought, I can't handle it. Maybe it's sympathy, but I don't want her fucking sympathy.

My eyes are sick, they keep closing but I'm not tired. I don't want to sleep. My head's on the pebbles, I don't care about the tar in my hair. I'm staring up at the sky, which looks weird, smeary, there's a mist building up or something. I've watched Nick and Jessie, they've gone off like the chosen two, all of Jessie's stops pulled out as a result of our little run-in. Even John must feel small. I think he gave Caz a quick one in the chalk cave at the end of the beach, but it can't have been anything monumental: she's lost all interest now and he's louder and more aggressive than ever—actually, I think, quite nervous. But Nick and Jessie must be moving the earth. They've been gone ages and the gathering has passed the joky stage, people are getting a little edgy.

"Must be a grubby one," says Toe-rag.

"Swimming in the quim," says John, opening the last beer.

"They'll wear the beach out," offers fat Colin.

"Children," Caz's friend says.

And they behave as if I wasn't there, as if it's not my sister who's bonking the balls off their compañero. I drift in and out, flames flickering in my eyes, blankness, a sort of half-words, half-picture image of Jessie and Nick as a humpbacked whale—two whales, I suppose— humping on the beach, the pebbles rolling up and down noisily, knocking against one another, grinding in the wash of their sex—not that I know what it's like. It's hot, I know that. It's sore, something is very sore, like my cock when I play with it too much. They're burning up, Nick and Jessie. It hurts, I can feel the hurt, sharp and well defined, small and far away. My feet are burning. That's it, my feet are burning. I can smell the rubber of my running shoes smoldering. That bastard John has put my feet in the fire! I must be half asleep because it takes an eternity to move them out. It's an effort of will—move, legs, move. Then they hurt more! I want to cry out, but that's just going to give him what he's looking for, so I grit my teeth and kick the shoes off. John watches me, laughing as I rub my toes, while Caz talks about the most disgusting thing she can think of to eat.

"A shit sandwich," butts in Toe-rag.

"Too obvious," reckons her friend.

"Food," says John, his intellectual prowess clearly boosted by the pain he's inflicted on me. "That's pretty disgusting."

"Your prick," Caz says, looking at him, but perhaps I misheard, it's not the sort of thing she would say.

And Jessie and Nick come back. I'm rubbing the soles of my feet, wondering whether the ocean would make them feel better or worse and not wanting to seem like a crybaby when I'm already the kid here, though why should I care? They look the same, Nick and Jessie, except they look as if they've taken a drug none of us know about.

"Give me that," whispers Nick, draining the dregs of the beer from John's bottle. Jessie sits the other side of the fire from him, sliding in comfortably between Caz and her chum.

I feel sick. I'm not part of life, it's not going to work for me. This is all my continuing punishment—my burned soles, the fact that my sister hasn't left me anything at all, she's using it all up—life, sex, energy, despair.

I feel flat. Nothing. My toes hurt.

■

11

Five o'clock in the morning and we're in deep shit.

It's light, but the mist and heat are spongelike, wrapping round us, clinging to us as we walk the last half mile or so to the cottage, Jessie having thought better of it than have Nick and the boys drive us to the door on their motorbikes.

"We're in deep shit, you know that?" she says, the two of us united again now in joint defense of our misdeeds, except that I haven't even enjoyed mine, whatever they were, and how can I trust her when she's wrecked or is wrecking all our futures, even if the wreckage doesn't show yet? "We've just got to stay calm and bluff it out. This is probably major coronary time. What did you tell Dad? How long did you say we'd be?"

"I said it was just a ride, I didn't give a time." I watch her. She's not really bothered, she's just going through the motions. Jessie can get away with anything and she knows it. Mum and Dad are going to be furious, but they'll get over it and so will Jessica. "There's death," she says when she's reasoning her way through a problem, "and there's being crippled or disfigured, but apart from that there's nothing much, nothing much they can do to you." She doesn't think in terms of humiliation. "Everything else passes. People forget. I do." I believe this last bit especially. Jessie forgets. She has a highly selective memory, good at remembering useful information but even then not infallible. She doesn't care, she really doesn't care. Even a grudge she might wish to repay, a score to be settled, will be forgotten if something more interesting comes along. She lives for the moment.

And that moment is now. We're at the front door and Jessie looks wrecked, I hadn't realized how wrecked until now. Maybe she did do something with Nick other than fuck him? But do they know about drugs down here? This is palookaville, not London, where even your average council estate kid can tell the difference between smack and crack, between street-grade heroin and something special. Jessie has a thin smile on her lips and pink eyes, but perhaps she's just tired and well pleased by Nick's attentions. Certainly she seems to have put our conversation out of her mind.

"Look repentant but not too much so," she advises. She digs in her jeans for the key. There's a gash on her mouth where I scratched her. And a series of red gouges decorate the calves of her legs where her jeans finish halfway down, which are nothing to do with me. "We just lost track of the time."

■

If Jessie looks wrecked, Mum and Dad look worse. Mum looks pale under her tan, still dressed in the clothes she was wearing in the pub last night, any relief she might feel at seeing us totally wiped out by the anger which has kept her going until now. Dad has sharp gray lines in the skin at the corners of his eyes which normally appear only after a night up working or a night out drinking with his partners.

"You two," Dad says as we walk in the doorway and they both materialize from the kitchen, "are spoiled little arseholes."

It's dark in the hall—the cottage seems darker than it ever does at breakfast time, not that breakfast time is ever this early—but Mum and Dad's faces are clearly visible, their eyes raking over the two of us, checking us for damage, speeding ahead of their mouths in accusation.

"What the hell did you think you were doing?" Mum asks, staring at me but addressing Jessie, the older, more responsible one.

"I'll tell you this"—Dad speaks slowly, trying to find the measure of his anger, close to taking us both and shaking us until it hurts either us or him—"if any of your motorcycle-riding friends comes round here looking for you, I'm going to take him off his bike and break both his bloody arms."

"Where were you?" Mum has the aggrieved tone I've heard her use with her clients when they do a runner, fail to show up in court or for their probation officer. "Your father's been out all night driving around looking for you."

"It was our decision," Jessie says, answering them both, making a show of strength which she knows will only count in her favor. "Well, not a decision really. We had a party on the beach. We just lost track of the time."

"It wasn't much of a party," I add, seeing the next question forming on my parents' lips. "We built a bonfire. And went swimming."

"Moron," Jessie whispers, crushing my burned toes with her shoe.

"Swimming?" my mother echoes, a new look of horror transfiguring her face. "Do you have any idea how dangerous it is swimming off the shore here at night? What if one of you had got caught up in the current? Or swept against the rocks? What would you have done then? You couldn't even see each other."

"There was a moon," Jessie offers, but she knows we're just riding this one out.

And we're still standing in the hall, no one's moved, the light hasn't been switched on, we're locked in this tableau of recrimination, but the gears are changing, the initial anger is running down, we're bumping toward a new area of judgment and penalty.

It's Jake who breaks the spell that holds us all fixed to the spot by crying out with his eerie "I'm hungry" call, the ghost of a cat's wail, a sound which always leaves me feeling uneasy when I'm lying in bed at night. Mum turns and runs up the stairs to see to him and Dad, who isn't nearly as ready as Mum to let go of his rage, ushers us into the kitchen, his silent, watchful gaze ominous as far as our getting off of this lightly is concerned.

He indicates two chairs where we should sit. This is the courtroom, we are the accused, but where's our solicitor? Mum's still upstairs. His back to us, he puts the kettle on. Jessie arches her eyebrows at me across the table, a look of superiority to everything, me, him, the situation. Dad's hair, from behind, is sticking up on one side at a weird angle, like one of his architectural drawings gone wrong, as if he's snatched an hour's sleep in a chair at some point and it's traumatized his hair, ironed it stiff in the wrong direction.

"I called the police," he says, and my heart sinks, I can see this is going to take a great deal more explaining than either of us thought, we're going to have to deal with the filth's patronizing reprimands as well. "But I thought better of it." Dad still has his back to us, as if it's more than he can do to look at us at the moment. He rinses the cups. "I thought, why bother them at this time of the night? If my children are stupid enough to go off with a bunch of Paleolithic bikers—and

I'm stupid enough to let them"—he turns and looks at us now—"then why waste the time of the authorities?"

I have this strange wish suddenly—strange isn't a strong enough word—that this could be a schoolday, that we could get through whatever lecturing we're going to be forced to endure, eat a token breakfast (I don't feel hungry, I think I'm hung over) and then take off for school and a day of dozing through lessons and dropping subtly misleading hints about the night's activities to whoever will listen. Except that I don't have a school right now; I'm stateless, I've got the horror prospect of starting a new one in September on top of everything else.

Dad finishes with the cups and stands watching us. He says nothing for a moment, lets the intensity of his examination pin us to our chairs, a needlelike ray that is all the more powerful because we know in the more boring, rational parts of ourselves that he's right, we were stupid, anything could have happened to us—and, in Jessie's case, did. This is what I fix on suddenly, that he's not so much angry with both of us as furious with Jessie for taking off with a reject Hell's Angel.

"You ought to have more sense, Jessica," he says at last. "Even if you think you're old enough to stay out all night flirting with the local rat pack, you should have thought about Tom. One o'clock I could have taken. Half past one, even. But you've pushed it too far. There's no point in us treating you as an adult if you're not prepared to behave like one."

"Time just ran away with us," I say, in an effort to see how much this is simply between Dad and Jessie.

"You've both got watches," he responds, his tone no less testy with me than with her.

"You don't understand what it's like," Jessie says, offering her first real defense, although she seems anything but defensive, more like the roles are reversed and she's explaining life to him. "You can't constantly look at your watch. Either you're having a good time or you're not. If you didn't want me to take Tom, you should have said so."

"Jessie," Dad says, his voice harder. "Don't try me."

"We were in good company," Jessie goes on. "It could have been a lot worse. Nick's great. He doesn't smell and he's got a job. I would have thought you might have liked him."

"If he's who I think he is," Dad says, conceding nothing, "he looks ten years too late for life. Did he give you that?"

"What?"

"That cut on your face. That didn't get there by chance. Is that his idea of a good time?"

Jessie looks at me and I look back, a dread building up in me, not that she's going to say anything about what we said but that what I'm witnessing here is somehow more fundamental than what I saw in the bathroom. Whatever Jessie thinks this is about, this is about possession. Dad thinks he possesses her, not just in the normal way that parents delude themselves that they possess their children, especially daughters—it's more complicated than that now because of what has happened. He's frightened, I can see that, and it's not something you want to see in your dad. He's frightened he's going to lose her. Or maybe he's just shit-scared about the whole thing. But he's also enjoying it, he's like her, he's high on the danger. And where am I in all this? Do I count? What does he feel about the rest of us now—are we still a family? I don't even know if I want us to be.

The kettle boils and cuts out. Jessie has taken a long time to answer. "Oh, that," she says. "I got a branch in my face on the way down to the beach. It's nothing."

Mum comes back down, Jack hanging on one tit, less bothered than any of us that the night is on its head—it's bright outside but we're all totally knackered. Dad puts tea in the pot and milk in the cups, a kind of ugly hard edge detailing every sound, even the closing of the fridge door.

"You didn't get that from a branch," Mum says, standing by Dad, supporting Jack in one arm, solidarity against the wrongdoers. She glances at me, searching for the truth, but I stare at the table, trying to find the stack of torn envelopes and postcards and the cup rings on the old wood interesting.

"Can I have a glass of water?" I ask, suddenly conscious of how foul my mouth tastes and wanting anything that will distract from the matter at hand.

"There's a glass on the drainer," Mum says, shifting to one side to let me up.

I fill the glass, turning the tap too far and spraying a fierce jet of water over the sink, the wall, me. Dad pours three cups of weak tea, too impatient to wait for it to stand, and looks inquisitorially at me as I sit back down and he hovers over a fourth. "Do you want one?" he asks. I shake my head without meeting his eye.

Mum sits down, maneuvering Jack into a comfortable position on her lap while watching us like a border guard trying to decide whether to shoot us now or later, when our backs are turned. "I think we should all drink our tea and get to bed," she advises, a trace of our grandmother's, her mother's, Polish accent slipping through as it does sometimes when she is tired or pissed off.

"Not before we've discussed precisely how we are going to resolve this," Dad says, allowing no room for argument. "You may think this is just bad news, coming home like this, and that it will pass. Well—" He looks at Jessie first, then at me. He knows how our minds work, how much we're anticipating, the short, sharp shock—no funds, no TV, how bad can it get? He goes on, "This time you're going to have to pay."

Yeah? Well, bollocks to that! I've been through these before and so has Jessie. I can't really see what the big deal is here. Compared to setting fire to the school, this is nothing. It wasn't even a good time. But Dad is enjoying it. Even in my current fallen state, I can recognize a crap line when I hear one and this is an act. Dad knows we know we're guilty; we're not stupid. Mum's right, we should go to bed and they can keep the screws tightened for a while when we get up. But this is what I thought: this is between Dad and Jessica, and I'm just caught in the crossfire.

"You're both housebound for a week," he announces. "No exceptions. No trips out, no shopping, no visits from friends, no telephone and no drinking." A frown in my direction, but I'm incidental. "And Jessie— no Nick. I know you're going to be able to do what you like in a few weeks' time, but that's then and this is now." A glance at both of us. "Is that clear?"

A moment's pause. It sounds fucking terrible to me, but I'm not going to give him any satisfaction. So we're dead for a week—so what? I scowl across at Jessica, trying to look unmoved. Her expression surprises me. She is staring at him with what at first might be hatred—instant hatred, the kind you can whip up pretty quickly when you need it. But it goes deeper than that; it's a kind of interest, I can't put my finger on it but it's a kind of excitement.

Mum, Jack and me are the fools. We might as well not be there. I don't know if Mum suspects anything—maybe not, because there's nothing obvious and it's the last thing she would suspect, I'm sure it's never even crossed her mind. But I'm stuck with it. I'm stuck with the knowledge and it turns everything to shit. I can't even get angry with him in the normal way, I can't even resent this punishment. Nothing's normal anymore.

Dad puts his hand on Mum's shoulder, breaking the spell with Jessie, resisting the impulse, thank God, to ruffle Jake's minimal hair. Mum looks tired and tense. She is usually the one who mediates in these situations, giving shape to Dad's anger, which is erratic and short-lived. But she's feeding Jake and she looks ready to accept anything that will cut this drama short.

Then Dad makes his mistake. And mine. "Have either of you got anything to say?" he asks.

Another silence. I hear myself breathing from a long way away. Saliva forms in the bottom of my mouth. My tongue prods against my teeth. My lips peel apart. The kitchen divides into irregularly shaped pieces: the pots and plates on the old enamel drainer, the dead flies in the light bowl, the cups on the table, the ponderous drip of the cold tap, the cracks in the flagstone floor, my family's faces, the ivy at the window. The fragments split and dance in space, jostling with swimming purple flecks of light.

"Yes." The whole kitchen explodes. "Go fuck yourself."

■

12

Sometimes it's worse when they don't get angry. You provoke a response, you demand attention, emotion, balls. You have to give a little bit of your life to get angry with someone. When you cross the edge and nothing happens there's something wrong. You don't want permission to piss around.

So Dad must really be off course not to rise to that. If Jessie had said it at this particular moment, I think he would have slapped her, which is not something I can remember him doing in a long time, but the rules have changed, they look like they want damage, those two, they're locked into something like two fighters circling each other, jabbing for first blood.

But I said it, and Dad's self-control is the last thing I want. He stands there, waiting, letting me reflect on my words, watching Mum to see if she's going to comment but she's less excited by language than action. "You're tired," he tells me finally. "And it's our fault. Go to bed."

■

And in the bathroom, trying to clean the shit out of my mouth, Mum makes a point of hugging me—sternly, to let me know that this has been a hard night all round, but a hug just the same. "Why do you always make things worse for yourself?" she asks, the voice of my childhood when I used to drive them both wild ripping up papers, drawings, court documents.

I almost want to cry and I swallow some toothpaste trying not to. It would be so easy just to sink into her arms instead of resisting the cuddle, maintaining my stance, the struggle, my independence. How can I tell her that nothing is all right, it's all bad and getting worse? Would she believe me anyway? Do I want her to know? She ought to—I need her to, I need her help. I don't know how much more I can handle on my own, but the weird thing is I don't want it to stop. Not now, not at the moment. I'm tired and my eyes are stinging and the toothpaste has burned my throat, but when I'm not tired, when I'm fresh and awake and reasonably conscious, what I have to fight, the feeling of my life slipping away and the summer holidays sinking toward term time and hell, is Dad and Jessie.

Mum has stopped holding me. She's standing watching me in the mirror, loving me, she never stops loving me. But she can't stop the system that grinds us all down and maybe Dad and Jessie can, they should be able to fuck the machinery if anyone can. I don't know what I'm thinking anymore, except that I think I need the idea of Dad and Jessie in my mind like I need London. While it's only me who knows, in a way I control it.

The birds are singing outside. Mum's in the mirror and so is the bath, but this is a different angle and Dad's still in the kitchen and Jessie's upstairs and it's not raining and she's not sloshing water over his peeled-back foreskin.

I could tell her now, but I don't.

13

Sometimes when the cells in my body are really buzzing and the blood's pumping and I'm feeling truly insane, I know that the weather is just another part of my dream. I create everything—you, me, my parents, day, night, this shitty cottage, the mosquito spattered on the bedroom wall, the ugly old woman from the village who walks past our scrawny front garden at least three times every day and squints in with eyes diseased with resentment and age and a life which has either turned her into an aching sour cunt or was something she never understood, never grasped, in the first place. Is this suffering all my doing? I must have tumors warping my brain. I want to start again, clean. Scrub this out, dig the pen in deep as I scribble over and over and over again, eradicating it, removing the pain.

So the weather's my fault too. And it's weird, it's like me, up and down, changing every minute, blowing hot, cold, gray, black. I lie on my bed trying to listen to a tape or read a comic book or squeeze my eyes shut and make myself stoned, and the weather keeps getting in the way. Sunlight flashes in through the window like photographic arc lamps, blazing hot for a moment, then dimming as the sky darkens and a wind shoves dishwater clouds across the sky. Minutes pass and it's bright again and I can feel the heat nudging me, edging into the room. Then thunder, great intestinal cracks from the sky, and it pisses down, torrents of rain beating against the earth, smashing the grass down, pummeling everything in its reach, wanting—and I understand this—to hurt.

Lucy comes, soaked to the skin, and rattles on to Mum for hours about her aunt in France and then starts vacuuming, and I wish I could control her, my creation, better. I've been shut inside for three days, allowed out only within a short radius of the cottage like a dog on an extending but finite lead, and the flashes of light have just been false holes in the prison sky, impossible to get to grips with, insufficient to recharge my failed batteries.

Her hair smells when she comes into my room and she seems to have grown larger, firmer, as if she's been exercising, toning up for more vacuuming or whatever else it is that she does with her time. I don't shift from the bed. If Lucy is my invention, her damp and wrinkled clothes will simply cease to exist, her jaw will lose the bored, slightly clenched set it has to it and she'll vacuum me with her mouth, the cord tying us together in an unmanageable, flailing heap. But she goes on and I lie there listening to noises coming through my headphones, music starting and starting again, jerking forward and back like my life, words drumming in my head meaning nothing. "You can't tell me what it's like to be black in England," I think, as I listen to a singer using New York music to describe Notting Hill. "Because you've got a fucking record contract and you wear a baseball cap with your band's name on it."

"What?" I hear my own voice, muffled, a surprise. I don't know what I'm saying.

Her mouth moves again. Sadly, not on me. She shouts, "Feeling sorry for yourself then?"

"Not very."

She doesn't switch off the vacuum cleaner. I don't turn off the tape. "I hear you had yourselves a party."

"Oh, yeah?"

"You didn't invite me."

She stands, arching her neck to get rid of an ache, eyes tired, no longer looking at me. I keep the headset off my ears for a moment, but she says nothing else, sticks the vacuum head under the bed, knocking the dulled metal side quite aggressively, breathing over me a dry waft of stale cigarettes, her eyes meeting mine only once, no message I can discern. If she's my invention, she doesn't know it.

■

And where's Jessie in all of this? How does she take to her incarceration? Like a bat to water, like salvation to a crime. She switches into a different mode, using the time available to even things up with Mum, sticking and unsticking an endless flow of disposable nappies, singing to Jake to knock him out, generally being more companionable than she has been of late, though not so much that it's obvious.

I watch her with Dad, to see if it's a cover, to see if they're just faking this punishment—she's taking it too well, there must be more to it. But they keep their distance, not showing any particular resentment or interest, no sustained, message-laden eye contact that I can catch, no sudden flare-ups, not even much body contact, which in itself is unusual for Jessie. She seems suddenly domesticated, teenage-mum time again, like one of those awful ex-punk blondes (not that Jessie could ever be blond) who discover family life. Jessie has a side to her that could almost settle for a Chelsea existence, married to a stockbroker or some other wimp criminal from the City, except that I think she'd chain him to the bath taps after three weeks and go mad after four. The domesticity is a pose and it's one I can find only two motives for.

"You're either feeling guilty or you're groveling and it's a sickening sight," I tell her in one of my more foul-tempered moments locked inside the cottage's storm-blackened gloom.

But Jessie is unreachable. "You're not handling this well," she says. "It's like pain. Go with it. Enjoy the punishment. You have to want denial. Otherwise it's boring."

The ultimate sin. Nothing is boring for Jessie, she won't allow it. I don't even know if she cares about not seeing Nick or if pretending she doesn't is a way of double-thinking Dad, making him feel more uneasy than if she were fretting over the situation. If Dad is what's important to her, she's not showing it—unless she is by not showing it. Maybe she's sucking up to Mum to freak him out? I don't know. I just know she is not my invention. Lucy, I might have managed, but Jessie, no way. I couldn't invent her. She cannot be another part of me because I haven't got it, I don't have her cool, it's all head-on confrontation for me—but Jessie, life bends to meet Jessie's will, life is something she strokes until it comes.

■

14

Day five of the life sentence. Late afternoon. It's rained all day but suddenly the sun has come out and it's hot, so Jessie and I have set ourselves up outside. She's got her ghetto blaster playing endless bloody reggae and I've erected three deckchairs because Mum is going to join us, we all want reconciliation now. Dad is inside, intermittently screaming down the telephone at his London office, barricaded inside the living room against what is apparently a real crisis, as opposed to the crises which occur once a month. He still loves it, fuck him. He loves the attention, even if it comes as trouble.

Jack is wailing upstairs and Jessie has gone to sort him out, all part of the war effort. Mum flaps down the kitchen step, having failed to find the other wooden sandal she's been searching for, and sits next to me, impressed to find me reading.

"What's it about?"

"It's about death. Drilling holes in your head." Actually it's about cricket, but even that seems like a form of death right now.

"Why don't you read the books I buy you?" Mum sips the drink she has brought out with her. I know there is nothing I could read that would shock her. I bought *The Story of O* when I was ten, but her only reaction was that I'd find it too intellectual.

"Because you buy me books I don't want to read."

Jessie appears with Jack's carrycot and hovers over us, supporting it awkwardly with one hand underneath, the other holding the straps.

"Do you think, if we put a towel underneath it, it would be dry enough?" she asks, dragging the grass with her bare feet and finding it wet despite the sun.

"Wait a moment," says Mum and she goes off to get a bath towel, which I could have done only I'm not into Jessie's play-ball-with-the-screws number.

"You know Jack's secret?" Jessie asks as Mum returns, spreading our ropiest towel on the ground in the shade of one of the chairs. "He wants to be at the center of everything all the time. He was screaming because he was upstairs on his own. The best place for him would be in with Dad, listening to the bullshit." She sits down. Mum is fussing over Jack, who throws an ugly glance in my direction. Jessie pouts at him, pulling her T-shirt over her head to point her brown tits at the sun. "He's totally sweet."

"He's part of the same disease that we are," I say, staring at Jessie's skin, which is dark, foreign, usable—not like my prissy English anemia.

But Mum and Jessie ignore me, Jessie turning up the Rasta music she uses like a drug so that Mum can't even hear me. Mum sits down again, stretching her legs out and reaching for her glass. There's a dead fly floating where the ice cubes have melted but she doesn't seem to care.

"You drink too much," I shout above the noise, looking for an argument, conversation, anything. "You and Dad. You're always drinking."

She smiles, puts the glass down beside her. "Are you surprised? It's parenthood. You try it."

"Jessie'll get there first at the rate she's going," I say, suddenly struck by the horror of the thought—I wasn't thinking specifically of Dad, but what if his sperm made a baby inside her? No, Jessie takes microestrogen or something. Does she? I'm not sure. Anyway, no one listens.

I stare at the book in my lap. I've got my swimming trunks on and there's a spot on my thigh just where the corner of the book is touching it, headless, the muck spread out under the skin in a welt, impossible to squeeze. Jessie talks to Mum over the grinding reggae, every track the same, and I tie a line between the rotting cells in my leg and the tree by the collapsing stone wall at the end of the garden. It had leaves less than a week ago and now it's dead. The few that are left are gray and yellow at the edges, their texture turned to paper. We're not halfway through August and something's wrong, not just with my life but with all the systems, natural, man-made, whatever. Or is it me, am I the only one, is everyone else having a ball?

"Penelope's brother is selling his car," my sister informs my mother as Jamaican poverty thumps out of Japanese plastic on a Devon lawn.

"It's a brilliant soft-top Morris, lime green, you saw it when she came to pick me up that day. Do you think there's any chance . . . ?"

"Yes?" My mother sounds only half interested. She has her eyes closed; she looks beautiful like that, vulnerable.

I sit musing over how Jessie came by that particular piece of information about Penelope's brother since we're banned from using the phone and she hasn't received any letters that I'm aware of. But Jessie always has ways.

She scratches one armpit, then on down to a rubbery nipple. She looks at me. I look away. "Well, Dad said that, when I can drive next year, you'd get me a car. I know it's a bit early, but it's the only one like it, I used to see it all over London, you could spot it everywhere, I don't think they can clamp it. It's perfect."

She waits. Mum doesn't open her eyes, but she tilts her head in Jessie's direction, "I wouldn't mention it at the moment if I were you," she says. "Not quite yet."

And Jessica bites a finger, running her teeth thoughtfully up and down it in the absence of anything else, timing this conversation perfectly, helped by the insistent distraction of a driven black voice intoning a song which seems to consist entirely of listing the chapters and verse of the Old Testament. It doesn't ring true. She doesn't. It's as if she's trying to react as she normally would in this situation, trying to reassure Mum that she's got the same preoccupations as any girl her age—any spoiled middle-class brat, as we both are.

"Do you think Dad means it about Nick?" she goes on, closing her eyes now, screwing them up as she faces the sun. I move my legs, impatient with her, and knock my book on the grass, tipping Mum's drink over.

"You know your father as well as I do," Mum says, watching me right her glass and not offer to get more. The music rocks on, music to praise Haile Selassie to, music to start a riot. "You haven't mentioned Nick before, have you? What's he like?"

Jessie frowns, eyes still closed, the toes of one foot clenching and unclenching on the ground, wearing away at the grass, digging a hole with her big toe. I get up.

"He wasn't interesting before," she says.

■

And upstairs I'm on my own. Dad is shut away below me arguing over steel or titanium cladding or something, dredging out the drawings and files that had been dumped in the musty under-stairs cupboard when we arrived here. Mum, Jessica and Jake are safe outside, baking now that we're back to fission heat, not likely to move except to pee and, later, get dinner. I'm on my own and I know what I'm doing. I'm not a victim, I'm not going to be a victim, I've got to take this matter in hand. Jessie is confident about every situation, except sometimes she's not, just occasionally there's a chink in her armor when she thinks she's not beautiful, when she thinks she's not blessed, when the world falls apart and she can't fight it and she's alone and anonymous and the smallest thing could crush her, reduce her to nothing, a hole, a mistake, a blob of human fear. I know that feeling—I can't say I have it all the time, but I'm familiar with it, far more so than her, and it's because of that that I'm still frightened by the possibility that Dad may be the one, that Jessie is wrong, this is his sickness. I don't know which is worse, whether I want them both to be guilty, or one, or whether I really think they're guilty or sick at all. So far they haven't hurt me, not reached out and torn my skin, burrowed into my head with a power drill. They're in my head but it's all inside, it hasn't broken through the bone yet one way or another—and it's what happens when it does that worries me. But maybe it's not sick, maybe Jessie's right, there shouldn't be any boundaries. Maybe incest is safe sex in the world of AIDS.

But I've got to move forward, I can't just sit back and let it all run away from me. I need to know what's happening, it's worse not knowing. And at the moment I don't know. At the moment Dad and Jessie are playing charades for Mum's benefit, and maybe for mine—does Dad know I know? Jessie won't stop. Even if Dad started it, she won't stop. However it started, this is too dangerous for her to want to give it up. I could see Dad chickening out—maybe—though he's a lot like Jessie, she took his madness and amplified it. But not Jessie. I've got to stop it.

So I'm looking for clues. I'm alone in her room feeling a charge in my heart as scary as if I were committing a real crime. I'm sweating with the excitement, leaving little damp patches where my soles have been, but it's too urgent to put some shoes on now or to grab some jeans to stop the trickles running down my legs. She's a few feet away, diagonally down in the garden, and she's extra sensitive, Jessie. If I'm not careful, her antennae will prick and she'll know better than me what I'm looking for and whether she has anything to fear from what I might find.

The room isn't a mess but somehow it isn't tidy either. I pass it all the time and yet now it feels more foreign than ever, I'm trespassing, I am the intruder. The bed's rumpled and she's left a pile of her jewelry in the middle of it, some the stuff she makes herself—all spikes, teeth and coils, like a tribal punishment—and the rest stuff that Mum has given her or men have given her or she's stolen. Her cardboard boxes are all round the room, waiting to go back to London and art college, and there's a new picture stuck on the window, cutting down on the light coming in through the small panes, giving the fleeting impression of a shrine. I haven't seen it before and it's amazing—a head-and-shoulders portrait of Jessie, clumsy, like a graffiti cartoon, yet it's her, there's something in the daubed mouth and slashed eyes which is Jessie when all the hunger's there, when nothing is enough, she can't push herself far enough. It's signed "Sonny" and there's the Greek infinity symbol underneath the name. It makes me feel strange, that someone else can see her like that, paint her that clearly. It makes me feel as if she's watching me now, watching my smallness as I slide out the drawers of the old dresser which still has the lace cover that was here when we came, part buried now under a pile of Jessie's makeup and cassettes.

I go through the drawers quickly: two filled with clothes, nearly all black, some underwear, boxes of tampons, unopened packs of tights and ankle socks, a tin of oil pastels and scalpels, more makeup. The bottom drawer has a different character to it, stashed with Jessie's shoes and belts and two packs of condoms and a pair of what look like elbow-length black rubber gloves that I didn't know she had, plus a buff-colored envelope which may be the treasure I am seeking—letters, information, evidence. But there's nothing inside of much use, just some unwritten postcards from various galleries, empty envelopes with foreign postmarks and pointless messages scrawled in a variety of hands—"The burglar alarm just went off, LB"; "Keep crossing the

Albert Bridge"—and books of matches from cafes and bars I've never even heard of.

I shove it all back in and go back to the drawer above, drawn there suddenly by the tin of crayons and blades. It doesn't fit somehow. I take out the scalpels and dig underneath, the crayons rattling against the box. There's pencil shavings and other shit at the bottom but there's also a folded-up wadge of paper which when I open it out contains cocaine. I taste it. I've had it before—I think. I was never sure if it was the real thing. This seems to be, and this is something—the fact that Jessica keeps cocaine in her bedroom might be something, but it's not what I'm looking for. I'm not sure what I'm looking for but I'm looking. I fold it up and put it back, my tongue wiping my teeth, numbed.

The reggae pumps up from the garden again after a pause in which I die for a moment and Jessie changes tapes. I glance at the picture of her, which seems bored now, as if I'm wasting her time. I close the drawers of the dresser and look around, deciding that to go through the cardboard boxes is just an impossible task. Trying not to let the floorboards creak too much, I go down on my knees and peer under the bed, my ear and nose brushing against the slightly sour-smelling old rug which, like everything else, came with the cottage.

There's nothing under there, just more shoes and a heap of Jessie's paintings, all different sizes and scraps of paper piled up, the bigger ones on top sagging over smaller ones underneath. I pull them out, disturbing a spider which nearly scares the shit out of me. I would have left them where they were but the one on top is just weird. In fact, it's a very dull picture by Jessie's standards. No figures, no flesh, no pain. Most of Jessie's pictures are like her—all impact. She wants to worry you, she wants to get you going. This one does, but in a different way. It's just a railway line, wasteland, dingy houses, under a drunken mackerel sky—but it's my railway line, my sky, my London. It's like looking at a moment in time that was mine, not hers, and I'm fucked if I know how she knew about it. Jessie doesn't see like this, I'm sure of it. She's too busy being Jessie. So why did she paint it? Am I that transparent? Does she break into my thoughts while I'm asleep?

I quickly sort through the others to see if there are any more little surprises for me. The paper is mostly stiff with paint and smells funny, dry, powdery—memories of flames licking the art department stockroom. There are some houses on top, all done in Caribbean colors but without the brilliance of the head-and-shoulders of Jessie that Sonny or whoever it was did. Still, this all comes as news to me—I didn't know Jessie did houses, I didn't know that anything that couldn't sweat or fuck interested her. There are a couple of collages in the middle, cut out from magazines, the images small and oddly disturbing, twisted and contorted in intricate patterns, but they're nothing special. I almost give up, then I lift a crumpled and dog-eared sheet of dull green paper and underneath find the gold, though it doesn't look like gold—it doesn't look like anything much at first. It's a chalk sketch, the soft, grainy white lines leading nowhere until I realize that the scribbled mass is hair and the rest of it takes on a solidity that is a cock in close-up, extreme close-up, sort of halfway through raising itself, neither limp nor properly hard, the foreskin still folded hoodlike over the end.

It's not just this one—one would be nothing—it's what follows that freaks me out. To see a prick the way she sees it, and she's really studied them. This is something she cares about, these pictures aren't for effect, she wanted to get at something. There's a whole stash of them and the detail turns me cold. It's too much. Whose are they? Is it all the same one? A couple have a hand in them, beautifully drawn, drawn better than I thought Jessie knew how. The prick—or pricks—are unidentifiable, but the hand is Dad's. The skin is old, older than Nick's or any of Jessie friends' (unless she has some buzz for older men that I don't know about; anything is possible), but the clincher is Dad's ring, clearly visible, tight up against a familiarly swollen knuckle. The hand isn't doing anything in one of the pictures but in the other it's holding the penis and that makes me sick. It's posed, he sat there or lay there while she sketched it, holding his dick for his daughter to draw. I'm stupid, I'm naive, I don't know how the world works. Maybe all dads are like this? I don't know him, maybe I don't know anybody. There's a gulf between us all—me and him, Jessie and me, Mum and me—but it won't swallow me up like I want it to, it won't open its jaws wide enough to take me in, it just makes me feel more outside. I can't feel the horror enough, it's a failure in me—I want it to hurt and it won't. Not enough.

The music has stopped. I feel panicked again—Jessie could be on her way up here now. I leap up and cross to the window, the pictures heaped on the floor in two piles—the prick pictures and the others.

Down in the garden, Jessie is still in her deck chair, sitting with Mum and Jake like a normal daughter, soaking up the sun. No danger. But there's a fourth figure, the old woman from the village, standing by the wall on the road side, staring at Jessie's brazen bare tits with evil eyes and cackling to Mum with words I can't hear but can imagine. Mum is mediating in her best fashion, playing it quiet and slow, and Jessie's obviously enjoying the old bint's nuttiness, though she looks just a little uneasy. The fact is, although the old woman is something of a local curiosity, she's part of a trend. We're not really liked here—not really liked. They're polite and all that, but we don't quite fit in, not even among the other aliens, the rebaptized city dwellers who've come to the country to renew their bigotry. We're a little too odd, a little too private—already I know that I'm going to have to put up one hell of a show at school to convince them that I'm a real scumbag, it's something I've worked for, not simply my birthright. We haven't taken down here as a family and, quite frankly, I'm not surprised.

I feel safe now. I feel in charge—a moment's pause makes all the difference. I gather up the prick pictures and push the others back under the bed. This is going to give Jessie something to think about. When she finds what's missing, she's going to shit a brick.

It's my game now and we're going to play by my rules.

15

Jessie's room again. It's dark, two o'clock in the morning and everyone's asleep except me. Her windows are open, the curtains half drawn to let in some air, though there's a stillness in the room to match the stillness outside. No sounds, no dog barking, no village traffic, not even a far-off owl or twittering bat or any of those country sounds you're supposed to be able to hear. London is not like this. In London, there's always someone walking the street, a thug, a partygoer, some poor homeless sod whose life is now a can of Carlsberg, a filthy coat over his face and his hand down his pants trying to scratch away the lice. This village is dead, it makes me care about nothing, I just want to get out, I don't care what the rest of my life is like as long as it's not lived here.

Jessie is sleeping in her bed, her face turned toward me. She's asleep. I can't but she can, that's how it works. She looks a step ahead of me even in sleep, her mouth curled down and open slightly over her teeth, ready to launch any argument I might present into space and convince me that nothing is what it seems. The pictures must still be under the bed—the ones I left. I don't know if she knows I've got the others yet, but if she does she's given no sign of it. I hestiate, standing over her, scanning the room in the darkness. Mum and Dad are asleep the other side of the landing and I don't want them to hear me. I especially don't want Jake to hear me. I've pushed the door shut but have wedged one of Jessie's shoes between the door edge and the frame. I'm wearing nothing but a pair of running shorts but I'm sweating despite the fact that a chill blade of fear is working its way between my bones, making me feel that this is a mistake, I should forget about everything and turn a blind eye, things can only get worse for me.

But that's what I want. If I'm stuck with it, it must be, right? I must want life to get worse, it's only by getting worse that we'll get away from here and everything will change. Jessie, you make life difficult for me. I fucking worship you and you mess us all around. You lie there sleeping like a perfect being, immune to the chaos you create, and I have to decide what to do. There's no one to turn to on this, so I'm blaming you because you're the only one I can reach.

There's no light in my hand but I switch it on. The glare is powerful, blinding, the heat instant. I ram it in your face—spit it out, make your promises and your repentance! She's only half awake and already I'm slapping her hard, sharp, a quick blow across one cheek, a heavier one across the other. The cut is still on her mouth from where I scratched her on the beach. I should have scratched harder. She won't understand unless I can make her feel the pain—and I can't feel any until she does.

I take her by the shoulders and shake her. She lifts herself off the bed, bleary-eyed, listening to what I'm saying. If only I had that light I could press it in her face, sweat it out of her, make her see what this is doing to me, to all of us as a family.

She sits up. I shove her back. "You're weird, Tom," she tells me. "It's not happening now. Go to sleep. I won't let it hurt you."

Why should I believe her? "Have you told Dad I know?"

"I'm not crazy." She sits up again, brushing me aside, turning and digging a determined elbow into her pillow. "Of course I haven't."

Her voice is a whisper, hoarse, sharp, she wants to get rid of me. I sit on the bed. She lies back wearily, keeping her arms above the sheet which is her only covering, pushing it down to her navel to cool off, maybe to reinforce the suggestion that she wants to be left alone to sleep.

"How can I trust you?" I ask. "I want you to say it's stopped, but how can I ever believe you again?"

"You've got to find a way."

"Why should I?"

Jessie's head is on the pillow. I have a view of her chin, then shadow and just the glint of her eyes. "No one was meant to know about this, it wasn't meant to hurt you." She cranes her neck to look at me, tries to sound close, like we used to. "This is between Dad and me. It's over. If you can put it out of your mind, it's as if it never happened."

What she's saying is true, but it doesn't help. Because it's not true, it's only true on one level, it's convenient, but she's a liar and a cheat and she's betrayed everyone closest to her. They both have. How could they do it? Sex must be better than love, better than money, better than anything for them to have wanted to do it this much. They must have wanted to, they must have thought about us and said, "Yes, fuck it, let's do it. Let's do it anyway. They'll survive, they'll never know."

I'm quiet. I keep my voice low. I don't need histrionics, I'm in control now. I throw myself over Jessie so fast she's stunned. I pin her to the bed, pressing her arms down by her side, moving my mouth so it's over her face. I could bite her nose off, it's in the way, it's getting between us, obstructing what I want to say to her. I let her wait, listening to my own breath, listening to her silence. She doesn't struggle, this kind of thing must happen to Jessie all the time, the way she behaves.

"Jessie—" My voice is dry. I try to squeeze it out of my throat, make it sound threatening. I am threatening her, I mean it. "I've seen the pictures. The pictures you did of Dad. I've got them."

"Yes?"

"I want you to stop. You must stop, I'll make you. I'll take them to the police. I'll tell Mum."

"The police wouldn't be interested."

"I hate the bastards. But I'll go if I have to. I think they would. I think especially here, they'd love to bust open a family like us. They think we're sick already."

She's hot beneath me. Her arms are rigid, maybe ready to throw me off, but I've got my hands locked over her wrists, she's not going to get anywhere without a struggle and that would wake Mum and Dad. I sense a movement in the curtains, but I wait and it's nothing.

"Get off me, will you?" She tries to lift herself up a little. I don't let her. "You're acting like a child."

"I'll tell Dad if I have to. I'll tell him I know and I'll tell him I've got the pictures. I'd rather tell him than Mum." I'm working this out as I go along. "And I'll tell him about the coke."

This doesn't worry her. What proof would I have? She could get rid of it before I'm even past her door.

"What is it you want me to say? I've told you we've stopped."

"No, you haven't." What promise can I extract from her? There isn't one. I force my weight on her, pushing my bony chest onto her ribs beneath her breasts.

"Look," she pants, "it hasn't happened much. It was something we tried. I wish we hadn't. It's too complicated. I'm more interested in Nick. You think Dad's that exciting?"

"You told me he was. You told me he was brilliant. Either you were lying then or you're lying now."

"Why should I want Dad when I can have Nick? Dad's old."

"He's not that old."

I think about this. She's starting to confuse me. I relax my weight a little, my grip. I feel her breathe, sucking in air, forcing my chest up with hers. She looks at me, eyes like slits, her voice different, less worried.

"It's not going to happen again," she says. "I promise. It'll be all right. It's Nick I'm interested in. At least until London. I mean he's not perfect, he's incredibly insecure, but he fucks well. He's great physically. The minute this stupid week is finished, I'm seeing him, he can't stop me. You know that—he can't stop me?"

Suddenly she's talking about Dad the way she always has, as a force to be manipulated, to be defied or won over. Maybe she means it about Nick. They were gone long enough. But I can't imagine him insecure. The thing about Nick that comes into my mind if I think about him is a quiet calmness. I would have thought he'd be very sure with Jessie—out of his depth, who isn't, but still very strong and confident.

I lie on her thinking this through. She's quiet, she doesn't interrupt. I can feel her breathing, relaxed now, waiting. The room is still, not the slightest waft from the curtains, just the two of us stretched on the bed, no movement, no creaks.

But then there's a sound outside on the landing. Someone is getting up, they must have heard us. No. The steps are on the stairs, going down. I can't tell if it's Mum or Dad. Jessie and I are frozen, holding our breaths to hear. There's a knock from the bathroom as the loo seat is lowered, then a tinkling sound, more a falling than a jet so it's probably Mum. She flushes. Water trickles from a tap and there's a muted thumping from the cistern or the tank as it fills up. Then silence and Jessie and I tense up. Nothing for a moment, then a click as the bathroom cabinet is closed, I think. Silence again. More steps on the stairs, coming closer now. The room hangs in the air as she comes past. Will she look in? No. The steps turn away, there are some dim, muffled sounds, then a murmur from Jake, half a cry, not much, then the sense more than the sound that he is feeding.

My mouth stretches into a strained smile of relief, though my heart's thumping and I don't know what I'm relieved about. Jessie eases me off her and I don't resist. I straighten up on the bed and sit over her, but then she slides out and gets up, moving silently to the window. She stands there naked, her back to me.

"I've still got the pictures," I whisper, barely audible but needing to reassert myself somehow. "Don't forget that."

"I won't." She glances back at me.

Maybe she'll try to find them, I think. But they're well hidden, not even in my room, down behind a pried-loose panel of wood at the bottom of the stairs—next to where Dad's work drawings are stored, but not actually in the under-stairs cupboard.

I get off the bed, looking round the room as if there's something I've forgotten. Jessie is still at the window, in front of the dark rectangle of Sonny's portrait of her but her head angled past it, staring out at the village. I move to go. She turns.

"You're thinking about this too much," she says, her voice almost a hiss. We can hear Mum soothing Jake. "I'm worried about you."

I stop in my tracks. It's another one of her classics, not really believable. "You should be," I tell her.

"No, I mean you're concentrating too much energy on the wrong things. This is something that's over, it can't be changed. You ought to concentrate on your own life more. I know," she says before I can stop her, "this is as much about you as me and I'm sorry, I am sorry. But you should be careful."

I feel awkward suddenly. She can do that to me. I feel a hole somewhere gaping in me, an emptiness. "What do you mean?"

"I mean you're too serious, you're too hostile. All right, I deserve that at the moment, but it's not good for you."

I can hardly hear her. I'm not sure I want to. I cross the room back toward her, just to say this: "You're really concerned about what's good for me, aren't you? You and Dad. Did you ever think about the rest of us before you started? I don't know how the hell it did start but you certainly weren't showing how much you cared for me."

Jessie faces me in the darkness, leaning down to scratch her leg. She's totally naked but she might as well be driving a tank for all the impact I've made on her. But I've got the pictures and that must make a difference.

"Life doesn't have to be a constant battle," she whispers. "The week's almost finished. Get out. Spend some time with Caz's brother." She looks at me, right through me. "Go and see Lucy." I blush. She sees everything, she gives me a sick feeling in my stomach. "I think she might be interested if you approached her right."

"Fuck off!"

"Do you want me to have a word with her?"

She's doing it again. I thought this was my confrontation, she's meant to be on the defensive—but she's turning the tables. She can't let it stop until she feels she's on top. I walk away. Jake is wailing now in the other room and Mum must have her hands full trying to quieten him. Jessie takes advantage of the cover to throw a thought at me, spoken so I can hear it clearly, so it knocks around my brain.

"Do you think she wanks in the toilet?"

"What?"

"Lucy?" I can feel Jessie smiling at the back of my neck. "Do you think Lucy wanks in the toilet when she's feeling neglected? I do." And she scratches her pubic hair as I turn, to point out to me how it's done.

I struggle to block my mind from thinking about anything but Jessie and the power she has over me. I don't want to hear things like that about Lucy—but I do, and about herself, I like her to try and shock me, to open doors I didn't know were there. She's an evil little cunt but she's my sister and all she's doing is driving me nuts.

Jake has stopped crying. Mum must have heard us, some of it, but if so why hasn't she come through? If she came through now, it would all have to come out, there'd be a way of telling her, I'd have to, but she doesn't.

I'm at the door. There's no one on the landing. Mum and Dad's room is quiet, no voice asking, "Who is that? What are you two doing out there?" Jessie is back on her bed, sitting on it, one leg on the floor, the other curled up, her foot almost in her lap.

"Remember, I've got the pictures," I say and I go back to my room, not even very quietly, the floorboards creaking and my mind all over the place, not caring, making myself not care. That's the thing: not to care.

16

So Mum asks me what's wrong. "What's wrong?" she says when I spend a couple more days moping around the house even after our internment has ended. "What is it? Is it being here? Is it really that bad?"

"Yes."

We're on our own together. She's sorting through a stack of photographs of Jake, choosing ones to have copied for relatives. The TV is on on the kitchen counter, an Australian soap opera with some young beach blonde in her knickers but they all look the same. Mum's face is alive as she looks at the pictures, a delicate smile hovering on her lips, real delight showing there, this is her escape, this is her baby, she doesn't need the rest of us. She looks at me, reading my thoughts— everyone can do that.

"Talk to me, Tom. Is it the baby? Does that make you feel different?"

She's astute, my mum. She likes people, she's genuinely fascinated by them. I wonder if she fucks her clients? I've often thought she must, she and Dad have their own lives so much and he's always been a bastard, I bet—I mean he used to seem like God to me and still could, almost, but he's also like Jessie, selfish, able to justify anything to himself. If Mum did make love to one of her clients I think it would be important to her, it wouldn't be something she'd enter into lightly. With Dad it's just greed, he's a slobbering prick, he doesn't give a shit either.

"I know this hasn't been a good summer for you," Mum says, watching me, making me want to cry stupidly but I don't. "You didn't want this move but you're stuck with it and you've behaved pretty well, really." Have I? This must be a mother's eyes. Whatever, it's distressing to hear good of yourself.

"It won't be forever," she says. She holds a strip of negatives up to the light to identify a frame. "We'll go back to London. That's what you want, isn't it?"

This sounds surprisingly definite. But perhaps she's just trying to make me feel better. She doesn't know, how can she when I won't tell her?

It's all nonsense, like the shouting match on TV, two bad Australian actors trying to act emotional. It's all crap, except the part that hurts and that doesn't fucking hurt enough.

"What's the point of me going through the horror of starting a new school if I have to leave the dump after a term or two?" I ask. "I mean I know I don't exactly have the most brilliant record with educational establishments, but this is doomed from day one."

"I know." She puts the negatives down and writes numbers in a box on the flap. She looks at me, her mouth open in a pout that's a lot like Jessie's for a moment, only more concerned. Mum cares, she feels for me, but just not enough to go to war on my behalf. "It's a good school," she says. "You might like it."

How can I tell her? She doesn't want to know about Jessie and Dad, it will destroy her. She's got her baby and she's got her career and she thinks she's still got us in the background and she's probably happier now than she has been for years—I ought to be glad that someone is.

Why? "I might be miserable," I point out, no surprises, she's used to me like this. "I'm good at that. I get a lot of practice."

■

I'm not alone, at least I know that. Other people are unhappy, maybe more so. This village is a sham, the quiet lives everyone leads. Only this evening the television news had the story of another village, not so different, where someone went mad with a gun and topped all the old familiar faces—his neighbors, his teacher, his parents and finally himself. Was his dad skewering his sister, or did he have another excuse? What good is life if everyone else can lose theirs so easily? It's rubbish, it's more Australian soap opera. I sit in my bedroom with the lights turned out and the window open and for once I think I can hear the sea and I wonder if I could do it, if I could just get a gun and open fire indiscriminately, and then I wonder why I don't—is it just some chemical in my brain and in most other people's that stops us from acts like these? Is it just some component of my blood preventing me from crossing the edge, or even now are Dad and Jessie not clear enough targets for me?

■

17

Jessie is seeing Nick but that means nothing.

■

I'm playing cricket. I'm doing what she suggested, hanging out with Neil, Caz's brother, knocking a ball about with his mates. There's a green of sorts down behind the car park on the approach to the beach, flatter than any other spot in the village and well placed for watching for approaching problems if we decide to break for a quick spliff. Neil's mates seem virtually subhuman, hopeless cases, but they can play cricket and Simon, whose brother's a fucking police cadet, seems to have an excellent source of shit, no doubt recycled from the porkers' training college.

My side's just about bowled out when Jessie and Nick appear on the bike, rolling into the car park as I make a run, so that I glimpse them through a haze of sweat and spliff-brightened colors and think—even in that instant—that this is a setup, she's brought him here for the sole purpose of being seen by me, she watches my movements as much as I watch hers. I slide into the wicket, wrenching a muscle in my leg, only to find that I'm too late, I'm out, my concentration's gone, I must have walked the last two yards.

Jessie is wearing her jeans with the seat cut out and, while I try to ignore her and keep my back to her, half the team is glancing her way, unable to keep their minds on the game.

"Your sister, isn't it?" says the Einstein of the bunch.

"I wish she was my sister," Simon says, rubbing the cricket ball against his leg.

"Yeah?" I say, trying to watch her and not to watch her. "Come on, let's play!"

But my mind is working overtime, struggling through its stoned clutter to decide what it is Jessie wants me to think. She knows I'm not going to be easily convinced by a chance appearance right under my nose. Unless I'm being too complicated—but I don't think so. I move next to Neil as we wait to take over the bowling and position myself so that I can see Jessie and Nick walk on to the beach, climb the first ridge of pebbles, then drop out of sight.

"Fuck, you look rough," Neil says to me as I aim a ball of spit at the grass. "Are you sure you're up to bowling?"

"No problem," I say, trying to clean my mouth out by sucking air hard through clenched teeth. I can see them both now on the next ridge, against the sea. He puts his hand on her shoulder, she slips hers round his leg.

Simon nudges me on the back, passing another joint. "I wouldn't want to get high with you in a boat," he says and laughs.

By the time I've had my over, Nick and Jessie have come back from the beach and climbed halfway up the hill toward the cliff, my sanity haven, she probably knows about that too—if this is all a put-up job she'd add her little twist to it, bonk him in broad daylight in my most private spot. But they disappear before they get there, they just step out of view over the edge, which makes me think for a moment how steep the hill is there, are they nuts enough to jump? That doesn't fit with anything, though, so I cool it for a few minutes and pretend to watch the ball, then I say to Neil, "Yeah, I do feel a bit rough. Think I'll take a walk. My mind's just not there."

Neil and the others hardly notice as I take off, walking backward for a bit toward the car park to show I'm still interested. I stagger on to the pebbles, feeling weird, watching for Jessie and Nick, but they're still out of sight so I may have lost them. Then I start jogging along, clumsily, lurching into dips, and I see how steep the hillside is as it becomes a cliff and realize that there's nowhere they could have gone, they must be there somewhere. I hear a final distant whack as the bat makes contact with the ball and I see it spinning like a planet in front of me, even though it's way off out of my range of vision, it seems to draw me on, sweeping over the pebbles, bouncing across the water.

Then I twig it—where Jessie and Nick have gone. Right on the edge of the hill, on a ledge cut out of the earth but totally overgrown now, about a hundred feet or maybe a hundred and fifty above a bunch of clapped-out beach huts, is an old wartime shelter. I've seen it when I've gone up there, but I've never given it much thought. It's set right into the hillside, a low-built slab of weathered concrete with slits for windows and a clear and unassailable view of the coastline in both directions. I'd assumed people just use it to piss in now, though I haven't needed to myself, but presumably once it was a significant strategic sentry post with some duffer with a rifle or maybe some serious dude with a machine gun defending our shores from Jerry. It's perfect for my sister and Motorcycle Boy now, I'm amazed it didn't occur to me before—the perfect mix of dirt and danger, the risk of being caught at it in a semipublic place. She'd like that and she'd particularly like the fact that I'm thinking about it now down here on the beach, staring up with the seagulls crapping all around me. Performance is all to Jessica; she likes an audience.

But I have to keep asking myself, "Why am I here?" She got me here, I'm sure of it. It can't just be to drum in the fact that she and Nick like screwing. I don't even know what I want to think. I've got the upper hand, I keep telling myself that again and again in my head. I've got the pictures. If she and Dad aren't going to let it happen again, then there's nothing to see, so why am I watching her? To make sure. To know. Or is it because, whether I believe her or not, and I don't, it doesn't feel like it's stopped? It all seems to revolve, like the cricket ball spinning, whirling into an impossible blur of motivations and possibilities. I stand under the cover of one of the beach huts and stare up. Does she really know I'm here? Is she watching me through one of the slits—would she tell Nick? Maybe they're both making a joke of me, the prurient younger brother: "Oh, Tom's just weird. It's a difficult age. He doesn't get any. The little voyeur."

No, this is Jessie I'm dealing with. Nothing simple. Nothing straight-forward. I think—and this is real madness now, this is just my head, this is the most desperate part of me trying to find the sanity in this situation—I think she's led me here because she wants me to see the shelter. I think she comes here with Dad and she wants me to know that because she wants me to stop it. She can't stop it. She doesn't even want to, on the surface, but underneath she's in trouble. Or maybe she's not in trouble, but she's not strong enough to stop it, she wants to but she doesn't want to enough. Shit, this is all nonsense. Jessie knows her mind better than anyone on earth. She loves danger, she loves the thought of doing anything other people would shy away from, anything that says "Fuck you!" to normality.

I'm here, that's what I've got to concentrate on. I'm here and Jessie's up there. If I doubled back along the beach, scrabbled across the ditch and up onto the path, I could be standing at the edge looking down on the shelter within three or four minutes. I could get closer. If I was quiet, I could peer in through one of those slits without them even knowing I was there but Jessie and Nick doesn't interest me, I know what I need now if I'm going to save us all.

I need proof. I need something even stronger than Jessie's pictures. Proof that will scare all of us—that I'll use if I have to.

■

18

The video camera just about registers in the dark of the shelter but it's not much, in fact it's impossible to make out any detail, so I probably won't get an image but the sound track will do on its own. If I get one, the sound track will burn with the truth, they won't be able to hear it without knowing—even fleetingly—what it feels like to be me.

It stinks in there. It smells fouler than I could imagine—years of urine and cat shit and rat shit and God knows what else, like milk and piss turned sour and mixed with a fishy smell and the tight stink of hardened crap. I cannot imagine that Jessie would want to lie down in there, no matter how funky she thinks she is. There's dirt and stone and dry leaves and an old stained and ravaged mattress, and when I kick my feet round the floor the cigarette packets and odd, gritty condom make it obvious that Jessie and Nick or Jessie and Dad aren't the first, though nothing suggests frequent use, which doesn't surprise me.

The slits of light worry me most. It's like a prison cell or a church, dark and claustrophobic, an unsealed tomb where you could bed down in the soil and get eaten alive by worms. The problem is visibility. If I use the camera through any but one of the slits, I'm going to stand out against the light like a sore thumb. The one slit that's almost blocked off by ivy and some kind of tough, reedy bush involves climbing out along the narrowest part of the ledge, where only the knotted roots of the brambles stop the earth from crumbling away entirely and dropping onto the beach huts below.

But I'm born to this, I realize that now. Jessie is pushing me further into it, but I'm good at stealth and observation, at getting where other people wouldn't go. I think about the noise the camera is going to make when I run it, but reckon it won't carry inside. I'm aware of the risk I'm taking leaving it hidden here—both of it being found by someone else or missed at home—but I can't easily walk around with it, it attracts too much attention. I know I've got to keep the battery pack recharged or I'm buggered. And the last thing I need is for some ramblers or locals or tourists to show up while I'm taping and ask what I'm doing or what time it is or if they can walk to hell and back from here, before I can duck out of sight. This is a popular hike, up the hill and along the cliff, but this must be an issue for Jessie, too, and presumably she'll choose her moment or Dad will.

That's if I'm right. Maybe I'm crazy. Maybe Jessie and Dad have stopped. Or maybe they never come here, or won't come here again, or I'll miss them—I can't keep track of them both all the time. But if they are still doing it, they must do it somewhere. I don't think they could go to a hotel. They could use the car, of course, the torn leather of the Bentley's back seat would be a different world from this shit hole. Or there must be a thousand other places they could go. But this is one of them, this is it. Jessie has shown me this for a reason. And I'm not going to waste it.

■

So I wait. I watch and I wait. I watch Jessie most, because I can read her better than Dad—I think. Anyway, he's foul-temperedly working again, hunched over his computer with a Scotch most of the time, swearing at himself or, like this morning, at everyone else as he tried to send graphics down the phone line to his Docklands office. "What's the matter, Francesca?" I heard him ask his assistant the other end, no humor in his voice, no let at all. "Is it your period or did you hit your head climbing out of the pub toilet?"

He seems changed to me all the time now. Even in the few weeks we've been down here, he's lost the heady calm he had when we arrived, the excitement he seemed to feel about Jake being born. Or perhaps it's just the way I see him. Him and Jessie is new to me—it makes me want to kick the fucker every time I see him, it makes me not want to look at him or be looked at by him—but is it to them? I can't believe I wouldn't have noticed before, but I don't know. I don't know anything.

Jessie gives me nothing much to go on, as if her appearance with Nick at the beach was all I'm going to get on a plate. She cadges a lift from Mum into Exeter and starts talking about spending a couple of days in London before she goes back there full time for college, but otherwise she's on the phone most hours of the day or in Sidmouth with me, sitting on the sea wall or the beach, both of us playing it innocent, working hard to pretend there's nothing to say except the things we always used to talk about, and making fun of the local morons who can't think of a better pickup line for her than, "You look foreign, darling. Where you from—Malta, Tenerife?" or asking if she's the waitress who spilled ketchup over them in the Devon tearoom up the street.

Except I can't resist asking, "Are you seeing Nick?" Because I sense there's something different, they've had a row or she's got bored. "I saw you at the beach the other day, all lovey-dovey by the water. Is it still going well then?"

"He's a Buddhist," she says, as if that's an answer. "He chants. Can you imagine? They are all bloody hippies down here."

"Does it make a difference?"

"He's serious about it." We're on the wall, eating ice lollies. She has to purse her lips to help her teeth cope with the cold so it's hard to tell whether she gives a shit about this, but my guess is she does: Nick interests her more than either of us thought. "He wanted me to chant with him."

This makes me laugh. "Did you?"

She slides the last of the orange ice off the stick with her lips, then chucks the stick down on the pebbles, where a wasp immediately lands on it. "I told him I'd chant, yes. But I don't think he felt my heart was in it. He's not used to meditating doggy-position." Doggy-position! I want to ask what that is exactly, though I can guess. Just the words fill my mind with weird images of her. "He said I had no balance or something, I'm an unsettling influence." She smiles at the wasp, circling some litter now, brilliant yellow in the sun yet somehow dirty-looking, corrupt. "He's really not that sure of himself, you know."

"Yeah, you said," I tell her, wondering if it's true and feeling strangely disappointed. I think I'd like someone to take Jessie over and give her a run for her money; she needs it. Maybe we all do, but she really needs someone to straighten her out.

I wait and nothing happens. I kill an afternoon with Neil, cycling into Seaton to steal stereos from grock cars, wondering all the time if this is it—if this is when Dad and Jessie are going to get their act together and I won't be there to accuse them, to watch them, to pin them down. It's only when we run a close one, when we tamper with a quartz job in a Mercedes outside the boat shop and some yuppie with a beard and his debbie fuck come charging out after us, it's only then in the heat of action that I know I'm going to get it, I know I'm right, I've just got to be patient.

And then it rains. It pisses down for a whole day and we all stay inside, the whole happy family. I have moments of paranoia about the camera—that it's already been taken or that the plastic carrier bags I've taped it in will leak and wreck it—but I also have the sense that it's going to be today. Dad has stopped fucking about with his grand design and seems in a better mood, lighter, as if he's actually trying, which he probably is. He takes me with him in the car when he goes to get some beer and we chat a bit and once again I feel guilty, I remember how much I can like him, that it was him who gave me the video in the first place—I'm the traitor even though I know I'm not.

"You're not worried about school, are you?" he asks, racing Mum's Volvo down the hill into Sidmouth, memories of Nick's motorcycle, the night helicopter patrol. We do have an off-license in the village, but Dad suddenly decided he wanted a local bottled brew and remembered they were out of stock, though this all seems to me like an elaborate ruse to avoid being seen by the locals today—just in case it might make a difference in him being recognized walking on the clifftop later on. "Your mother told me you were still anxing about it."

"What's changed?" I say. "I wasn't happy about the idea before. Why should I feel different now?"

"Just don't burn this one," he tells me and smiles. We enter town and make an illegal right-hand turn which nearly panics some old codger in a VW into a fit. "I didn't like school much either, but let me tell you, the one thing it is is a training ground for dealing with the pillocks you encounter once you've left."

I've heard this speech before and it didn't convince me then. Dad was brilliant at school and had everyone fawning over him. His idea of rebellion was weaseling exemption from religious instruction to fit in an extra afternoon's rugby practice a week.

"I'd just prefer the pillocks to be London pillocks." My familiar refrain.

We park up on the curb outside the off-license. The window looks sickeningly dull—the same posters and logos as London, but stuck there forever to fade and peel.

"I'm sure you'll find someone who fits the bill," he says, no hint that there might be some foundation in Mum's mention of going back. We dive through the rain and enter the shop, a dad and his son, makes your heart weep, doesn't it? "Pillocks don't vary that much from county to county."

■

The rain stops. Jessie goes out to see Caz, which is the first signpost, because Jessie and Caz aren't that close, Jessie doesn't turn to Caz for anything much other than a cover for seeing Nick or, if this is it and I know it is, for this.

It's six o'clock. The TV's on, the news. Jessie goes out and for ten minutes or so, nothing. Mum's feeding Jake. The news drones on. Dad's washing up—this is really significant, this is preemptive guilt, not that he never does it, but not at this time of day, more likely first thing in the morning when he gets up. It's all coded. Not one action is simple, unconnected. It's all part of the dream I'm moving through, every detail dull with reality, I'm being tested, this is all a test, a run-through, but soon my real life will start and that will seem like a rehearsal for something else, too.

Where is Jessie now? She's been gone twenty minutes, maybe more. She could be anywhere in the village. She could have met Nick at some prearranged spot and hopped straight on his bike, they could be in Sidmouth by now. But they're not. She's not. In my mind I can see her and she's waiting somewhere, she's between two stools, vacant, emptying her thoughts of any awkward emotional bonds she might have which could get in the way of what she's about to do.

The local news begins. The telephone rings. A signal? I want to get it, but I can't reach, I'm too far up, I'm on an elevated column, totally remote, looking down at my family in a zoo, running through the corridors. I can't reach out to touch them or anything near them. I'm moving, getting higher all the time, more and more precarious.

It's for Mum. Dad plays with Jake while she talks. How can he do that? If this is it, how can he play with Jake one minute and then . . . ? He looks relieved when Mum rings off. Far away, he looks relieved. She takes Jake. "Who was it?" he asks. He's not really interested. A friend of hers from London who's just had a baby too. He picks up a newspaper, puts it down, turns a half circle, looks at Mum, tit out to Jake, looks away. His head is below me, at the foot of my column; I could drop a rock on it. "I'm going for a run," he announces, glancing out the window. "It looks all right out now." These words are coded. Listen to the radio, a state of war exists but only I know it. "I'm out of shape. Do you know where my sports socks are?"

■

He leaves little to chance, my dad. Before he goes out, hairy legs looking too old or too hairy for synthetic blue running shorts, his face wearing an odd, slightly puzzled, slightly pained expression, he tells Mum he's not taking a key, will she be here? Of course she will. Where's she going to go? Take Jake for a drink? He looks at her for a moment longer than necessary before jogging out the door and then I watch him, a forty-year-old man, or early forties or whatever he is, pumping away, running over bumps and gravel and grit, running steadily up the climbing village road, a steep overgrown grass verge on either side, the hill and the cliff ahead, the sky orange and purple, stretched out with cloud, on fire after the rain. I watch him. His mouth turns grim with the effort, he stumbles a little over a ditch, then rights himself, not losing pace, running because at the moment he thinks he's got something, he can't recognize the taste of shit in his mouth.

And then I follow.

■

19

It's my place. Not right here, not the shelter, but this stretch of hill and the cliff are important to me. It can be so fucking beautiful, it is now—it's just that they're inside together and I'm right when I really would have liked to be wrong. I would have liked something to scramble it all up and say, "Look how stupid you've been, you arsehole, you joke, you waste of space."

I'm cold. There's no wind, it's August, the sun's still highish, and I'm numb, no sense in my fingers or my back, it won't come back, I know it, I can feel where the nerve cords have severed themselves, my body is crippling itself to match my mind.

I can taste metal in my mouth. Everything's metallic. The fields are liquid gold, even the sheep, but it's not a pretty color, it's not like one of those shitty commercials where everything has the same quality, where cow crap would look as glorious as a steaming plate of instant anything. My body is wrecking itself, molding itself into the twisted shapes cars make when they run under a lorry. The camera in the bag is one more part of me, screwed up in supermarket plastic, incomplete. I remembered the battery pack. Even though it was in my hand, I couldn't feel it and I kept telling myself that I'd forgotten it but I hadn't, it's here.

■

Dad walked some of the way. There's this prize at the end of it for him, his daughter waiting with wide-open legs, and still he can't make it, he can't run it, he has to take breathers every now and then. He didn't look back once. Maybe that's part of his deal with whatever drives him, not to look back, but I was there and I just hope to fuck he felt something was following him, I hope he felt a little uneasy, a little dirty about this.

They're in there. Jessie must have got here first; I didn't see her enter, but she's there, I can sense her as much as hear her voice. I'm outside, on the ledge, moving like a ghost despite my paraplegic body. I'm careful. Having come this far, I want to get it now, I want to nail it, I don't want just to disturb them and get some fucked-up, feeble excuse.

I breathe. I touch the concrete wall of the shelter, my numb fingers resting on it, telling me from a long way away that it's chill beneath what's been warmed by the sun, drawing the dampness out from inside, trying to touch what's there, to know what they feel. I move round, sucking in as I dodge past the light slits, wanting to look but knowing I must wait for the farthest one, the one that's covered. Every inch, every step seems to produce a million sounds all orchestrated at once: the brush of my jeans on the wall, the wet rustle of the bushes being drawn aside, the slow thud of a misplaced foot hitting the earth.

I've got the camera in my hand, it's heavy, it's an unnatural weight throwing my balance—the ledge is narrower than I thought. I breathe carefully. I do everything carefully. Something sharp, a thorn or something, scratches my arm and makes me want to cry out, but I stifle it and when I look and see my skin bleeding it seems fine, I can't feel it, it should bleed some more. Finally, I get to where I want to go, I lower myself into the bush by the stone slit, holding everything, bracing myself and the damp branches to minimize the noise. Down below, the beach huts glow in the sun, looking less ropy than they do usually—hard, distinct shapes to fall onto. Would it hurt very much? I'd like to know how it feels, I'd like to see myself splodged all over their peeling paint and weather-stained roofs.

I can't hear anything, that's what worries me. The sea gulls have stopped, I can't hear the sea up here and whatever insects there might be have shut down suddenly or died or are colluding with Jessie and Dad to make my presence known. That's what worries me—I can't hear them, I can't hear what they're doing inside. Are they listening for me now, do they know I'm here and are crouching together, waiting for the moment to surprise me, ridicule me, make me the fool, the criminal?

I look. I press my eye to the slit and look. It's real. It's nothing. They're in there together, two strangers, my sister and my dad, people I don't know. I know every line on their bodies but I don't know them. Jessie has her back to me. Dad's face is wrinkled and shadowed, he needs a shave, I could touch that skin, tear it like the rubber mask it is.

I'm outside. Ouside again. They're in there and they're kissing, that's why I haven't heard anything, nothing to hear. They're in that shit hole and they are kneeling, shins buried in the scummy torn mattress, bodies pressed together, praying in the half-light, eating each other's faces, slobbering and sucking, spit running down their chins. Jessie's got her jeans on but they are half off, rumpled round her knees, her knickers a bit above, the crease marks visible even by the light in there, ugly grooves cut into her skin, the elastic somehow making everything seem a mistake—her body, her life, this.

Dad's still got his shorts on, but his T-shirt is off, spread on the mattress behind Jessica, presumably to lie down on, to create some kind of a barrier between them and the spongy, infected foam. He's clutching at Jessie's back, shoving her shirt up, forcing the flesh into two vertical folds which he holds as if he wants to hurt her, he must do, she doesn't have that much flesh to spare.

And then someone comes. A voice calls a dog, whistles, "Here, boy! Come here!" Tensing, I duck down, shrinking into the bush, willing the animal not to come near, not now, not after all this. I put the camera down, not even sure if it's of any use—even if this arsehole goes away, they haven't said anything yet, I'm not going to get a picture in there and maybe all they'll do is mumble and fuck, it won't mean a thing.

It's a man, not anyone I know. I can just make him out as he steams up the hill, bloody singing to himself now, the dog nowhere to be seen. He's about ten years older than Dad, his face is craggy, dull, I wouldn't want him to be my father, and his hair is long, almost on his shoulders, he looks ridiculous. He's nothing, he's not important to me, so long as he goes away. The dog is still out of sight, but it could be anywhere, it could be nosing about right in front of the shelter—there's a whole area I can't see from here. I can imagine it, cocking its leg by the entrance, scenting something odd inside, sticking its mutt in, seeing them there with those puzzled dog eyes, baring its teeth, ripping my father's balls off with one swipe. And what are they doing, Jessie and Dad? They must be every bit as alert as me, more so. Are they pulling their clothes on, nervous, excited? Or are they frozen like me, waiting for this to pass, knowing it will, it must?

The man walks by, his pinky-brown trousers taking the steps cut into the earth like clockwork, his hand slapping the dog's coiled chain-link lead against them as he climbs. I never see the dog. It must pass out of my line of sight because I hear his shouting, decades later, while I'm still keeping covered, warning it not to go too near the edge.

■

Time passes. I cannot move. My life can just end here, that would be fine. There's nothing. I'm nothing.

I force myself forward. I have to be strong now, if only because I need something to get me from this moment to the next. They are doing what they're doing and I can stop them, I believe that, but whether it matters anymore is something else. Don't think, just move—move arm, move leg, get back to the crack in the concrete, my window, made for me. Lift the camera, turn it on, I don't care if they hear it, I don't give a shit, I could whistle a tune, blow snot through the slit, this is playtime, we're all mad.

They had pulled their clothes back on, but they must feel safe now. Safe and scared. Turned on, I don't know. Maybe they don't care either. I don't even use the camera properly, just the microphone, and the motor whirs in my ear, deadening my hearing, but they carry on anyway, caught up in their own little world, their own little performance in the middle of a shit hole.

My sister talks. I try to listen, to know what she's thinking, but it's just mechanical, an instruction: "Don't! Bend back a bit, you're hurting me."

Her body seems at odds with my father's. Each time one of them moves, it seems to throw the other one off. "Kneel," my father says. He seems to be having trouble balancing. He pulls his shorts off, getting them caught on one foot. His prick doesn't seem so surprising this time. It just looks ridiculous, it just makes my stomach turn.

I must be sick, watching this. I must really be sick. I shouldn't be here. Whatever they're doing, I shouldn't be here, but it's my right, I'm part of this too, I want to know what to think when I burn them in their beds, when I smash the camera down on their heads.

"Your stomach's going," Jessie says, quite nastily. She's right, it is. She pulls her jeans back down. She could get out of them, but Dad stops her, makes her keep them rolled halfway down her legs.

"Turn over, OK?" he says.

She twists, turning herself with her hands, keeping herself up so she's kneeling in front of him, hands on the ground, off the mattress, looking my way for a moment—does she see me?

He shuffles closer to her, moving on his knees, planting his legs firmly on her jeans, recoiling for an instant when he kneels on something hard, her jeans buttons or maybe her keys, I hope they dig straight into his fucking nerve. He forces her legs apart, although they can't go far, pulling her to him, his hands on her hips, maneuvering her bottom so that that stick prick ducks down between her cheeks.

"And you still don't eat enough," he tells her, pushing, shifting his weight from one knee to the other, working on her, leaning forward over her. "Otherwise, you're fine."

I feel dizzy. My ear throbs, a muscle in my neck pulses. I can't breathe, but when I do it's fast. Everything is different from how you imagine it to be. I can't see, but I know what he's doing, where he's going.

She doesn't answer him. Jessie's mouth is open, half grimace, half pant, like a dog, like her eyes, which are wide open, button bright, like the bitch she is.

■

The camera falls because I don't have the guts to jump. It's like everything else: disappointing. I chuck it out but it's no distance, it falls back in and knocks against the side of the hill, not even rock. It hits earth and bounces a bit, then comes to rest still in one piece behind the beach huts, where I hope some fucker finds it.

■

20

start back to the cottage, which is not my home, which is one more cell, another shit hole, but I turn, hesitating, thinking I should storm right in there and confront them with it, see the look on their faces as they try to pull apart, dog on dog, I know what it is now—except I wouldn't know what to say and I don't have the strength to hurt them as much as I want to, there isn't that much strength in the world. I can see them dead but I don't know how, all there is in front of me is a blurring pitted grass field, no gun or knife or brick, I need someone to lay the weapon out for me, guide my hand, show me what to do. I can't even walk, I just stumble, not wanting to go anywhere. There is no one. I am totally alone, I realize that, and one day I'll die. I just wish it could be now.

■

Finally, the cottage. I hate it. I hate every drab, weathered stone in its walls. I hate the ground it stands on, its gloomy roof, its oldness. It's evil, but it's a shapeless evil, it can wreck your life but it can't scare you, just depress you. I want to weep. Suddenly I know the difference between crying and weeping, like I know the difference between London and this death trap. In London I would know what to do, I would know how to cope. In London the rest of my life would not look so unutterably hopeless; I could escape somehow, somehow this wouldn't be a blank wall.

The back door is open. I pass through the kitchen, empty, into the hall, a dull, dark tunnel at the edge of my vision. Mum is on the floor of the living room, her back to me, sponging up a pool of something Jake has brought up. She has tiny flowers on her dress. Her arse sticks up at me like a part of the furniture, a flowery cushion, not like Jessie's at all. I want to cry when I see her, but I don't want to look at her face, look into her eyes, speak.

She hears me. The light in the living room is fading, thick, a shadowy mist. Everything is gloomy, compressed. She turns. I'm on the stairs before she calls out my name.

Upstairs, I ram the door of the bedroom shut with my bed. She must hear the shunting noise as I shift it across the floor, but I don't care. No one else cares. I'd always imagined I might persuade Lucy one day to do this with me: put the bed against the door and screw on it. But now I don't think I'll ever do that myself. Dad and Jessie have done all the fucking for me. "Otherwise, you're fine." His voice creeps into my head, like he was appraising cattle or something, gripping her rump on a monthly or weekly basis or whatever it is and grading the meat. He has had Jessie where she craps and I don't think there will ever be anything as disgusting in my life again.

■

I do not cause a scene. I just need time. I just need a hostage and a gun and I could be happy.

They come back—singly, Jessie first, then Dad—but not before Mum has asked me what's wrong. She knocks on the door but knows better than to try and open it. "Leave me alone," I tell her. "I want to think." She persists for a few minutes, but gives up and goes back to her baby. I can't protect her.

I am going to kill them. I don't know what happens after that, but until then every road leads to that door, until then I can face anything because I have a purpose, I have a reason for still being here.

■

21

Next day.

I am the same person. I let the milk soak into my Shredded Wheat. I step into my underpants wondering whose legs these are receiving messages from my brain, my foot going through the hole with remarkable precision, then holding my weight as I repeat the exercise with the other.

Breakfast is a bit dead. No one speaks much, or is it me who thinks that, is breakfast always a bit dead because we're all a bit dead first thing in the mornings? We ate last night too and no one said much then, but Dad claimed he was tired by his run and Jessie said she'd eaten at Caz's but I know she'd done coke, she tried so hard to be relaxed about everything when in fact she sounded flat, lifeless. I hardly looked at her. If I think about her too long, if I get too close to her, I will lose my resolve. I try to concentrate on her hole clenched tight round Dad's pole. His penis is the foot of a chair leg in my mind, I cannot explain, it is just a chair leg digging into the ground. The thought of them both in the ground frightens me but I'm going to do it. Mum, I'm sorry. I'm sorry we're all failing you at once. I don't know what you've done to deserve this but either there is something you're responsible for or life makes no sense, it really is just shit and only other people escape the pain.

■

"I want to talk to you." Jessie is on the stairs, going up. I've filled the deadness in my stomach. I want to get out of the cottage. Even to me, my voice is an absolute, it cannot be denied.

"Yes?"

"Not here. Outside. I'm going up the hill. Follow me in a minute."

I open the front door and walk out. It opens easily, which it doesn't usually. It's bright outside so that I have to squint at first. I walk in the road, waiting for the sudden impact of a car's bonnet from behind. The world seems spread out before me. There is the cottage, here is the village, my cutout family is behind the cardboard walls, school lurks at the edge of the cereal packet base, the full meaning of which will be revealed if and when I go there in a week and a half's time and burn it or break it or just shovel earth over the headmaster's dog.

I walk alone in the sun, almost enjoying its heat. The sheep look beautiful. Strands of barbed wire link wooden stakes, but no blood—this is not Beirut, just part of a pattern of the country that I'm not a part of myself. Tranquil Devon: gin and tonics, Range Rovers and sheepdogs. And then you die.

Jessie might not follow me, but I think she will. I know what certainty is this morning, I am drawing things on, but not in any way I have ever wanted. I wait at a stile two or three fields down from the shelter, turned away from it, unable to see it anyway behind the hedgerows but sensing its presence, watching the village roads below me, the car park, the beach.

Eventually she comes. She climbs the path with no particular excitement, a bored look on her face, a bit pissed off with me for making her walk up here, but also wary—bringing her here must make her more than wonder.

"You lied to me." I don't give her time to say anything.

She stops a few feet away, a mound of dead brown grass between us. She frowns, licking a little saliva from the corner of her lip, out of breath from the climb. Her mouth looks weak today, as if someone's broken it somehow and put it back together wrong, but it also looks as if it could get strong very quickly if it had to, she looks ready to twist my words, turn hard, shut me up.

"You fucking lied to me."

She looks away, older sister time, only she's not so sure. "Boring."

"I don't know what boring is. Everything seems the same to me. Have you been to the toilet yet this morning? Does it hurt? I bet it does."

This gets her. She turns and confronts me, angry fast, guilty. "What's wrong with you?"

"I don't know," I say, hearing how bitter my voice sounds for the first time. "Cancer? AIDS? The fact that I've got a sister who lets her father have her right up her arse?"

I stare at her, not giving her any help, making her react, waiting for her to look away before I do, and I feel like everything changes in that moment, I can do it, I can hate her to her face. She shifts her eyes to the sea for a moment, looking troubled, looking more troubled than I can remember her looking, so that I start to feel sick with love and guilt and want to touch her, until she looks back and her mouth changes, protecting herself, not allowing herself to hug me and be my sister and cry because we're all fucked up, lost, but instead pretending it can go on, she can deal with me.

"I saw everything."

She stares at me. She can hate me too.

"I watched you."

"You filthy little creep."

"Look who's talking. You love it."

"You're weird, Tom. You get off on all of this, don't you?"

She's desperate. She's nasty, she has a really deadly edge to her.

"Come and look! Come here!" I grab her arm and pull her. She could fight but she comes with me, not caring, just thinking her own thoughts, working out where this leaves her, whether anything's really changed, how far I will go. I take her up to the shelter. I'm not even sure myself what's in my mind. I'm not going to kill her like this, I want them both. I want them to feel what I feel, I want her to be outside this shit hole and imagine how it was for me. She's not short of imagination, Jessie.

The sea is there below us as I push her out along the ledge, above the matchbox beach huts. It looks unreal. It looks massive, flat, cold, sparkling. If we could leap across it to the horizon, maybe we could escape. If life worked like that, if we had that power, that size, we could just go on, blank out the past, harden ourselves. But we can't and I shove her face up against the stone slit, her short hair bristling under my hand, her head compliant, weak, no will of its own.

"Look!" I tell her. "Can you smell it? Can you smell the sickness in there? I watched you, Jessie. I watched you go down on your knees like a fucking animal and like it. Both of you, you both want it." I'm blubbing, but I don't give a shit, I just swallow the tears and let my face burn and feel twitchy, wired, scared. I could do it now. One push, we could go together.

"Are you sure?"

"What?"

She's got a different face looking at me. Humiliation, sadness, different steps in her eyes down to a cellar, I don't know what it is. "Are you sure we both want it?" She leans away from the stone wall, pushes a branch out of her face.

I feel uncertain. My body's light, shaking, no weight in my legs, no certainty in my brain—already I've lost the clarity. "I don't know," I say. She's telling me what I want to hear, I know that. "I—"

"Yes?"

I'm careful. I know her. "Do you need help, is that it?" Those eyes. She is totally alive. She can take it all, she wants it all. "Is that what you wanted? I thought maybe you were scared, you wanted it to stop but you couldn't say it, that's why you showed me this place with Nick."

She looks at me with a long laugh. This is a good one. Her eyes are sparkling, like the sea, it's mask time, where's Dad? I stare at her mouth. She likes taking the piss out of me—but gently, she's my sister, she's just breaking me in for the kind of superior cunts I'm never going to meet. "You're mad."

There's nothing to say. She's playing games with me. I'm back to square one, zero option.

"Look," she says, getting serious. "You shouldn't have got involved with this. I love you, we've always been close, but this is different. This is fucking dangerous and it's not something you should even be thinking about."

I screw my eyes up, wanting to scream, digging my fingernails into my palms, trying to hold on, trying to wait, this isn't the moment. "What do you expect me to do?" I ask, beg.

"Nothing," she says. "You can't do anything. Anything you do will damage us all. You don't want that. Talk to Dad and you'll freak him out completely, he doesn't know you know anything. Talk to Mum and you destroy us. What do you want to do?"

We're still on the ledge. I'm between her and the hillside but there's no point in threatening her, threats don't work, only action, and this isn't the moment, not for me; if my whole existence amounts to ending theirs, I'm going to get it right. "I'd like to fucking kill you!" People who say that don't do it. Let her feel safe.

Another face. Close, like when we used to share everything—or when she used to, I didn't have much to share, I think she got a kick out of telling me things, exciting me. She takes my hand, clasps it onto her arm and drags it so that my fingers scratch her. White tracks appear, then red but no blood, so she does it again, harder. This time the skin breaks in a couple of places. "Hurt me," she says. "Try it, I want you to. You'll feel better."

I'm tempted. But I want to go all the way. I really would like to hurt her, even killing her isn't going to hurt her the way I'd like to—I don't know the way. I take my hand back. A layer of her skin is wedged under my nails. Red droplets materialize on her arm, wet, finding each other. She holds her arm in front of me for a moment, smiling, then shifts past me along the ledge as if we've had a chat and now it's over, everything sorted out.

"Wait!" I scramble after her, grabbing her arm again, spinning her round. "I do want to hurt you. You're right."

She looks surprised for a moment, not very much, but surprised, I've actually managed to surprise her. She stands, waiting for what's coming, still confident, watching me as I take a box of matches out of my pocket. Those surprise her a little more, but she still doesn't flinch, Jessie is totally cool, she's even smiling.

"Sit down," I tell her. She sits on the grass. I kneel next to her, taking her arm, not the one she made me scratch, the other one. She's got some kind of a Spanish shirt on with short, puffy sleeves. I make her roll the sleeve up onto her shoulder.

"You're sure about this, are you?" I ask, not really caring what she says.

"Do it."

She looks at me, ready, not smiling anymore but keeping her face still, waiting to feel something.

I light a match. It takes three before I can keep one going. With cupped hands I slowly move the tiny flame toward the top part of her arm, the softest part, just where the hair she doesn't shave peeks out. I feel weird. We're on the grass, on the hill, in bright sunlight, and as I watch and think about what I'm doing I hold the burning match to my sister's skin, keeping my hands round it to stop it from blowing out, and let it burn a small blister there while she jerks back for a second or two before tensing her arm and holding it still for me to finish. From the side of my vision I glimpse her teeth and the wetness of her mouth as she gasps and bites her lip, but my attention is focused on her arm, on the redness, the skin wrinkling and raw.

I press the match against the burn to stub it out. Jessie lets out one small cry, but otherwise says nothing, watching me, watching my eyes, gazing at her arm, her shoulder, then away and back to me. I throw the match on the grass and stare at her.

"You're stupid, Jessie, really stupid. I can't believe you're really like that."

"No?"

"No. You're fucking yourself up. Why are you doing that?" I don't feel any different, just disappointed with myself that I couldn't wait, that I had to do something now—and something so small.

"You're pretty fucked up yourself, aren't you?" She looks at the burn on her arm, fascinated for a moment, her mouth twisting with the effort of straining her neck round. She pulls the sleeve down over it and stares at me, right into my eyes, there's a hint of concern in hers. "Well, I suppose you would be."

And she leans across, hand on the grass, and does the last thing I expect. She kisses me. A sisterly kiss, brief, warm, touching. But it comes with a price: "Don't try to stop us, Tom. Please. We've only just started. I want it to go on for the moment."

I know that if my resolve should fail she will give it back to me. She is perfect. Even in being fucked up, she is perfect—she is perfectly fucked up. I can't stop them. I can't blackmail them or threaten them or expose them. Whatever I do, they'll find a way. There's always a way. The corner I'm in is the only one, made to fit. There's only this moment. I want to think about what her arse looks like to Dad when it's red and sore, whether she's lying again, whether he did this to her when she was a little girl, when we used to have baths together and the world always felt strange, like a collision course someone else had set up for you to run through. I want to think about what it would be like to hit them both with a cricket bat or something else hard, swinging it down on them as they dog-fuck each other, except dogs don't do it that way, dogs aren't nearly as fucked up as they are. But there's only this moment. All I can see is Jessica sitting on the grass in front of me; the sun is sharp, the sea is wide behind her.

I am going to do it. Some other time. Soon. Together. "Did you really?" I ask her, schoolboy in the playground disbelieving someone else's boast. "Did you really just start? I think you've been doing it for a long time. I think you've been doing it all my life."

She half gets up, crouching with her arms resting on bended knees. She looks like she's going to tell me something, then her face clouds again and she smiles that nasty smile, games-playing, we've used up our free exchange. "Maybe," she says.

"Who gives a shit?" I stare at her, she can't control me anymore, I can fight her and keep on fighting.

She stands up. "Look, just let it run its course. Things end. This will." Yes, it will. Her eyes seem to be searching mine, honest again, looking for an opening. "Do you want me to get you something? Something from London?"

"What are you talking about?" I know, but I want to see what she says. She can't really believe she can buy me off. I get up too.

"You know what I'm talking about. What do you want—do you want to come to London? We're going tomorrow."

This is news to me. "Who is?"

"Dad and me. He has to go. I'm going to see Sonny. Do you want to come?"

"I can go to London myself if I want to." I press her. "What can you get me—cocaine, dope, money, crack, sweeties? What's on offer here?"

She is looking at the shelter. I catch her, but she goes on looking anyway. We start walking down the hill. "Come on, what can you get me?"

She reaches over and lifts the hinged lid off my head. I'm a robot for her, she thinks she knows me so well.

"I can get you laid."

■

22

We're in the Bentley. We're safe—I mean, even though it's a heap, it has the power and lines that fuel this country's divide, it can drive right over your child without stopping, it can part the way through police on horseback with visors over their faces at a football match. You can do anything in a car like this, you can fuck your daughter, you can knobble a judge or an MP, you can shoot horse and you won't get caught. It's not loud, that's the secret. It's not even clean. This car knows what it's about.

It has taken us up through Devon to skirt round Bristol and follow endless feed roads onto the M4. It all looks the same. At this speed only the trees look alive and not all of them. At this speed there's only signs and barriers and hard shoulders and the lines diving under the bonnet, and it all looks flat. The trees that are there don't fit and won't be there for long, this is In-between Land, no reason for it, this is dead time. If there was a way of getting from nowhere to somewhere—to London—without traveling, this land would not even exist.

The Prick is driving, wearing a suit and setting himself up for what's ahead, confrontation time, he's grim-mouthed but he's looking forward to this. He talks to us from time to time, but we're not there, he wants to get to the site and say his piece, and maybe if he shouts loud enough and gets worked up and shoots the Texans down he can have his daughter for dessert on a nice cozy hotel bed, they'll get shit stains on the sheets.

And she is next to me, a world away, listening to her stereo, going through her bag, glancing at Dad in the mirror, but coolly, as though he's an encumbrance at this moment, she's in a different mood and he's not part of it. I stare at the meaningless stream of traffic, bored with the silence in the car, it's a phony silence, they could talk but they can't with me here. A container lorry drags past, going backward from my point of view, then two cars and a coach. A child's face peers down at us from the lap of his hawk-faced grandmother. He has a gun.

We stop at a motorway service station. I need a piss and Jessie wants a magazine so she goes in the shop. The whole thing is perfect for the

In-between Land, for my state of mind. You could die here and not even know it. The bogs are awash with blue disinfectant yet still they stink, as if it's just colored blue, it doesn't do anything, it just tints the diseases. The food shop—the pantry!—has the same kind of bluish-green tinge as the disinfectant, they probably flavor the force-grown fruit and chemical pastry with it. And in the gift shop, where I go to look for Jessie, it's Christmas all year round, shiny paper and tinsel over everything, toys and tourist tricks that you wouldn't give to charity.

She's there, with him, with the Prick, at the till, hanging on his arm just the wong way, like a tart, like a fuck, like something he's picked up on the road. They're playing a game: maybe they look like father and daughter, maybe they don't; maybe he's the freako businessman—menopausal-punk hair, soft, weathered face, suit—and she's the antidote to his life, she lets him feel human or dirty or whatever men like that need to feel, she can give him a thrill just out of buying magazines and chocolates and crap key rings.

Except he doesn't look too happy about it. He looks more than a little uncomfortable, the Prick, testy, as if she's trying his patience. He wants to push her hand off his arm, but Jessie's clinging tight, I see her fingers buried in his sleeve as I approach past the cellophane-wrapped funeral wreaths.

They both react when I appear, Jessie holding tight but altering her expression in some subtle way which makes her look the affectionate daughter, flirty but not unnaturally so—a hungry schoolgirl proud of Daddy. The Prick, for his part, frowns and prises her arm off his, being the adult, being the responsible one, and looks straight at me, his eyes telling me what to think, warning me off, saying, "Tom, do you want anything?"

So I stare right back and don't even look at the counter or the bored, mind-fucked girl on the till ("Where do you work?" "I work on the M4") or the travelers who clearly buy their clothes and eat their food and make their lives at these places, and I say, "Why? It's all shit," and then walk out to the car.

We go on. I listen to Jessie's stereo because I haven't brought my own. She sits glancing at her magazines, full of packaged artiness, hip wank pictures and hip wank writing. Dad drives, moving from lane to

lane just to break the tedium, letting the weight of the Bentley barrel
through the formations, the retired minds in the slow lane, the serious
movers in the fast, none of them equal to his determination to maintain
speed without actually arriving, his need not to get to the next moment.

No one speaks. We each inhabit our space in the Bentley, plotting
our sex and our murders and our own destruction until, as the suburbs
of London begin and the pattern of the motorway changes—more signs,
more slip roads, the necks and heads of streetlights and streets and
houses in the afternoon quiet—Dad says, "Fuck it, I didn't have to
bring you two! This is a boring enough trip as it is without this conspiracy
of silence. I can get depressed without your help."

So something's working. Something's getting through. I almost smile.
"I didn't have to come," I say. "It was Jessie's idea."

"Tom needed glue or paint thinner or whatever it is he sniffs," Jessie
says in a bored voice. Her hand finds mine on the car seat and presses
something small and hard into it. I finger it for a moment before looking
down. It's a bottle, a little black bottle of American air freshener, amyl
nitrate. I try to give it back—I hate the stuff, it gives me headaches,
and I don't want any of Jessie's bribes—but she pushes it into my pocket.

"Tom doesn't need anything to get high," the Prick says, as if I'm
not there, as if he feels safe, he's got me sussed. "His mind is strange
enough to start with."

And I lick my finger and write "Fuck you" on the seat, meaning him
but meaning Jessie too. She sees it and stares at me, really stares, longer
than I can bear. It's not an angry stare or a disdainful one or anything
I can adjust to, it's just bored and unbeatable, as if she's got the time,
she can wait me out, she can fuck me over in ways I can't even imagine.

We go through the center, past the airport, past the warehouses and
odd light industrial factory unit, past the hotels and the hoardings, up
the ramp and into the heart of my world; chaos, fumy and bright at
the same time; short-fused snarl-mouthed achievers bullying past spacy
dong-faced tourists; tatty high-street secretaries, magazine gloss career
women and the others, the boys and girls like me, street fucks and street
fighters, all adrift on a set of poncey old buildings and banks and shops-
with-no-name; trendy, hip, faceless. Sometimes when I dream at night,
when I can, when it's not blocked by my twisted emotional musings,

I see it all burning—like the Great Fire, only better. It's not the people I want to burn, not especially, but the city would look brilliant all ablaze. I'd love it.

The Prick likes it too, that's why we go this way, why we don't skirt round it. It torments him. He loves to sound off about it, to pinpoint its madness, the crap that's preserved, the total shit that's been built in his lifetime, the detritus that's going up now. "We have political and aesthetic masters," he says, sliding the gearstick like it's some part of Jessie, "whose idea of taste is anaglyptic wallpaper in a nice house on a mock-Tudor estate. What can you expect?"

And we're into the City, the nation's hard-on, where all the little semen squirrel about trying to find an egg to crack. I see them from the car—not many, it's not chucking-out time yet, they're still at their screens, on their phones, in the toilets with their rolled-up notes shoved up their nostrils—but there's a few around, holding hands and talking, trading the world.

Then a hiccup. The old London, like the old New York, like the old quarter in 1984. Right next to those slabs of money, just down the street from those monuments to decency are the boarded-up shops and slum-holes of the proles. God, they let them get close. It must have been a mistake. Or maybe they knew they were no threat, they could be contained easily enough. Beaten old farts sit in the scummy windows of an establishment which offers—get this—reconditioned toasters, electric razors and irons. Wire grilles front a shop selling guns and knives and implements of torture—the only one doing well, the only one with anything to steal. I should tell the Prick to stop here; I could use his cash to buy the instrument of his death. Panels of chipboard or something stronger patch the broken glass of a Chinese social club. It looks disused but I hope it's not; I hope all kinds of crime goes on behind there, I hope they stick bamboo shafts up the City's arse.

The docks next—no longer a part of this world, but not anything else either. The Prick drives the Bentley over polished cobblestones, past tarted-up workshops and offices, round the dismal hulks of Victorian warehouses, beautiful in their ugliness but losing it fast—some being torn down, others cleaned up and renovated, turned into flash power bases, media fiefdoms, million-pound apartments. The Prick's wharf is like the rest—half built. Across the water the shell of a part-demolished warehouse looks like a funky nightclub, a great bite chewed out of its massive floors, twisted metal and rubble and hanging-off windows leading the way to a pillared dance hall, dark, totally empty—the sort of place you could take your father and your sister and beat the shit out of them, then slide them down the old tobacco chutes to nowhere.

But the Prick's little toy is growing, not crumbling. The pyramid is going up, sticking its nose up onto the skyline, dwarfing everything around it with its newness and its meanness. Even covered in scaffolding, it makes me wonder what the fuck Dad thinks he is doing here. This is his statement, this is his finger raised at everything that's been built here ever. But it's the same, it's no different. It's another fucking ego trip, another pile of emptiness erected with a huge concentration of effort and no real fucking reason. This is what Dad does. He builds things. Why? Because he has to put food on our plates—and because maybe the supercharge he gets out of designing something other people have to live with, have to confront daily, something that attracts attention in all those self-obsessed architectural journals and even the junk press, maybe it all gives him a feeling of specialness, a feeling of righteousness, a sense that, "Yes, I shape people's environments, I define their lives, I am different, I am special, I can fuck my daughter and keep it quiet from my family, I can keep my wife and baby on hold, and my son where he belongs—outside, in the cold." When Dad is gone, when Dad is cold and in the ground, one day this will follow—this monkey puzzle of steel and glass, this cage. There'll be another pile of rubble and another son staring.

Jessie gets out of the car first, attracting whistles and catcalls from shirtless construction men high on girders. The site foreman, Bernie, comes to meet us, issuing hard hats and riding the storm as Dad plows into him before we even reach the site office.

"What's the story, Bernie?" Dad slaps his hand on Bernie's shoulder in a determinedly unmatey way. "A fucking holiday all round?"

But Bernie can take it, Bernie can take most things. He's a hard-nosed bastard, a thug in a suit with a harelip and a lisp and the eyes of an ex-boxer, smooth as shit when he wants to be, which isn't now.

"They want to get paid for what they do," he says. "That's all."

"You'd better wait out here," Dad says to Jessie and me as we reach the office, which is a joke, having come this far, but he seems decided.

He opens the door of the transportable shack and goes inside, followed by Bernie, who winks at Jessie, breathing through his mouth as though he's going to tell her something but doesn't.

So we stand in the sunshine, not wanting to talk, not really wanting to be with each other at this moment. The water at the edge of the wharf is dark and deep and freaky, not like the sea, without that size, and one of the boys tells us—tells Jessie—that a crane driver died in it the week before, just came off his lunch break, sober, took a dive off the crane and never came up. They never found the body. It makes me feel like I'm wasting time; it makes me feel like I'm losing the edge: hanging on to Jessie and Dad, not looking for an opportunity to do it but rather an excuse not to.

Time passes. One of the security guards, Jason, shows us the cosh he carries—"Just in case things get serious." He got it in New York, it's spring-loaded and telescopes out to become a terrifying weapon. I could use one of those. Dad's voice is audible even outside the shack. He shouts, then it goes quiet for a few minutes; it's like a piece of music. Finally he opens the door and comes out and I glimpse a girl in a skirt so short it's not there on her knees on the floor picking up the pieces of a scale model of the site. A wire-faced bearded Irishman in sunglasses watches her arse. Neville, Dad's job architect, runs after us and catches his arm. Dad turns, like something spring-loaded, like Jason's cosh, and explodes. "Never," he pauses, riding his own emotions, "give them the whole fucking picture. Am I clear?"

We drive back, past a hoarding which says Docklands is going to be London's Venice and New York rolled into one. I think my father would have fitted into Renaissance Italy fine; they all fucked their daughters and each other in the line of business. He doesn't say much in the car, just drives aggressively, stopping punchily at lights and then gunning away. Black spray from the road hits the windscreen and he leans into it, driving faster toward the red lights of a lorry in front. "They're bankers," he says, "they're fucking bankers and they don't understand money."

■

We check into a hotel. The Prick has meetings fixed for the morning to play big boys with the Texans and their money. Jessie is seeing Sonny.

I could go and see Luke except that I don't want to spend any time with my old friends, there's nothing to talk about, nothing I can talk about, and anyway Jessie says she's set me up.

"I'm not interested," I tell her, but I am, she knows that. I want to take back everything that she and the Prick have taken from me. I want to meet this person who can paint the greedy black hole Jessie is. Sonny is part of the tunnel I'm in, I'm convinced of that—part of the pipeline, where time is counting down, where I don't even have to follow my own reasoning, each moment is the last, nothing is repeatable.

"Sonny's brilliant," she says, and then with a laugh: "Golden showers!"

"I don't need your help."

■

We go to dinner. The weather changes abruptly, lightning flashing across the sky and rain tumbling down moments later. I think about the last time Dad and Jessie and me had dinner together in a London restaurant. Mum was there; this time she's not and everything has been fucked in the meantime.

Jessie sits next to me. Some kind of weird thin black jacket is all she's got on over her black stockings and she keeps nudging me with her leg, as if we're sharing a joke or flirting or something or she just can't keep herself still. It starts getting to me, really annoying me, because I'm thinking about Mum at home cut out of all this, and Jessie and Dad are drinking wine and acting cool, he's the proper parent and we're the kids mucking around, he keeps us in line, he's a wonderful father taking his two kids out like this, we're a wonderful family, really close, really open with each other—he can talk about his problems and the need for a dynamic architectural language in Britain and we can listen to the bullshit. Until I turn and say, "Look, fucking cut it out, will you? You keep knocking my leg!" And Jessie stares at me as if she genuinely didn't know she was doing it and the mood of the dinner changes somewhat.

We go back to the hotel, the rain crashing down on the Bentley and the sky flickering neon-white, only it's weirder than neon, starker, lighting everything. Jessie rides in the back with me but hangs on Dad's seat, so that he tells her to sit back because she's obstructing his rear view. The traffic is chaotic because of the rain but he seems steady, as if he's resolved something in himself about the Texans tomorrow, his irritability only returning when Jessica suggests we go to a nightclub.

"I'm not interested," he says. "Tom can't go to a nightclub." Thanks, Prick, for your sympathy and concern.

"Yes," Jessie says, "yes, you are," leaning forward, pretending I'm not there—or pretending she's pretending. "A friend runs it. It's only two nights a week. I can get you in and you can leer a lot and dance and make me sit up on the bar and protect me. It'll be brilliant."

"I don't want to go to a nightclub!" my father snaps, turning round, flashing anger. "Shut up, Jessie, you're drunk."

At the hotel, Jessie and I share a room and she stands staring out the window for a long time, still in her jacket and stockings, watching the storm light up the river, looking like an image from one of her hip magazines. She doesn't say anything to me and I don't say anything to her, I just get into bed and lie there wondering if she's waiting for me to go to sleep so she can creep into his room or whether she's thinking about something else. I feel confused. If I'm going to do it, if I'm going to kill them both, I'm going to have to choose a moment and this would be as good as any. I don't know what I'm waiting for. I don't seem able to plan it.

The storm moves away for a while, the thunder still close but not overhead. It comes back, circling round, and Jessie pulls a chair to the window and sits. I listen for her crying, because it feels as if she might be, but I don't think she is. Then she wakes me, shaking my shoulder as I'm drifting off.

"Have you still got that thing I gave you?"

"What thing?"

"In the car. The amyl nitrate."

"I chucked it," I say, but I'm too tired to argue and she knows I'm lying so I tell her it's in one of my pockets.

She finds it in the dark and takes it back to her chair. "Do you want some?" she asks.

"No."

Outside, a burglar alarm goes off, followed by another. Jessie opens the bottle and the sickly synthetic smell fills the room. Thunder cracks overhead and I listen for sirens but there aren't any. I get a headache and seem to fall in and out of sleep, but the storm is a separate force waking me and I glimpse Jessie in dramatic, broken flashes of white at the window and hear the alarms and feel confused and wonder where we are.

When I wake in the morning, she's gone, but she's just in the bathroom and I don't know whether she slept or not or if she spent part of the night with Dad.

■

23

The air in London is black, grainy, as if you can touch the carbon monoxide or whatever it is that settles on everything, layering it with dust, running streaky when it rains. We walk down the Embankment tube station steps, not really communicating but moving as a unit, a brother and sister, through the bewildered foreigners and dossers and shoppers up for the day, clutching their maps and bottles and asthma inhalers and stepping back as diseased mice dart out from wire-grilled no-go areas and dive under the rails, missing that middle one, the burner, the one with the charge.

The tiles in the station are new, shiny, characterless—a toilet that no one wants you to use, that's been built just to prove everything is clean, above board. The whole of the West End has been renovated, laundered, shined up, rewired, re-alarmed, so that you can see how thick the walls are and the color of what's inside. They don't hide the problems—they police them out, they keep them across the river, where we're headed. It must be a lot like Nuremberg was. Or Munich. Or Disneyland.

I watch Jessie and me at the platform's edge on a wall-mounted video screen as the train comes in. In the picture, we're flat, lifeless, green. In the picture, I push or pull her, taking her with me. On this video screen I could show my home movies, if I'd taken any. The shoppers and dossers and foreigners could watch as my father parted her bum and stuck his thing between.

The doors close, the walls move and we go under the river. The train stops for a long time and I feel the weight of water above us—if that's where we are—and sit staring at the three other passengers in our carriage, condemned by their awfulness. An old man sits alone at the far end, his mouth propped open by some tube down his throat, gasping at the air and staring glass-eyed at nothing. A woman with glasses and an evil, hating face looks up from her yellowed paperback book and mentally sorts me out. I'm her son, she will beat me until I bleed and then go on forever. A skinhead with a blotchy cherry birthmark and a

knife scar down his neck sticks his boots up on the seat across from him
and stares away from us, frightened by something in his head, moving
his lips silently and clutching a brown leather sports bag to his chest,
clinging to its scuffed, Union Jack-emblazoned bulk with a curled intensity which only a couple of well-placed kicks to his kidneys would
push over into total despair. Jessie sits beside me, her shoes off, a faint
sicky smell like the amyl nitrate rising from them to mix with the stale
air of the carriage. She rubs her toes, massaging the digits through the
filmy black net of her stockings.

"I'm unhappy." My voice sounds strange in the closed environment
of the carriage. I don't know why I'm telling her. It won't make any
difference to either of us.

"Oh?"

"I've never been this unhappy."

She works her toes, poking her finger and thumb into the nylon,
forcing a channel to touch the tiny cunt between each one. "I can
understand that."

Can you? Thank you, Sister.

"Sonny will sort you out."

The train moves again.

∎

Clapham North. We come out of the tube and set off on foot, Jessie
leading the way, looking oddly at home here—I didn't know this was
her territory. We cross the road from the station, running in the path
of a huge articulated truck which deafens us with a slow wail of its
horn, the narrowness of our escape showing me a picture of Jessie
dead—by my hands, not the truck. I don't know death, but it doesn't
seem so far away. The Prick's mother died, but she was just someone
from my childhood. She was a grandmother, a warm presence at Christmas, someone who hugged me, but she was old and smelled of oldness
and old perfumes, she was a bit dead already. Jessie walks in front of
me now, the truck forgotten, wearing black stockings, a short checked
skirt and the jacket from last night and I think about her stiff, cold,
still. Her body would look sad, dead—I would have to join it, to follow
her; I think I'd float her in a bath and climb in beside, slopping water
over the top, using her cocaine blade to slice little chunks off myself

under the surface. I know I want to kill them, but it worries me sometimes whether I can. Killing Dad will be a struggle—his surprise, his
resistance, his refusal to bend to anyone else's will. I'm smaller than
both of them, though not much smaller than Jessie, but I'm expecting
a superhuman strength. The thing that frightens me most is not being
able to finish them off. I know I can start it, but can I keep it up—if
I use a knife will I lose my nerve once it's in, will I do one and not
the other, or will I just fall back when they try to fight me off and
collapse in a corner, regretting my whole fucking life?

We walk to Brixton, my eyes on Jessie's legs, the side of her head,
the heat and the movement around us. An army tank rattles down
Railton Road, charging along, clearing everything in its path, an army
goon standing up in the turret, imagining himself in Belfast, the Falklands, Beirut, Libya, the Gulf—somewhere where he can open fire on
the bastards. A bunch of school kids watch him from a wall, turning
up their ghetto blaster and jeering, sticking their heads into brown paper
bags and sucking the glue in, chucking the petrol bombs in their brains
instead of on the streets. Two Rastas walk toward us, a huge dog on a
leash tugging at one of them and a woman walking alongside in high
heels, a bra and tiger skin shorts. She stares at Jessie as if she can't
decide, but then she does and cracks a thin, sharp-cornered smile.

We cross and head up toward Herne Hill, the traffic at a standstill,
the sky a chemical green, hot, threatening rain. A bus has broken down
and a ripped seat has been stuck out on the road behind it. Fat women
with prison faces wheel shopping trolleys in and out of the legs, the
litter, the broken pavement slabs. A businessman walks in the street
shouting obscenities at the thin air. Cracked toilet bowls and old sinks
are piled outside, offered for sale. BUST THE PIGS is spray-painted in
pink across a solid post office door.

Jessie leads me up a side street, past the barbed-wire-topped fence of
a dismal school playground, down the side of two houses and through
a rickety back garden gate to a kitchen door. She knocks and we wait
but no one answers. She tries it and it's locked, but Jessie seems to be
expecting this. She stands back and aims her foot at the bottom right-
hand panel and kicks. The first kick doesn't do it, so she kicks again
and then twists the handle and the door pushes inward, jamming on a
mat.

We go inside the kitchen, a piss hole of a place with cups and dishes stacked up alongside rusty house-paint pots and rags. The walls are peeling and damp and the floor is covered with grit and bits of rubble where something has recently been smashed. Jessie takes me through the house, up the stairs to a landing with three locked doors. She tries one, but this time when it doesn't give she leaves it and takes me back down to the kitchen. So far we've hardly said a word since we left the tube. She starts digging in the cupboard under the sink and asks me something I don't catch.

"What?"

"I said, 'Coffee?' "

"Yeah, OK."

She finds some and retrieves a kettle from behind a black plastic rubbish sack. She fills it and puts it on to boil, tipping coffee from the jar into two of the cups and hunting round for something to stir it with. I watch her, thinking she's a stranger, wishing she was, wishing she was just someone I'd met who'd brought me back here—then, even if she was meeting the Prick and I was going to watch, it wouldn't be so bad, the betrayal would seem almost normal.

"Will you tell me something?" I say as she pours hot water on the coffee and stirs it with a discolored spoon.

"No milk." She holds out a cup.

"Did you fuck Dad last night?"

The cup burns my hand. I let it. Jessie leans against the sink and looks at me. She doesn't say anything, but I think she wishes she could be rid of me, her eyes have that hard look. It's not hard enough, though—she doesn't want it enough to do anything about it. I'm just making her life more difficult.

Then we hear the front door open. It slams shut and someone mounts the stairs. Jessie calls out "Sonny?" and dumps the coffee down and vanishes into the hall. I tip mine into the sink, regretting coming, feeling that even by going along with Jessie this much I am weakening my drive, dragging out the inevitable, but I'm desperate to taste what it is that's so all-powerful, that's rammed the Prick into Jessie with no regard for anything—what sex is. I'd rather do it without Jessie's interference, but there's not time. I don't care how it happens, how anything happens. I don't care.

At the top of the stairs a door is open and in it Jessie stands apart from a beautiful black girl who has one hand on her neck. They are leaning back from each other, taking each other in, staring at each other in a way that doesn't surprise me one bit, though it's something I understand almost without understanding. She is stunning. My heart sinks at the thought that I'm the joker here again—she's Jessie's girl-friend, why bring me?—but Jessie must know something, she's promised me this payment, this bribe.

Sonny is taller than both of us. Her legs—long, slender, shiny—disappear into a strange frilly outfit that's like a 1950s bathing suit and I can't take my eyes off them, their length, their color, their finely honed muscularity–like my mother rather than Jessie: Sonny is someone who works on her body.

She catches me looking, hovering still at the top of the stairs, and scowls, spinning her eyes to Jessie, then me, then Jessie and back again. "Definitely related!" she says with a slow laugh and some kind of won-derful mixed South London accent. She shows us into her room, which is stacked high with magazines and newspapers and dominated by a huge canvas, unmistakably the same style as the picture of Jessie, this one a six-paneled group scene of floating women's and men's torsos, the women all loaded with tits and the men's dicks each bloating into a goldfish bowl.

"Sit down, boys and girls," Sonny says, standing in the doorway where we've passed her, staring at us, staring at me, the door still open. Her eyes are liquid and yet I feel like I'm being medically examined, sliced up and peeled apart, searched for further evidence of closeness to Jessie.

"How have you been?" Jessie asks, sitting on a mattress in a corner of the room, picking up a large, newspaper-size magazine and opening it.

"I'm good." Sonny shuts the door and turns away from us, walking through into what looks like a tiny kitchen and loo combined. I sit on a chair and watch her legs while her back's to us, feeling sick with myself just for being here, for getting excited like this, getting a hard-on. "I've just seen Jazz," she says, bending to open a midget fridge, my eyes following the line of her thighs to the two fingers of blue, polka-dotted bathing suit that meet where she meets under the frills. She turns and peers over her shoulder. "I'm getting a car, can you dig it? Sonny's going to be driving!"

She comes back into the room with a bottle of wine and a corkscrew. "Here," she says, giving them both to me. "You're the man." And she laughs.

"If the car is from Jazz," Jessie says, turning the pages of the magazine, ignoring me as I struggle with the bottle, "I wouldn't count on doing any driving."

"No, it's great, I've seen it." Sonny flits back into the kitchen, a thick, flower-sweet perfume wafting from her. "It's wheels, anyway. A car with no name. And no owner. Probably have different number plates front and back—"

"If it has them at all."

"—if it has them at all." Sonny emerges with two glasses and a paper cup. She puts them down in front of me and shoots me another fierce scowl as I struggle on with the cork. She retreats over to a small stereo system on a table by the window and turns on a tape. Something old comes on, music I know but can't place—American city music, conjuring TV pictures of summertime ghettos, spouting water mains, beatings from visored cops.

She sits on the bed next to Jessie. "And Martine's been messing me about again," she tells her, leaning her arm and chin affectionately on Jessie's shoulder, so that a thought I've been fighting since the first moment I saw them together returns with a vengeance—the physicality of their relationship, another part of her world that she's kept me out of, another dimension to Jessica that seems to diminish rather than increase what truth I know about her. "She is so immature." Sonny pulls back and seems to study Jessie's ear. "She has a real nigger attitude, do you know what I mean?"

"She's a cow." Jessie turns and I hardly recognize the look: jealousy, a kind of one-sided hostility that expects to bite more than get bitten.

"I know you don't like her much . . ." Sonny leans back and gets her cigarettes and a mirror and a paper sachet. "But she's beautiful when she's not coming on like some smug Thatcherite bitch."

I finally manage, flushed and straining, to force the cork out of the bottle and pour with a shaking hand two glasses. I hand them over with a stupid terror—I am headed toward oblivion, yet here I am desperate before a stunning black dike whom I'd love to fuck but whose only interest in me is probably as some sort of cat toy for her and Jessica.

"Do you have any beer?" I ask.

"Beer he wants!" she screams. "Look in the fridge." And without missing a beat, to Jessica: "You look great."

"So do you."

I go to the fridge, which is almost empty, but there are two cans of beer there so I take one and hold back a moment, drinking it and glancing at the toilet, the basin Sonny uses as a sink and the postcards covering the wall, dozens of them, some just straight-on shots of ugly hotels, others more touristy, exotic. There's a couple of art cards and a bunch of Polaroid pictures of Sonny and friends and a picture I recognize of Jessie when she was about nine or ten, which freaks me out, it's like seeing a part of my childhood pinned to a foreign wall in a dream. Then I see a shot of Sonny naked, bending over and peeking between her legs while a white girl who's also naked except for a Fulham Football Club hat rests a long spiritlevel on her arse. The two women together look somehow complete, like the Prick and Jessie, like the rest of the world enjoying things I know nothing about. I stare at Sonny's tiny ridge in the photograph and the black hair and her dark brown skin and the pinkish lips and feel she's expecting me to look at this, or Jessie is—it's all part of the game and I'm determined to break it, not to be a part of it.

I go back through. Sonny and Jessie are laughing at some private remark and doing coke, so I walk right over to them and say to Jessie, "This is boring, I'm going to go."

And Sonny looks up at me, dabbing her tongue with the coke on her finger, and says, "No—wait. Have a toot. Relax." Then to Jessie, "Does he?" And me again: "It gets better. I've got toys to play with."

Her mouth is in my eyes as I look away—wide, smiling—and I know she resents my presence, whatever she pretends, but something about the curve of her accent as she says "toys" sparks a dull electric charge in my gut and in my prick, and maybe the coke will numb it, will help me just to stop caring, so I crouch over the mirror and snort, feeling cold, wishing I could bash Jessie now—and Dad and Sonny—and crawl into that lifeless bath with her.

Sonny leans across to reach a small cupboard door with a key in the lock. Her thighs are virtually in my face now as I hover over the mirror and I can smell her skin, the focused finger points of her perfume, but it's Jessie she's leaning on, Jessie her blue frills are crushed against, Jessie she wants to touch. The key is just out of reach and as she gets up to go to it their eyes meet. "You think he'll like them?"

"Tom's up for anything, aren't you, Tom?" Jessie says, rescuing the magazine that Sonny's been sitting on, pushing it at me. "Have you seen this?"

I take it and sit on the floor and stare at the ad it's open at. A large photograph of Sonny, the full height of the page, confronts me with what looks like Paris in the background and the brand name of a tequila.

"Fueling the capitalist machine," Sonny says dismissively, glancing over as she turns the lock. "But fucking it too." She grins. "A dozen crates of that stuff and you could overturn an economy—shit!" The door is jammed and she has to brace herself against the skirting to pull it open.

My head is starting to feel sharp as Sonny unloads the cupboard, kneeling by it and removing weird solid shapeless white objects that I find I can focus on to the exclusion of everything else. I stare at them where they litter the floor round Sonny's knees and feel a kind of ruthless certainty that I'm going to screw her, whatever she's interested in. She struggles to lift a larger, heavier one, swinging it onto the floor closer to me, and suddenly it's obvious—this last one has hips and thighs attached and rests on its arse, the legs reaching out into space, then stopping where they're cut off.

"My pussy collection!" Sonny confirms and Jessie pisses herself laughing. "What do you think?"

"It's brilliant," I tell her, not really sure what to say but not caring either. I'm going to fuck her. "You do a lot of those?"

"They're like beautiful sea creatures," Jessie says, picking one up and fingering it. "Where's mine?"

"It's here, God love you," Sonny says, finding it and passing it to her. She turns to me, her voice deepening and sounding grand as if she wants to convince me, though I know she's taking the piss too: "These are a national art treasure. To redress the balance. I take plaster casts of my friends"—a glance at Jessie—"and one day when I'm ready I'm going to dump them all on the Royal Academy."

"The Royal A-cunt-omy," Jessie corrects, handing me hers.

"Right."

I turn Jessie's cast over in my hand and feel a chill. It's all there, all the detail of her cunt and arse, Dad's playground, like a relic that will be left when they're dead. I feel her watching me and stare at Sonny, who seems to be enjoying this, sitting on her heels with a big sculptured torso between her legs, the white of the plaster a shock against the smooth brown of her thighs. She runs a finger down the tract in the middle, stroking the molding with a tiny circling motion performed deliberately for me. "This one's mine," she says and I see Jessie watching me still, drinking her wine.

"Show it to him," she says, putting the glass down.

"I am."

"No, I mean show it to him," Jessie says, getting up off the mattress and onto her knees. She looks at me and with total confidence puts her hand to Sonny's groin, sliding the plaster torso aside and slipping her fingers under the tight blue polka-dotted gusset of Sonny's costume and pulling it back, stretching it taut to reveal—what? Black bristles, pinky-brown lips, a sort of affronted vertical gasp that closes again as it adjusts to Jessica's pressure on it.

My eyes fly between Sonny's cunt and her face, wanting to look but wanting to look away too—Jessie is playing with both of us, but we're letting her, we could stop it if we had the will.

"Tom's interested all right, aren't you?" she says, grinning at me and resting her other hand on Sonny's shoulder, massaging her neck. "He likes to look."

"You ever seen one like mine before?" Sonny asks, and the flash of her eyes convinces me that I do hold some interest for her—as Jessie's brother, as a sort of male arm of her. "Chocolate fudge split." She draws the words out, accentuating them, and suddenly I'm more embarrassed by her own reference to her color than I am by staring between her legs.

"I'll take the fudge," Jessie says, rolling down a strap of Sonny's suit and unpopping a tit which she kisses immediately. "And Tom can provide the cream."

"Oh, God, Jessie," Sonny groans, dipping down to meet her face with her own and laughing. "You can get out of here right away. You know I'm not into that."

"But he's my brother," Jessie croons in her ear. "Close your eyes and you won't know the difference."

I feel like a dumbo. I feel more out of it than ever—watching Jessie like this is almost worse than seeing her in the shelter because this is her trick, her taunt, this is the proof of her total control over me. I am not as strong as her, I have to take account of that—I should never have come along, I have to make her an abstract entity, someone I can deal with at a distance, someone I can force through to a tortuous death without entering into conversation.

"I'm not your fucking puppet!" I tell her, erupting out of my own thoughts into their snogging and pushing myself up, ready to kick them both where they are and get out of here.

"Calm down," Jessie says sharply, pulling back from Sonny as if she can switch gear whenever she wants, we're all just balls in her juggling act. "This is going to be worth it for you, I promise. You need to see, Tom, what your life is about. This is going to open your eyes totally." And she sounds for a moment like Mum wanting me to be there when the baby is born.

Sonny looks at her, one tit hanging out, the dark brown nipple wet where Jessie has been chewing on it, and then she grins at me and starts rocking and singing, "It's a fam-ly affair . . ."

I feel shock for a moment and wonder how much she knows but decide she's just thinking about this now, Jessie, me—though why it shouldn't be more, I don't know—maybe she's totally clued up about the Prick, maybe she and Jessie get together and act out an all-girl version of their scenes, what do I know?

Then Jessie takes her hand and plants it on the fly of my jeans, jerking our strings some more, pushing Sonny's fingers between the buttons, and I'm standing here—two good strides would take me out of the room—and I can't leave: if I leave Jessie will think I'm scared; if I stay she's won but if I go she's won too. Sonny's hands pull my fly open with no great excitement—this isn't where her interest lies—so I shift my anger to her, my mind drumming "I'm going to fuck you, whatever you want" over and over, my hand pinching her other strap down, uncovering the second brown tit as she uncovers my dick and holds it like a wet fish flapping in her palm.

I grab her waist, pulling her off balance, but she's bigger than me and she shoves me, complaining, "Take it easy!" There's a numbed simplicity to everything that must be the coke and I put my mouth to her tit where Jessie's saliva is still damp and see Jessie's hands roll down the rest of Sonny's bathing suit and linger in the space between her legs even as she warns me, "Treat Sonny gently, Tom—she's got a fierce temper!"

And they both laugh and Sonny turns round, virtually kneeing me in the groin as she thrusts my jeans down with her leg. Then she steps out of the frills Jessie is holding and over to the stereo, which has been quiet for some time. Jessie crouches in front of me, the only one of us who's still fully clothed, and tugs my jeans over my shoes, glancing at my prick as if it's some kind of toy version of my father's—a cheap, molded plastic imitation. "Just be patient," she whispers up at me. "Don't blow it."

Sonny turns the tape and goes through to the kitchen-loo, swaying to the music, totally relaxed and happy naked because of Jessie, not me. I crouch on the floor, my dick dangling, and watch her as she opens a drawer, her arse bobbing to the beat, her breasts dancing on their own, the nipples drawing a line across my brain like a flesh-brown jet trail. I feel condemned, the way I did in the tube carriage, only different—dumped in a room, a music video set in a riot zone, only there's no riot; another pathetic empty box where my life moves from *a* to *b*: this is where I experience sex, if you don't count watching my father bugger my sister; this is where she looks on as I get my dick up some friend of hers whose cunt she no doubt knows better than I ever could.

Sonny comes back through, clutching a handful of black plastic rubbish sacks, humming a sort of counterpoint to the music in a rich, clear voice. I stare at the dark ridge of her cunt as she walks toward me and think about the picture in the kitchen and Lucy—I wish this was Lucy and I was alone with her now—but then I'm distracted by the bags and wonder what the hell they mean as Sonny tells Jessie, "Help me spread them on the floor."

They lay them out, lifting the plaster cunts and using them as weights, then Jessie tells me to take my shirt off and lie down, but I crouch there not moving and watch as Jessie starts to perform for me with Sonny.

"Go on," Jessie urges when Sonny, finding herself behind her, cradles her bum with the fur of her crotch, rubbing against the back of Jessie's skirt with an exaggerated circling motion aimed, like their eyes, at me. "This is Tom's education, he needs to lose his fear. He doesn't think women function like boys do, he needs to see how we work."

That's not the truth and she knows it, I have other fears, other horrors to haunt me—she has taken everything: all the love, all the feeling, all my worth. She eases round in Sonny's grasp and draws Sonny's head down to her skirt where Sonny's hands have already been playing. They get down onto the floor and Sonny draws Jessie's knickers off, casting them in my direction where I gaze at a vague golden stain inside their front and at Sonny's angular, high-boned face plunged between the elastic tops of Jessie's stockings, lapping at her cunt.

"Wait," Jessie says, her eyes not leaving me, her voice a little throatier than usual. "I want Tom to try this too. Lie down," she tells me, "so Sonny can sit on you."

And we all move round like fucking musical chairs—Sonny and I have surrendered all rights to our will, to our individuality. I am led by my prick almost literally, by an overpowering need to do it now even if it means I'm a shit—even if it means my sense of righteousness falls apart next to Jessie's because she is always so clear and unsentimental about what she wants.

With the strange plasticky touch of a rubbish sack under my head, Sonny sits on my face and Jessie stands over her so that our two tongues can work at once. The force of Sonny's weight nearly blacks me out at first and I have to push her off and let my tongue strain uncertainly up into the arena above, my mouth and nose almost clogging with the sodden clash of tastes and smells—sharp, uriney, sweaty, then something sweet like jam.

I open my eyes to Sonny's chin and Jessie's arse and skirt overhead and think, despite all my wanking self-recriminations and doubts, that I can't hold out, I'm going to come in a moment, and I don't want it to be yet, not until I'm inside Sonny—but then she changes everything, lifting herself off me to examine the arm Jessie has just exposed from her jacket, saying, "What is that, honey?" in a voice of real concern.

It's a put-up job, another one, it has to be. Everything is arranged, everything is planned. It's all fiction—Jessie's fiction, not mine. I lie here, some kind of rank, porky smell on my lips, and Sonny poised over me staring at the burn on Jessie's shoulder. "What happened?" she asks.

"Tom did that."

"Tom?" She looks down at me in a new light.

"You wanted it," I remind Jessie, feeling defensive suddenly, feeling very young, lying here naked with Sonny's knees rooted firmly on either side.

"You enjoy that, do you?" Sonny asks.

"Not particularly," I say. "No."

"What are we going to do with him?" Sonny asks Jessie, settling her shins down into the flesh of my arms, her arse on my chest, so that I'd have to fight to move and right now I seem to have lost my fight.

"I don't know." Jessie is behind me, her knees edging onto the tips of my hair, tugging it painfully, but out of my line of sight even when I roll up my eyes.

"I think we got to do something," Sonny says, sitting hard on me, taking Jessie's outstretched hand above my head and kissing her fingers. "Maybe he'll enjoy this . . .?"

And I feel a thin trickle, burning hot at first, start at my chest and run down to my armpit, followed by another running toward my neck. I hear the music playing and feel Jessie's knees forcing down my hair and see the pouting, heavy lower lip of Sonny's broad mouth as she gazes down at me with a kind of consternation and realize that she's pissing on me, she's peeing all over me, lifting herself forward now so that my face is her target.

"Fuck off!" I manage, twisting my head sideways.

"Taste that," Sonny says, moving with me as I try to struggle out of range, spraying my cheeks and mouth. "It's straight from the source."

"Drink it, Tom," Jessie tells me, ramming her knees onto my shoulders but keeping my face clear for Sonny. "I know it seems weird to you but you need this. It's as natural as breathing, it will open all those strange, dark doors you keep locked."

I try to shut my mouth as hard as I've got my eyes shut but some of it gets in, I've got gulps of warm acid going down my throat and a taste on my tongue that's flat and dry, making me swallow, my mind reeling with a sense of humiliation at Jessie's hands—this is it, she has sealed our fate, all of our fates, she is no part of me, she's just an animal I'm going to smash.

Somewhere beyond the sick black walls of my eyes the spurts die to a trickle again and Sonny dumps herself back down on my chest, crushing my ribs, twisting herself over me in a loose rhythm to the music that's playing. I feel the hem of Jessie's skirt brush over my face as she moves forward, her knees cutting into me harder than ever, shooting veins of lightning across my head. I keep my eyes closed, hearing the music, feeling wet and uncomfortable all over, sensing the soft contact of their mouths and not wanting to live at this moment, not wanting to have to face them here in this room.

But Sonny's not finished. "You've been a good baby," she says, working her way down my stomach to sit on my dick. "You could get to like it as much as Jessie here—" And I open my eyes as Jessie takes herself off me and see Sonny lifting my prick and wedging it between her legs so that it sticks up as if it's coming from her. "If only you didn't have this thing."

And for a moment of blind panic I think they're going to do something really crazy, like cut it off. I force myself up onto my arms, as far as I can go, but Jessie's ready for me. She has a towel in her hands and in an instant it's round my head, tight, gagging my mouth, locked round my throat, my brow, the rough, furry weave rubbing against my eyes, her knees pushing me back down.

"Don't struggle or I'll pull it tighter," she says and for a curious, floating moment I'm back in our childhood together when we used to play games like this and sometimes take them too far. But this is now and we're older—we aren't playing.

"Jessie, you're a cunt!" I can hear the muffled fear in my voice. "I'll tell—" But who am I going to tell? Mum? The Prick? This is just another corner of the web.

"Is that a bad thing or a good thing to say about your sister?" Sonny asks, tweaking my foreskin back painfully with her nails, then grabbing my flailing arms with her hands.

"He loves me really," Jessie tells her. "That's the thing he can't stand. Listen—" I can feel her face close to mine on the floor, her breath hot through the towel. "I'm going to live up to my part of the bargain— you're going to get laid. Now you live up to yours. No running to Mummy or anyone else. No more watching us or interfering." For a moment I could almost convince myself that it is Sonny and her she is talking about, protecting the two of them, but that would be simple, that would be no problem at all. "It doesn't have to hurt anyone. It was never meant to—"

"What—" The towel tightens with the opening of my mouth, cutting a line across my neck, strangling my words. "What about me?"

"It doesn't have to hurt anyone else then. Tom, I'm truly sorry you found out, but try to understand. It's not so foreign to you—admit it. Let me explore." She relaxes the towel where it's garroting me, but only enough to let me breathe. "I know I can't scare you . . ." One hand is on my head now, stroking my brow, the line of my hair through the cloth. ". . . so try to understand and . . ." I listen to the words, trying to work out even now how much Sonny knows, whether it's everything or if she's lost, guessing or not caring. Jessie's hand abandons my hair, her voice retreating in space: ". . . sympathize a little."

There is an argument outside in the street, the abuse close through the open window. The music stops and the tape clicks off. I know Brixton is there, with its warring moods and chemical sky and the nasty houses opposite—and London, which is no good either: it's not interested in my protection. Somewhere, too, the Prick is with the Texans—or has he brought them here, all of them, now, watching?

I lie on the plastic sacks, mummified, sucking insufficient air through the towel. My back is dappled with patches of Sonny's urine, the bags sticky from my sweat where they're not wet. For a second she moves off me and Jessie lets go of the towel. There is a movement, a suppressed whisper—which one of them I can't tell. I could tear the towel off my face, get up, but I'm dead. And then Jessie's grip is back on it, tightening it over my eyes, my Adam's apple, her knees shifting round, thumping my shoulders. I feel Sonny lower herself onto my penis and start to rock and this is it, I am in an anonymous wet hole, my body functions and I am the same as them—Jessica, the Prick, Sonny, Lucy—killing will come like this, a brief spasm in someone else's being.

■

24

The Prick drives us back. This time, Jessie sits in the front. The towel has grown onto my face, bonding with my skin, entangling my hair, choking me still—but shutting them out. It's dark and it's cold tonight and the car is the same one Jake was born in. Do they use it? The leather in the back is sharp where it's torn and cuts against my fingers if I rub it right. It could tear little holes in Jessie where her stuffing would come out.

I feel the city leave us, like a physical presence that hangs back, like Jessie's and Sonny's hands fingering the mask I have on, holding on to me but letting me slip through. I have been to London and nothing has changed. London is with them, not me. Like everything else, it fucks around. Life is what it is. Only if the car crashes through the central divide and slams sideways into the paired lights racing toward us will things be made more simple.

In the timelessness of space, the Prick's voice comes to me: "I spoke to your mother today."

The car drones. Lights sweep toward us, silhouetting a blurred image through the towel of his head and shoulders and hers next to him.

"Jack managed a proper smile for the first time."

One push to his hands on the wheel. One.

"She said she couldn't find the video camera."

■

25

Jack is sick and Mum is in the hospital with him. It happens the night after we come back, in the middle of sleeplessness, when I have patrolled the toytown village several times in my mind and uncovered the plot, the truth that Dad is mad and this is where they send him. Or we are all inmates, me especially, and everyone else is a warder watching every move—but just not closely enough. Hours pass and no one is sleeping, or maybe Dad and Jessie are. There is a sense of urgency, of unease, in the cottage; I hear noises as Mum moves from the bed to the cot to the kitchen and back again.

I play the radio, headphones on, and find only foreign stations broadcasting to American soldiers, English farmers stationed in Africa, Dutch- and German- and French-speaking insomniacs. The village feels at the edge of the sea now, it's an island remote from the security of London, except that London has died in my imagination—I could have walked to London before in the pitch-black on bare feet just to enter the chaos, but now I would go there only to pour petrol over myself and light a match—to show it I don't give a shit.

I listen to a baseball game fading in and out from a lifetime away. I listen to an American preacher, his voice like the boom of Armageddon, talking about the holocaust and the judgment of the Lord and His justice, and I know that this man could build a pyramid in Docklands too, he could bugger his daughter, and if when the daylight comes the world is blistered and burning and sick, this man, this preacher, and my father will be the only healthy ones left and they will take turns with Jessie as she tries to remember what she will not tell me: how she started it.

Instead of sleep I feel nervy, unable to lie still, feeling my body spark and twitch at random. I take the headphones off and move round the room, not wanting the light on, wondering who on the outside would be left to inquire after us if we as a family ceased to exist—if, when morning came, we simply were not here.

I open the window more and breathe in the air and listen to what might be a cow miles in the distance and try to remember who I was only weeks ago and if that was the same life and the same me and wish I could go back.

Mum startles me with my name, looking in the door and whispering, "Tom—I thought you were up. Jack isn't well and I'm going to ring the hospital. Would you stay with him while Dad brings the car round?"

Suddenly my sense of unease seems justified—something is happening, but divorced from my thoughts, something else that has nothing to do with the cartoon blackness of my mind. I go into my parents' room, grateful to have something to do, and brush against the Prick on his way out. He looks worried, he has normal dimensions, he is not holding hands with the preacher—but I can't trust him. He takes his car keys off a chest of drawers and I stand over little Jack, who is red-faced and crying.

I watch him for a moment and feel his heat. He looks sick and I feel sorry for him and think maybe he's not so strong and wonder how the hell he's going to cope with everything he has to cope with and then his head jerks and a spurt of vomit or something comes out of his mouth onto the blanket. I call out "Mum!" not knowing what to do, but then Jessie's here, pulling on a T-shirt, and we act as if we hardly know each other, she looks at me and I look at her and then she lifts Jack onto his side and wipes his mouth.

This time, we don't go with them. Mum has found blood in Jack's nappy and the Prick drives her to the hospital with him because it's faster than waiting for an ambulance to come. Mum's eyes glisten as she carries Jack out to the car and I realize I love her and that Dad and Jessie seem like actors in a hospital drama, another Australian soap, going through the motions of love but being driven further into lies with every moment. The car disappears into the darkness of the village—you can watch its lights dip down and up the hill—and I wonder if anything really exists, if there really is a hospital at the edge of this blackness or whether Mum and Dad and Jack have simply faded out to leave me and Jessie alone.

The cottage is quiet, strangely dead with only us here. Jessie and I are still outside, shivering a little. My concern for Jack vanishes with the car headlights. He is there and Jessie is here and though I prevaricate and have internal debates and feel stupid some of the time and think normality is there—I can touch it, this horror is all in me, I'm the one—I know one thing that is constant:

"I'm going to kill you soon."

She is just going through the door. She doesn't even turn. "Oh, Tom—shut up."

Her hair, which is about half an inch longer than it usually is, is flattened on one side and bent, like Dad's is sometimes, so that she almost looks like a younger, female Dad for a moment.

"Does he do it up your arse all the time? Is that the only way you like it? With Nick too? Is it only Sonny who can touch your twat?"

Her body stops and revolves on its base like a shopwindow dummy to face me. The T-shirt she's got on is too big for her and suddenly it seems to swamp her, but it can't hide the nasty yet hurt look in her eyes, as if her only defense is attack. She might almost scratch her cunt. "You could if you wanted to."

The words confuse me. I can't cope with her, I should know that. "I don't!" I say hastily and close the door behind us, shutting us in.

"You really are constricted, Tom."

The cottage seems cold—like the cold cunt it is. This cottage bears a large part of the guilt for what has happened. I'd like to burn it. She stands, keeping me against the door. I twist a smile at her: "No, I'm not. You've opened my eyes, haven't you?"

"Stop trying to psych yourself up for some negative act. It's not in you." She turns away again.

"Wait and see."

"You'd have done it by now."

"Sometimes people wait years."

She's at the stairs. She glances back. "You do what you want. We all will anyway." She starts up the first step. "But when I try to show you that you haven't even begun to realize what you're capable of, you shy away from it—or you would have."

"You're a slag, Jessie!" I shout at her back. "A lying dike slag! What you do with Dad isn't special or anything—it's sick. Even biologically, it's sick. And Sonny's just as sick as you are."

She turns on me from the stairs. "Is that really what you think? Is that what your most profound and private feelings are—as predictable as that?" She pities me from halfway up, arrested in mid-step, one hand on the banister. "What's your life about then? What the hell do you think your next sixty or eighty years are about? Why don't you just go out and zap the nation with your mathematical skills or whatever you'll be left with if you stay at one school long enough to learn anything? It's perfect for you out there now—they like angry little bastards who want to nail everything down. I'll tell you something, Brother—despite all your anger, all that pissing about you get up to, essentially you want everything to be sweet. And it isn't. If you could face up to that, maybe you could relax. The sweetness is the lie they put out to make us all slave harder. Nature isn't sweet. I seduced Dad—not him me, whatever you may think—and no way was that sweet." She comes down a step, relishing this, enjoying her effect on me. "He stinks, Tom—he smells like no one else can. It's like fucking our childhood, all I can smell is his bloody hot buttered toast first thing in the morning, every morning for the whole of my life. I used to sit on his lap, years ago, and press myself against the pencils he always kept in his shirt pocket, digging them deeper into my arm—I've still got the marks, little lead bruises. He was such a fucking prince, even at five I wanted to be his princess! Now I'm his dog." She smiles at me as if she wants us to be in this together, us against him as it always was. "He made me and I've swallowed him whole—I don't care what's supposed to be, that is like fucking Creation! Otherwise everything goes on exactly the same."

"And this is better, is it?" This whole outburst—her whole energy—scares me like hell. I'm at the bottom of the stairs, I'm lost, I'm meant to be menacing her, not letting her squash me into nothingness, conformity, a living death at an early age.

"You'll never know."

I watch her and shiver and try not to see the soft stretch of thigh mocking me from beneath the sag of the baggy T-shirt. She stands there and I move forward, up one stair, trying to find a way to answer her. The thought of Mum and Jack at the hospital stabs at my mind and I know that if I kill Jessie and Dad it's for me, it's not for them—Mum would rather deal with a sick, deceitful daughter and a cunt of a husband than with their deaths or mine, but I feel selfish. That was the word Dad used, wasn't it? "It depends on how selfish you're feeling." I don't know when or if it had already started—but he and Jessie must know how it feels.

"I've thought about it," I say, two steps away from her now, no need to speak very loudly though there's no one else to hear. "And there's nothing you can do. Nothing you can say. I'm not interested anymore. What you and Dad do, however you do it, whether you enjoy it or not, is like running a knife up and down my back. I feel hollow—which is how you'll feel soon."

I think I frighten her a bit—my state of mind if not the buried threat. I put my hand out to hold on to her as I climb past on the stairs and she flinches a little, she jerks back slightly. That's good. I smile, feeling her warmth as I pass, smelling yesterday's dead scent, her slightly stale breath.

"Don't feel too safe," I say.

■

And then I'm cycling to see Mum. She's back at the same hospital in Exeter, which is quite a ride, but it's good to be on my own, the road is long and straight and I can stare at the ground and watch it moving under me, not stopping, nothingness rolling by like a belt. I pedal harder, working at it, trying to break through to a different level, one that will flood my mind, wash away my thoughts. I keep my head down, hoping to meet the raw edge of a metal bumper, a truck's rear axle, the tangled blades of a farm machine—lose my nose, my face, in a single slice.

It's the last day of August. The air is cold, really chill, though summer can't be over. There's a wind blowing in the trees and fields on either side that feels unnatural, that feels like the weird currents of air you get at airfields, that sounds—when it swings into me, switching from the push it's been giving—like the drowning roar of jet fighters flying low. I see encampments up ahead, old hill forts only there in the blackened roof of my skull, and my mind picks through the soil and flint and slime to find little bits of school—a broken chair, a desk— and my dead grandmother and Jessie's tin with the crayons and blades. The mounds are close and in the distance at the same time and they fill me with a sense of dread, so that I try to cycle faster still, thinking that will get me past them, but they move with me.

Jessie and the Prick took the car this morning, soon after I woke, which was soon after I slept. I wouldn't go with them. They need time together and I can't watch their necks in front of me, the backs of their heads. The cottage was a shit hole without them. It was the shelter, the same decor. I ate a bowl of cereal and left it in the sink where their breakfast things were piled up. I kept thinking I could hear their voices, then I did and I went.

■

26

They won't let me take my bike up to the ward, which almost provokes a scene when I try wheeling it into the lift, but the woman on the desk calls some uniformed Nazi and the bike suddenly seems very important to me even though I couldn't give a shit about it the rest of the time and don't even have a padlock for it. He holds it and I try to wrest it from him, and he's probably just a porter, he's not trained for trouble, but he looks like he wouldn't mind a shot now, he'll have a bash, but then I think, "Fuck it, don't attract attention, just forget it," and I let him have it and walk out of the lift and up the stairs instead, leaving him to hold on to it, and I know I'm going to have to face some kind of heavyweight crap when I get it back, but there's not much they can do.

Mum and Jack are in a cubicle in front of the nurses' station and news of my arrival can't have filtered up yet because they let me straight through, just asking me to wait while they wheel out a color monitor and a blood pressure machine, which makes room for me to sit down nicely but I don't. Mum already has a prison look to her, despite her tan and the short summer dress she's got on, and Jack is on a drip like some bag creature from a weird movie, but the cubicle has a sense of peace to it. I like it because it's nowhere, it's just a place where they watch you to see whether you live or die and the Prick's skills as an architect would get in the way here.

"How is he?" I say, thinking, "You're going to be OK, Jack—Dad and Jessie have seen to that, this would be too easy a way out."

"Did you cycle all the way here?" Mum says, hugging me. She feels warm, alive, anxious. I hug her back, wishing I could feel something. "Why on earth didn't you come with Jessie and Dad?"

"I fancied a ride," I say, wondering once again if she's guilty, what her crime is. You must have one, Mum—or several. Maybe you're too fucking perfect, too fucking tolerant. You've always tolerated me. Maybe you actually love the Prick. Or maybe I don't know you either, you also have a secret life I know nothing about.

You touch my chin before letting me go. "You look good on it," you say. A smile. You're so easily fooled—I feel dead, I feel only the hate in me is thriving—yet usually you're the one who sees through us all. "You must have needed the exercise."

Jack stirs and makes a strange snorting noise—the sound of someone blowing through a Christmas cracker toy. Mum turns to him and his face screws up and he wails and I think he's just a small animal suffering pain, and then I look at him and it's more than that, it's not just the physical pain, there's an intelligence working there and that's the disease—he knows. It's knowing that's the sickness; not knowing something, just knowing.

"Is he all right?" I ask.

"Poor angel, he's been peeing blood and it hurts." Mum opens the cubicle door and calls to a nurse, frustration and worry in her voice: "He's peed again and I wasn't able to get a sample."

The nurse comes in and for a moment I fade to nothing. They change him and I watch Mum, strong, rationing her emotions, saving her energy for Jack. She must have been like this with me once and yet I can't remember. I vaguely remember crawling into bed with her and Dad when I was very sick, but they were comforting forces in a giddying dream, they weren't distinct people and I never thought what it meant to them. I search my mind for a link between that tenderness and what Dad and Jessie have been doing together—could it be a small step, from that closeness of childhood into a deeper, more devastating closeness?—but there has been no tenderness in what I've witnessed, I think they're past tenderness into a doglike slavering for each other, a kind of supremacy over guilt. I should have put the Prick out of his misery while I had the chance—in his bed, in the heady flush of childhood sickness.

The nurse is still there, staying too long, taking precious minutes from my time with Mum, keeping me outside in the ether so that I may not be able to get back. "He looks cooler, has he been drinking at all?" she asks, and I think she means alcohol, the Prick's Scotch or his beer, and I want to blame him for this sickness even though I know it's one thing he's not responsible for.

Then she goes, which Mum hardly registers, standing over Jack for a while longer, rocking slightly on her feet, her eyes wishful, compassionate. "He's OK," I say, without much confidence. He's OK now, but maybe I'm the one who's going to fuck things up for him.

She looks at me when I speak, remembering I'm there. "Oh, Tom," she says. "Thank you so much for coming."

"We're in trouble," I tell her. Except I don't. I'm not sure how much I say anymore and how much I imagine, but I don't say this.

"I didn't hear you," she says.

"I said I needed something to do."

Now I sit down. The phone rings at the desk and I catch the sister or whatever she is glancing my way. She looks irritated by the call and watches me, but I stare back at her blankly and after a while she looks away. My mother fusses around a bit, pulling the cover down off Jack because it's hot in here, turning up the fan and moving a book off her chair and then putting it back because she can't find a spare surface for it.

"Would you like a Coke? Or a cup of tea? I could make you one."

"No, I'm not thirsty." A lie. I'm gasping, but I don't want anything that is going to separate us for even a minute.

She picks up the book again and sits, keeping the book in her lap. Her legs underneath it are someone else's legs, the legs of a woman in the street who's had a wonderful summer. My mother's had a good summer, but it's going to get worse. Her eyes seem lost in her face, unsure where to go, flickering back and forth to Jack in the cot, then settling on me with a concern that suddenly seems directed more at me than at him.

"Are we bad parents?" she asks and the question startles me. It seems to open the door to so many more.

"Why?"

"I was wrong, you don't look great. You look terrible."

"I'm just tired. I was up last night anyway."

"I lay here this morning thinking about all of you. Jessie—I don't know what's wrong between me and Jessie, but she resents me for some reason at the moment, doesn't she? She tries to disguise it, but I really feel it. Maybe it's just a phase—or the baby. Or a boy."

She seems almost hopeful when she says this, but I feel numb. My mind has already started to dive-bomb at the prospect of this all becoming a reality, becoming something we—Mum and me, we're all that's left—can say out loud. The nothingness of the cubicle intensifies. The edges blur. This is an experiment—I am a rat in a tank, some thought-drug has just been injected into my skull. I stare into the light.

"Has she said anything to you?"

"About what?" I sound hostile.

My mother's face is a couple of feet from me across the room. She frowns, her lips arch like Jessie's sometimes do. "I'm sorry—I shouldn't talk to you like this."

"No," I say, a dimness in my brain. "I want you to." Where does this go? Where can we get from here—is this the time to go all the way, expose it? I can't face it. Not here, not with all these watchers around, ready to intervene, ring their alarm bells, take it further.

"Is there a problem?"

"With Jessie?"

"With either of you?"

The sister outside the cubicle peers in, as if she's expecting to find a scene of bloodshed and mutilation, me reveling in the carnage like the freak I am. Her face is a thousand other faces—the mad old cow in the village, a face in the tube, a grandmother on the motorway—all watching, waiting for a slip. Mum has no idea, I'm sure of that. She may have doubts, feelings, but she's swimming in a different pool. In mine you can't come up for air.

"Yes." I watch to see if she's expecting something. Her face is alert, involved, her courtroom face. "No. I mean—you know my problem."

I can't fucking say it. The moment has passed again. On every front, I let time slip away. I want it to happen for me, but it won't—I have to make it happen.

She moves the book, bends her legs sideways, massages her brow above one eye with a hand that used to hold mine. "Can you give it till Christmas?" she asks.

"What's different at Christmas?"

"We could get our house back. We only have to give three months' notice."

"We could rent in London now." We're drifting further from the point. London is irrelevant; London has no power anymore.

"I'd like to stay here a little longer." Would she? "So would your father."

My father would like a lot of things, half of which you know nothing about, Mum. You could fuck a doctor, every patient in the hospital, I would forgive you—but he, he has wedged the knife in our backs.

Suddenly I feel angry with her. Maybe she's not so perfect. She picked him, she fucked him to make us and now she can't see the poison when it's stuck right under her nose.

I get up and go over to her. If the sister's watching, let her wonder. I lean over her. I'm shaking. I'm ready to run. I can't say what I'm going to say and stay.

"You're going to misinterpret this—" My voice is tiny, it sounds girlish to me, someone else's voice, far away. "It's not going to help you, stuck in here alone with Jack—" I touch her arm briefly, to convince me she's there. The words won't come. I don't know what to say. "Don't trust him."

I'm across the room before the words mean anything. I didn't think she'd take me seriously, but her eyes look panicked—maybe it's me she's worried about, my games are getting crazier, Dad and me have come to blows?

It's not enough, but it's said. Her mouth opens with a question, but I've got the door open.

"I'm sorry."

■

27

And I'm home.

I'm knackered. The ride back has finished me, I just want to be dead, but as I approach the cottage, standing on the pedals to force my bike up the hill, I spot the Prick in the garden trying to get a fucking barbecue going. I skirt round and ditch the bike behind our wall, avoiding him and climbing in through a window so that when I walk into the kitchen where Jessie is I can feel the pain smash into her chest when she turns and finds me there.

"Christ, Tom!"

I'd like to spit at her gaping face as she stands there staring at me, but I'm too busy taking in the detail—the pronged sausages on the board, the chopped onion, the fork in her hand.

"This is nice," I say. "Life goes on as normal. Mum's in the fucking hospital with Jack and you two throw a party!"

"God, you're a shit." Jessie looks different: a little cowed, as if it's all getting too much for her. Something's been said in my absence—I wonder what? "One day," she says to me, "you'll make somebody a lovely wife."

I ought to punch the coiled little navel that is poking its ugly mouth in my direction from between her black jeans and black hacked-off top, but I'm distracted by a spark of life outside—the Prick pouring paraffin onto the barbecue coals. The flames cough hungrily, the smoke thickens and Jessie bares her tanned, deceitful neck at me, the hair bristling, color rushing there like what's left when you take raw meat off a plate. She stares out the window and utters, in that dulcet, girls' school tone of hers, "Oh, fuck!"

I can hear what's happening before I see it—the uneven blast of Nick's motorcycle as he runs it at the stumpy tree roots guarding our path, the skid of his back wheel on the lawn as it churns up clumps of turf and throws them into the barbecue smoke. Then the sight of Nick's leather jacket shining, his smooth, sharp face staring first at the cottage, then turning to deal with Dad—a doomy prick playing with fire, preoccupied by some inner hole, unprepared for this invasion of his sovereign state.

Nick looks different from when I first saw him at the pub—his hair shorter like Jessie's, younger, as if he's not caught up in the game everyone else is of trying to look older. He stops the bike and steadies it, two, maybe three feet from the barbecue flames, the sputtering smoke wafting past him as Dad beats the tongs on an invisible drum, trying to adjust his mind to this confrontation.

"My daughter doesn't want to see you." The Prick's voice swings clearly through the open door as Jessie goes to sort them both out. He sounds like any other uptight, reactionary prick on a summer's evening—not the slobbering leech he is. He puts the tongs down on the grill and blocks Nick's view of the house—and mine of him—by stepping in front of the bike.

But Jessie is already there, wiping her hands on the seat of her jeans and advancing toward Dad's back as if he's something she can walk through.

"Brilliant move, coming here now, Nick—why couldn't you call?"

Dad steps aside to look at Jessie when he hears her voice, his eyes hard, his face corrugating into a real bastard's mask—the mask he uses on site.

"Go back inside, Jessie. I'll deal with this."

The force of his anger surprises her—but not that much. "Let me talk to him, I can—"

"I SAID GO BACK INSIDE, JESSIE!"

Now Nick is the voice of reason. He sits back on the bike, letting go of the handles, keeping its weight between his legs, his manner that of someone who has some kind of an ultimatum to deliver. "There's no need for argument," he says, his soft voice accented with his country twang, yet tougher for one moment than either of them—ruthless in its decisiveness. "It will take us two minutes alone to find out if there's even anything to argue about."

Dad stares at him. He'd like to swat him, he'd like to smudge Nick's fluids all over a rolled-up newspaper—I can see the fear in his eyes, the competition. "Don't try to be reasonable with me," he says, acting the affronted father but taking it past the accepted limits, locked into a hostile, patronizing style that he brings his own evil twist to. "Reasonableness is an insult to my intelligence. I know you've fucked my daughter and I want you out of my garden—now!"

I think Jessie gets a kick out of this. I think Jessie gets a kick out of seeing Nick's astonishment at these words, even if the openness of them worries her just a tidge. I think—and this is just my feeling, right, I'm just a sick observer in all of this—I think Jessie would like to get down on the grass with Dad now and do him in front of old Motorcycle Boy. But Dad's said his piece and he's obviously cheered by it, because he tells them, "All right, five minutes. You can say your goodbyes, tell your lies and see if you can pull the wool over my eyes."

He starts back toward the kitchen and I disappear fast. There is a truly ugly mood settling over tonight—he's cracked, something's snapped in him—and I want to be part of it, but at my own speed. The beauty of this is he doesn't even know I'm back yet; he's got that surprise to come. If I thought there was going to be some pain in the Prick's countenance while he times them out there, I might hang around, but on this one he's won—it's already over, any fool can see that, Jessie just wants Nick to go.

■

Upstairs I lie on my bed, my legs like lead from the bike ride, and try to rest a moment but Jessie won't let me go. The window is open and I could get up and shut it but I'm finished, so I lie there in the half-light—it's darkening outside; inside it's the same old Beirut bomb site—and hear their words, closer than I want them to be, the garden's too fucking small, I'm between them, particled in the air displaced by their breath.

"What's going on, Jessie?" This is said as if he's got a right to know. Nick's a trier—for a boring old hippie, he keeps on trying, but he's losing my sympathy fast. He should belt her.

"Don't ask me. You started it." Sister dear—definitely a bit defensive tonight. Could my warning to Mum have sparked a call? She's stuck there in the hospital; maybe she's had time to work things out?

"Want to come for a ride?" The motorbike is switched off at the moment, but I can picture Nick's hand on the key even as he doubts the point of this—he knows something or thinks he does. He's impatient for an answer.

Silence. I lie there but it's no good. I have to see what's going on. I stumble across the room, kick a chair leg and curse—I'd like to kick Jessie's guts. The air at the window is warmer than it's been all day. Everything's weird. I can hear the sea—a low interference noise in the background, lapping round England, keeping us apart, sloshing round the cottage, keeping our nonsense in.

What's the Prick doing while this is happening? Taking a slash? Watching the cooker clock, waiting for the buzz when their time is up? He's probably reading the fucking paper, his feet up, water on the boil to chuck in Nick's face, scratching his skull manically the way he does when he's under pressure so that he really looks crazy.

My angle on Jessie is weird—hair, brow, nose pointed at Nick, it's all lit by the calculation of how to get rid of him most quickly.

Nick's face I can see. "Let's go!" he tries, winding himself up, both hands on the tank now, leaning forward, though he knows it's a lost cause.

"You heard him." She is standing to one side, a distance between them.

Nick shakes his head. "What's wrong with you?" He wants to spit, I see it. He should. He mumbles something I can't hear. Then: "You're acting like a cow—is this what two days in London does to you?"

"Wait a minute—" Jessie is barely even listening. There has been a minor collapse at the barbecue, a limp combustion chucking out a few sparks and a billowing cloud of smoke which spreads over the garden, catching the weird dying light and bringing cancer to our already strangled and wrecked grass. In the absence of the tongs, which Dad has taken in with him, Jessie kicks the hibachi's legs to aerate it and turns back to Nick, her belly flashing, a sort of bored, half-interested mood to her now, as if she might come alive if he made the effort. "Come over here!"

Nick stays put, straddling the bike, and I suddenly remember Jessie telling me that he does Buddhist chants. If so, they're not doing much for him now. He looks distinctly rattled. He looks like he's half a mind just to take off out of here now and forget it, but then Jessie goes back over to him and wraps herself over one leg—a change of tactic; hard to tell who she's working on: him or the Prick in the kitchen watching. Her left hand delves down into his groin while her right embraces his neck. It all seems so transparent to me that I can't believe Nick goes for it for a moment, but he must be playing along because he says something and I catch a characteristically haughty "Yeah, yeah" from her. She whispers something close to his ear and blows it—because suddenly Nick pushes her off.

"I want to get things straight, Jessie, that's all." It's hard to stand up to Jessie when she's determined, she makes sure of that, but Nick is armed and ready. "I thought we were close"—his voice cuts through the evening air; he's nervous about something—"I just didn't expect competition from your old man."

If the Prick hears that, it must throw him. How do you handle this one? Rush out there hot with denials and fury? Laugh at the absurdity of the suggestion? Write it down and instruct your solicitor—in this case, your wife when she gets back from the hospital—in the good old middle-class way? It certainly must give Jessica something to think about, wondering how dangerous this is, whether the bomb's really dropped or if Nick is just stabbing in the dark.

He looks at her, standing where she's stepped back, having been evicted from his thigh. She looks cool, fascinated—this is just another night in her life, an accusation of rogering Dadda, so what?

"John saw you together," Nick says, weakening his case with explanation. "In the car—in Harpford." He's starting to doubt himself; she sees that. He takes hold again: "Of course he could be lying but I wouldn't say it was the kind of thing John's imagination runs to."

Can Dad hear this? I hope so. I hope it buries itself deep inside him and twists and tears there. On the lawn, Jessie is horrified—her Sunday school disbelief could almost fool me.

"You are a sick bastard," she tells him. "You and John! Go away!"

It's an impressive performance, but not quite up to scratch for Nick obviously. His eyes fix on her for a long moment and even at this distance I can see a kind of pain there. "Trust me, Jessica—" He reaches out and takes hold of her arm. "I know when you're lying."

"Fuck off and leave me alone!"

She pulls away but he grabs her with some force, swinging his head toward her from his heavy mount on the bike so that for one instant I think, "Yes! Right!" and I'm him, I'm locked physically with him as he rams into her, nutting her hard on the skull, sharing that splintering crack as his forehead meets her forehead and he says—the anger coming out now, forget all that Buddhist humming—"I fucking love you!"

She is not worth it. She pulls away and staggers back and I see her pass below me, out of my sight, leaving Nick on his own, stuck on the bike in the middle of our piss-awful garden, the barbecue chugging away behind him.

"Tell me to go!" he shouts after her, and it suddenly occurs to me that this little scene might be attracting the attention of the neighbors —I'm sure one or two lights have gone on down the hill—and I don't want that, tonight is mine, I can feel it, I don't want any poxy interference from the forces of sanity outside. "Tell me the truth!" he shouts. "I'm not leaving until you come back out here and tell me what's what."

The motor of his bike kicks into life, but he's not going anywhere, I know that—and I want him gone now too, I'm keen to be rid of him before he brings the bloody filth down on us. He overrevs it, tearing at the night air with the sound, so that I don't hear his mates' bikes approach until they're on the road outside—and neither does he.

"Here, Nick—" John's voice is like an old friend punching you in the cheek at the pub, it has the warm, sodden crunch of teeth, blood and alcohol about it. He sits on his bike at our gate. "Where is she then?"

Nick has already got his bike on the move, rolling it round the uneven turf of our lawn, circling the barbecue, guiding it carefully for the moment through the narrow gap between the grill and the trestle table. He ignores John, though he doesn't seem surprised to see him, riding close to the house now as he shouts, "You think you've got something so fucking valuable that everyone wants to take it!"

"Where's the perv?" I see Toe-rag's familiar twisted grin in my mind as I hear him call out behind John. "Pervy perv! Is he home?"

"Shut up," Nick says, but he doesn't really care anymore and he aims his bike straight at the barbecue this time, knocking it onto the grass, scattering hot charcoal and sparks and setting little patches briefly alight. Then John is over the tree roots and he's in the garden too, followed by Toe-rag, though I think ape-face Colin on his wimp machine stays behind. I run downstairs—I want to be in on this—to find Jessie struggling with Dad to stop him from going outside.

"Just ignore them, they're morons. They'll get bored and go away."

She doesn't sound entirely convinced of this, holding her head where Nick cracked her and trying to hold on to the Prick at the same time.

He looks at me quickly, his lizard face, the lines round his jaw tightening as he takes me in, sweat or saliva on his lip, his eyes like reactivated sheep's eyes in biology, two tiny torches shining through dead meat at the danger outside and—if he can read my mind—here in the kitchen.

"You're back. Are you OK? Did you come through that?"

He indicates the roaring bikes outside, one trying to outdo the other. There is a loud, splintering crash, followed by another, as John and Toe-rag ram the garden table from both ends. But I'm wrong—it must be Nick, because suddenly something hard flies through one of the small kitchen windowpanes, smashing the glass and breaking the plates on the drainer, and then the kitchen door slams open as the wheel of John's bike hits it and comes inside, his face following, bringing the sharp smell of the smoke with him, his mouth stretched wide, rat's teeth showing as he leers and shouts, "HEEEEEEEEEERE'S JOHNNNY!"

Dad swings round to grab his tire, but John is already rolling back out and the Prick has to let go or get his fingers mashed under the mudguard. He follows him outside but gets thrown off by Toe-rag, who drives straight at him, yelling, "It's Larry boy! Watch out, the dirty old sod's getting it out!" I just stand and watch as my father flings himself out of the path of the bike and recovers his balance with surprising speed. Jessie is at the door but he shouts at her to stay back and for once she listens. He picks himself up in the middle of the madness, looking crazed himself, his face gray in the lingering smoke, the bikes moving round him in a field of dazzling flashes and burns, lights streaking past the windows and door of the kitchen as Nick and the crew try to scare him shitless, running their bikes at him in kamikaze collision courses across the tiny lawn.

The Prick stands there, enjoying the chaos in a way, ready for this, steeling himself to lash out at the furies or whatever they are circling him, like the hero or poor diseased god he has been forced to play in some mental Greek myth. Jessie has been yelling pointlessly at Nick to go away and there's the faint peep of a siren audible in the brief lulls between the roaring of the motorcycles, but Dad doesn't want any help from anyone—he wants this fight for his daughter's cunt—and he dives side-on at Nick, taking him by surprise, knocking the bike over and throwing himself on top.

"FUCK OFF OUT OF HERE, THE REST OF YOU!" he screams, his head jerking round to show that he's ready to take on all comers, and then he lands a punch right on Nick's face as he struggles up, scrunching his nose down with a force that shocks me—its bite, the pleasure he takes from it.

Jessie is through the door in an instant and I follow. John and Toe-rag are down on him with their bikes like a ton of bricks and one of them obviously whams hard into Dad's back because in a moment he's on the grass reeling, spitting air out and coughing, then dragging it back in as if he's going to be sick. Jessie pulls him back from the tangle of Nick and his bike and I must admit I help, though he's still the Prick—part of me sides with him against these local wankers, the other wants to put the boot right into where he's been nicely softened by the bike.

But it's over. Nick doesn't want to fight anymore—maybe it's against his hippie principles to risk losing and try to finish it—and the others' adrenalin is draining down as he wipes the dark jam flowing from his nose and picks up his machine. The siren is down the dip of the hill now, getting closer and someone—it has to be Colin—points this out, so they leave the garden, the bikes revving and bouncing over the tree roots at the gate, and take off up the road to the beach, John pouting his rubber lips and waggling his tongue back at us in a totally obvious fashion while Toe-rag's accompanying animal grunts fade into the night.

There is a timeless gap before the police arrive, another moment of unreality in which I feel outside my life, the Prick and Jessie are just characters from a dream I keep returning to and anything that happens is fine because there is no code of behavior in a dream, you can fuck and maim and die and nothing touches you except the fear that every-thing is going to go on and you are going to come back again.

Dad is walking now, rejecting Jessie's and my support, holding his lower back and trying to straighten up, the effort making him sweat, streaks of it running down his lined madman's forehead and swimming down the sides of his cheeks. We make it to the kitchen as the piggy wheels draw up outside and Dad takes my shoulder and presses on it hard and I'm not sure how he's looking, there's an effort to conceal something—pain, maybe, or regret—but he's also trying to draw me into this by keeping me out. "Go upstairs," he tells me. "Don't get involved." And there's a kind of pleading there, like he needs my help. "I want to talk to you," he adds, and I think: "Fuck you—but fuck them too, the pigs."

And now Jessie's all over the place, vicious suddenly—even her fear is loaded—and she pulls away from both of us with a look of contempt, flashing resentment at me as if I'm the cause of all this, and she takes the board where she's been chopping the onions, pronging the sausages, and opens the cupboard door where the waste bin is and rams it all, board and sausages, into the bin, saying, "You didn't want a barbecue, did you?"

Then the police are at the front door and Dad answers and I crawl up the stairs, letting them see me, letting them see I'm not interested in what they can do. Jessie is still in the kitchen and one look at the complacent, family face of the mustached copper on the step lets me know that she'll take the fall for this—but not in any real sense: they'll take one look at her, her fierce eyes and her belly button mouthing "Fuck you!" and they'll put it down to boyfriend trouble that's got a bit out of hand and think the Prick's a prick for letting her out like that.

And I'm right. It takes forever and I wait in my room, waiting for one of them to come up and plant something on me—they don't want us here, they know who we are: tourists, and sick ones at that—but they don't even bother, they're not even interested in asking whether I've noticed my dad boffing my sis lately and then taking it out on the local scumbags. But I'm right. I hear the muffled voices, the Prick entertaining them in the living room—he knows how to handle tits like these: offer them a drink, nothing too obvious, they know you're patronizing them but they'll play along anyway—and I peer out the window and see the car with its reflective stripe down the side and the mad old cunt squinting at it, tottering past it on the other side of the road and nodding her head. She's probably the one who called them out, I'd love to tell her what she's really been missing, sell her a season ticket to the shelter—"There, feast your eyes on that, you old cow!"—she'd probably love it. I'm right. I hear the mustached one's voice in the hall, all forced cordiality, advising the Prick that perhaps the young lady should stay out of the local pub for a night or two so as to avoid any repeats of tonight's little flare-up, and Pricko agreeing that that's a splendid idea—but perhaps it might be more to the point if the local constabulary kept a watch on Nick and his companions and generally made life painful for them. And Mr. Bill times it perfectly at the door. He says, "You know, there's only three people from London I've met that I've liked—" and I can picture him standing there, his uniformed boyfriend already heading back to the car, leaving him to handle the local diplomacy bit. I bet Dad looks at him, wanting to get rid of him as much as I do. The mustache flickers up, a suggestion of a smile, this is community policing—imagine what it's like if you're black. "And now there's you, sir. Good night."

■

The door closes and there's a pause and then the Prick's feet on the stairs and he's at my door—he must be feeling guilty, he must be feeling terrible, even the pleasure he took from creasing Nick's nose can't wipe away the strain that's showing in his features now.

He comes inside, a hand on the door, hunched slightly from some evident difficulty with his back, his face gray and hollow, the lizard skin sagging, cracked and wrinkled though he's shaved tonight at some point—earlier, before the fun began. I stare at him and he keeps his hand on the door and I notice his trousers, dirty with grease and grass, and imagine the scruffily hairy legs inside—that sack of crap and cock that's had Jessie must be ready to drop, wondering what went wrong.

"Can we talk?" he asks and the gravity of his voice makes me want to puke or laugh. "Just tell me!" I want to shout. "I know it all anyway. Don't fuck around."

He shuts the door. I'm on the bed and I stay there—maybe he'd like me too? But he looks like a pensioner at this moment, someone who's lost all his balls. He moves to the window and looks out, as if he's never been in this room before, as if he's piecing together how much I've been able to see all along.

Of course, I could be wrong. This might be something else altogether. Mum could have interpreted my parting remark in a dozen different ways. Maybe she hasn't rung at all. Maybe she's too caught up in Jack even to think about anything else at the moment. But ever since I got back I've felt it in the air—this is when it happens, this is where I find my strength. I can feel the patterns changing, the walls moving back to show me the darkness. At the hospital, when I got my bike back, they treated me as if I was sick, as if we had just suffered a deep and damaging loss in the family. They humored me. They told me I was a stupid little boy, but they treated me like a joke. I wanted to grab them by their pudgy, authoritarian faces and ram them up against the wall, tell them, "Don't underestimate me, cunts! There's going to be damage like you've never seen before." And it's going to be tonight, I can feel it, I'm ready for it just as Dad was with Nick. We all have our mythologies to act out.

He keeps his face away from me and I glance at his back, the back that's giving him so much trouble tonight. He's outside the depressing ring of light my bedside lamp gives out and I wish he wasn't there at all because he's taking a lifetime to say something and, however he says it, he won't choke on the words the way I want him to. All I can think about is how stupid he is—how incredibly, inhumanly stupid—and how stupid he has been. I'm the fool for ever believing in him, but then I had no choice: he drew the lines for what honesty was.

"Well, what do you make of all this?" he says after a long time, a long time of standing there with his back to me and his hands creeping round to strangle each other against his trouser seat.

I bring my knees up in front of me and stare past them at the wall. I could take one of my running shoes off and throw it at him to wake him up, but why bother? What am I supposed to say—"I don't make anything of it, squire—you go ahead and fuck Jessica if you want to"?

"I think you need your head examined," I tell him.

He turns slowly. No anger, he's treading warily with me now. His face in the semishadow is all misarranged, like one of Jessie's paintings. "Do you?" His voice is trying to stay with me, but it's prissing up, it's getting pompous and superior, just like Jessie.

"If you think we've got anything to talk about, you do." I swing my knees round to block him out. I can do it tonight. If I had a knife I could do it now, but they're all in the kitchen. I know the one I'll use—smooth red handle, razor edge, with a neat little curve at the end of the blade to decorate his paunchy, desperately exercised gut before going on to autograph Jessie's.

He takes a step forward, but not too close. I remember a hiding he gave me, one of the few times I can remember him really smacking me. I was about six at the time and I can't remember what it was about, but it had something to do with a toolbox. Now his whole being looks like a pathetic apology, a nonperson desperately seeking absolution and admission to the world again. "Fuck off, my son!" I want to say. I've always fancied being a priest.

"I've been a prick, Tom," he mumbles—or is it just my imagination? If he gets any more humble, I think I'll kill him now and put an end to it; knife or no knife, I'll find a way. "I think you know what's been going on."

"Oh yeah?" I say, jaunty, trying to really screw him into a corner. "What's that then?"

"Tonight, with our friends on the motorcycles—"

"Yes?"

"Don't be a prat, Tom. You heard them, though I don't think you needed to. Jessie's a closed book where you're concerned, but I've felt you looking at me like a piece of shit—I'm not completely stupid."

He's right. Stupidity doesn't cover it; there's sickness, ego, greed, the fact that he's from another planet, his total inability to care about or love anyone but himself . . . all the great parental characteristics. And Jessie doesn't grass on me. I'll bear that in mind. I'll kill her tenderly.

"I—"

I can feel it coming. This is where my life turns, even more so than with Jessie, this is where the madness has to be confronted, its ugly adult form is showing its head. It's actually happening, it's been happening and we're not in some TV show, on some council estate with the kids screaming and the cat shitting and the smell of cooking and half a discount store of stereo and video and computer junk in a corner—see, I'm an elitist at heart, I revert to type. But this is my life we're talking about and it's tiny, flat and insignificantly fucked up.

His hand wipes his mouth, eradicating a smile, spit, nothing, he's just nervous. I had never realized how womanly his lips are—a female reptile's razor slit, pursing in an unlizardlike way. His voice is slightly huskier than usual, like when Scotch catches in his throat—or is it the fading memory of sluicing Jessie's juices, snuffling at her crotch, as he makes a grand gesture and gives up a part of it: the easy freedom to do it again? "I've been carrying on with Jessie," he says.

Right. Sid James and Kenneth Williams and Barbara Windsor probably got a look-in, too. Is that the best he can do? Can't he find a better way to put it than that? What is there? "I've been plonking your sister . . . getting my oats with Jessie when no one was looking . . . bonking her brains out . . . fucking her quietly with my song . . . banging her up the arse . . . enjoying a bit of rumpy-pumpy with your old cot mate"? It's all crap. It all slams into my face, missing the flesh but hitting the bone inside. It's a laugh, innit? Maybe I should use two knives, try to stick them both at once.

"Right," I say. My life is over; I'd like to spew up every memory I ever had. What I've got now is the thrust of my hate, like a cuddly teddy bear, my pristine vision of the Prick and Jessie as apocalyptic angels rolling around in the shit waiting for me to strike them down. Where is Jessie now? She's keeping out of this one. She's letting Daddy handle it. Maybe he's handled it all along; maybe we're all berks and he's the big bad demon after all, she's been fooling herself, he's ridden her from the start? Looking at him now, even in this most abject weakness and disgrace, I can almost imagine that, almost blame him entirely. But I don't think he can take all the credit for me and nor do I think he can even begin to control Jessica, she has her own charge in her that could blitz us all. If I kill him, I am his flesh, does that make it suicide on his part? If I kill her, I feel like I'm killing something from the stars, some megaforce that's lit by the sun's light. But he's just standing there anyway and I'm on the bed, both of us lost, two total pits of human refuse wasting the air we breathe.

"Tom—" A flash of anger, pain, some sort of near-human response. "I'm trying to find a way to . . ."

"What did you say? Just now? I didn't hear you."

Strained eyes. A frown. "Don't play games with me, I . . ."

"Get fucked." No emotion. I don't want to push it. I get up off the bed. "You're not my father and I don't want to have this conversation."

"Tom—"

There are no tears in my eyes, though there could be—there's a hollow draft burning my nose and a welling in my head that wants release—but I'm concentrating my energy on dealing with this now, getting him out of here, out of my room, leaving me alone. I push him and it feels good but he catches my arm and holds it steady, trying to transmit by osmosis or something the suggestion that we are not irretrievably torn apart, there is still some chance of repairing the damage. I'm not as strong as him but his back is a handicap now and a knife will help. Just give me a little time. I push him toward the door again and he surrenders a couple of feet.

"You should have screwed someone else the night you made me! Where was Jessie? Wasn't her cot close enough to hand?" The words just come out and he slaps me across the face, which is brilliant. I want more of it. I want to feel the crunch of my father's knuckles on my skin—I can slide so easily then into what I have to do.

I push him to the door. He looks at me, helpless. He could hit me again, he could reassert himself, he could beg—but I think he knows none of it would do any good. I get my hand off him. This could be the last conversation we ever have. If I was Jessie, I'd do it with style —I'd pull him to me and kiss him, just to see what kissing dead flesh is like, just to remind myself that I thought I loved him once. Then I'd stick the knife in. But I don't and my life doesn't have any shape or form except anger. Anger is the one thing I feel clean in.

"I'm sorry," he says, "I shouldn't have hit you." And just for a second—less—I remember two or three times in my life when I actually felt we made contact, when I thought for a moment I might have some clue as to who the fuck he is. He wasn't so bad at times—that's the joke. He hid it so well. "We must talk," he says, as if I'm one of his problems, something that can be solved. The door closes, shutting him out forever. "In the morning . . ." His voice hangs outside the room. He's waiting there, waiting for the knife or something else instead—he knows he's got it coming.

And I slide my bed up against the door, just to find some peace, to arm my mind for the night ahead.

■

28

Sleep would have been the only escape. But I'm in the kitchen. It's three in the morning and I've got all my clothes on, not simply because I haven't undressed but because I want to be ready for anything, inside or out. I need every advantage now. Jessie came to me, earlier, later, after Dad had walked away from my barricaded door and spoke to me through it.

"This is stupid." I heard her voice, a sister's voice, a voice I have heard every day of my life, playing, messing around, arguing, on the phone, happy, sad, whispering secrets and slander at boring receptions and inaugural parties Dad has taken us to. "I didn't say some of the things I said, OK?" She's alone on the landing outside my door. She's worried now, like when she used to go too far in her temper with me and smash up what she could of mine and then fret over the fact that I, twisted individual that I am, would want to take the blame for it, not out of any desire to protect her—she didn't need protecting, she was happy to accept the consequences of anything—but because I wanted to play some part in her emotional world, I wanted her to have some debt to me that she couldn't quite cancel out. "I go mad sometimes like you do." I almost consider letting her in—we could plot, as we used to, how we would survive if Mum and Dad broke up, died. "It's all gone too far. We're the guilty ones and yet somehow we're putting the blame on you."

"Oh, Jessie," I wanted to say. I wanted to push back the bed, open the door and hug her—but I wasn't sure she was there. I think she was. I think I could hear her scratching the names of my crimes in blood on my door: I invented Nick, I brought him here tonight, I recounted to Mum in graphic detail how her daughter had supplanted her in her bed, I went to Dad and told him the jig was up, that a sealed envelope containing a dossier of all their lurid copulations, including copies of Jessie's prick pictures, was at this moment in the post on its way to the hospital social workers, his partners at the practice, Jessica's college, the *Daily Mail*, 10 Downing Street. I heard her voice, outside my door. "Are you satisfied?" it said, with real loathing, with an honesty of passion rare in our family. "Did you have fun?"

■

And then I heard her go to him. Hours passed—though in fact we're outside normal time, normal time doesn't matter. I heard them both going to bed, using the bathroom, cleaning their teeth, flushing the loo, Dad first, then Jessie some time later. Some sort of strained conversation had gone on downstairs, I caught its long pauses, its leaden awfulness, but not the words. I don't think they ate; I didn't. I haven't eaten since breakfast this morning and the nagging tightness of my stomach, ground hollow by the bike ride, suits me fine tonight. I don't think I'll be eating for a long time.

They went to separate beds but couldn't sleep, I bet. I sat slumped against the door on mine, my ear pressed to the cool gloss paint, shifting slightly as cramp stabbed my shoulder or the door felt too warm, listening for the sounds of Jessica wanking herself in her room or the Prick trying to ease his back straight on the mattress. I could hear a tap downstairs, in the bathroom, I think, spacing time out—little bits of a lifetime slowly dancing together to form a whole, then hanging, kicking, throttled, before gravity cuts down the drip and obliterates it and the slow dance starts again.

There are twenty-four forks downstairs in the cutlery drawer, eleven of them dessert forks, all of them probably sharp enough to inflict a fatal wound or wounds if used with sufficient force and imagination. There are thirty-nine spoons, counting soup spoons and teaspoons, all virtually useless unless perhaps rammed down someone's gullet. There are forty-five knives, I've counted them, including cheese knives, steak knives, a huge heavy-handled carving knife, several smaller sharp blades and the red-handled one I intend to use. There are also two potato peelers, a manual tin opener and two or three sharpish-looking instruments, but I have made my choice.

Jessie's weight moves off the bed in her room—I hear it—and pauses for a moment. It's warm tonight, far warmer than for last night's hospital panic; she won't be wearing a T-shirt. What would she put on to go in to see Dad? Nothing. Why put on anything? Maybe her sun-glasses—but I don't think Jessie's sense of humor is her strong point just now.

The pause is much longer than I expect. Perhaps I'm wrong; she's staying where she is? I jam my ear to the door, making it hurt, sending black waves of pain to my brain, wondering how I'm going to move the bed, go downstairs, get the knife and come back up silently enough to surprise them both, one after the other. I need them together. I've always wanted them together for this.

Drip! The door numbs my ear. How many thousandths or millionths of a second does it take for the sound of water falling from the tap and smashing in the basin to climb the stairs and penetrate my door? Drip! Silence from Jessie's room. Maybe she's already gone in to Dad? But I haven't heard the creak of a floorboard, the oiled grind of metal upon metal as a hinge turns. Drip! Normal time is happening somewhere else—in the village, in the black empty mass between here and London, the streets there hazy from shopwindow lights and drunks pissing against the walls and dark, ratlike faces in waiting cars who know where the action is, know where the party's happening, know their lives are just starting and I'm about to add the royal crown to the fuck-up that mine is already. Still nothing from Jessie—is she asleep standing up or has she lain down again to spite me? Drip! Normality is outside, not in here, there's a force field round the clump of earth that's our garden, from the bent tree to the stone wall, twisting everything that's inside it. I am sweating. My bed feels like it's giving me friction burns on my hands, through my jeans, and I'm not even moving. I am inside the long death of a Sunday evening when school is looming closer and everything awful in the world seems to be sucked into the drain that is my life. But it's not Sunday and the days to school which I can count on one hand are meaningless at last.

Nothing. Even the tap seems to have stopped. But then I hear it, out of step, I think, although it can't be—a muted, echoing plonk as the bullet of water hits its mark. And a creak on the landing. Two more, the hard pat of a bare foot touching bare wood for a moment. Then silence. Where is she? I know it's her. I hold back from the door briefly, resting my ear, changing sides. I am going to have to move the bed soon—how can I do it quietly? Or maybe I can climb out the window and creep back in through the kitchen, fetching the slaughter weapon on my way? No.

"Dad!"

Her voice is quiet but not a whisper. She might be feeling sick. She might be unable to sleep, turning to him for comfort—but it's none of those things, she wants to talk on her own terms: the word is a command.

I think he grunts. Perhaps it's his back racking him. I can't hear clearly—the drip sounds sharper than him. The door clicks shut and I know she's inside. Like a moon walk, I move off the bed and start to inch it away from my door, scraping it across the floor with an agonizingly slow squeak, convincing me that I will bring one of them out here.

I open my door, adrenalin pumping, suddenly cold and wet with sweat. The landing is a huge, endless black cavern, dripping with stalactites, crisscrossed with ledges and needlelike rock bridges. Lucy is there, vacuuming the entrance to Jessie's room. Mum is on the stairs, sitting with Jack on her lap, eating cherries and spitting the stones past the line drawn by Lucy's snaking lead. I am bursting to pee, but I force myself to forget it.

The door to Dad's room is closed. I cross to it, better than Jessie at muffling my footsteps, the ridged soles of my running shoes absorbing the sound. I wait outside, smelling her in the air—a trace of the oil she calls New York for and orders on one of Dad's cards; for two years that's been part of her Christmas treat. There is smoke here too, the vague dungy essence of what came into the cottage and settled from the garden or traveled in on Dad's shirt and trousers. Perhaps when I'm done I can pour what's left of the paraffin round this shit hole and set a funeral pyre? I can be every bit as creative as Jessie.

I hear his voice, irritable, he's keeping it down but not as if she's close: "—feel like hell, I want to go to sleep."

"What did she say?"

"She hung up on me. That was enough."

He trails off. I feel weird out here, as if I'm only getting half the story, they're sitting in there reading a script round a microphone for some fucking radio play.

"Did she say anything about me?"

Silence. I think he moves on the bed. Where is she? Sitting on it? Standing? She's not close to the door.

"Well, did she? Does she know or doesn't she?"

The hall is dark but there's a crack of light under the door. In the corner of my vision I see something move and feel my arms and shoulders jerk back in a shiver that jolts my whole body. A garden spider—this fucking place is full of them—its spindly legs navigating round my foot, its indecision and sudden changes of direction filling me with a ridiculous dread that it's going to crawl right up me.

"I'll have to tell her. It will destroy her."

"No, it won't." Jessie sounds like a complacent little cunt. "What about us?"

"You know what I can't understand," he says, and I wish I had the knife now, I wish I could open the door and surprise him, wash that smug, frank defeat off his face layer by layer—the ease of it, the comfort of slipping into the wreckage. "I've been the biggest bloody fool on earth, but I still can't believe you came from me."

Jessie almost laughs. "I'm me," she says, "that's what you can't take." And I can't take any more myself so I go downstairs.

■

In the kitchen I can breathe normally, I don't have to think about each breath as I draw it in, hold it, let it out. My feet move silently, carefully, without any effort on my part. The room is half dark—a thin, spidery light comes from the moon and stars outside. The window is broken where John's rock went through it, the glass still splintered all over the drainer and the plates. I hear the sea and for the first time I take it for granted: it's there, it always was. I could walk out of the door and up the road the bikes took and cross the field and be there, on the hill, looking down, opening my eyes to the night, to the blackness churning on the shore below, long white lips of foam rolling in with their poison, their crap and junk, old torches, plastic bottles filled with petrol, scummy twists of plastic film, diseased fish—all the death we've brought to it, getting our own back and more for the dead it's claimed since time began. It's like the sky kissing London—man and nature meeting and wrecking each other. But there's the shelter and all the times they must have used it—even if it was only once I don't care, they've taken everything from me and they can't put it back.

The fridge clicks on and makes me start. There's a coffee mug on the table and a half-empty bottle of milk. The tap that's dripping is in here, not the bathroom. I could turn it off but it's a useful measure of the time.

The cutlery drawer slides open with a slight rattle, impossible to avoid but so slight that even I barely hear it. The tap drips. Silence outside —apart from the sea. Upstairs, I think I hear the murmur of voices, but they are less than the sea, dead sounds absorbed into the walls. I don't need to look. In the darkness of the drawer, in the compartment to the right, my hand finds the smooth rounded end of the red-handled knife. It buries itself in my palm as I pull it out and see the blade now, shining dully in the pale light. I am afraid of blunting the blade but feel compelled to dig it into the grain of the table top, carving three tram lines the length of an arm, my arm, past the coffee mug to the milk. A bird shrieks outside—a seagull at night?—and I'm suddenly conscious of time in a different way: that I might miss my moment, that perhaps already Jessie has gone back to her room, making my task more difficult, less symmetrical, an awkward inky dribble across the fine pencil lines of the architectural plan Dad might draw of their deaths.

I mount the stairs carefully, feeling ordinary, the knife in my hand only a minor variation on countless other stair climbs—though not these stairs—with cups, toys, books. Without excitement or even much interest, I imagine newspaper pictures and unreadable headlines, blurred photographs of the cottage, a particular school picture of me when I was ten, round-faced and staring at the camera with a grim smirk. Another family slaughters itself in the countryside. Why must my face look so dumb, so innocent, so much the kind of twerp I would beat the shit out of in the playground?

The landing again. Nothing has changed. The door has not opened. The crack of light is still there, spilling out over the floorboards, accentuating the joins and nailheads. The power point where Lucy plugs in her vacuum is loose on the wall, I know because I've noticed it a dozen times now and meant to tell Pricko or do something about it myself. I touch it with my foot, with the rubber cap of my running shoe, and feel the socket shift on its wiggly screws. I am tempted to wet my fingers—my other hand, the hand not holding the knife—and jam them down between the white plastic socket and the wall. I could take it. I could take anything right now. I hear the Prick's voice, impatient with her, untroubled by the tap the socket makes against the wall as my foot nudges it.

"Jessie—!"

"No."

"Go back to bed."

"No."

"You don't know when to give up. Don't make it more difficult—" He's pissed off with her now and maybe with the situation: having to keep his voice down, hold back from waking me.

"It can't be more difficult. It's impossible, so why stop tonight?" Jessie wants to be heard. She sounds reckless in the way that's always made me sick about her—there's so much more ground to throw away when you're a daughter, so much more room for easy damage, and even then she's always been so fucking protected. I grip my knife, let my foot shift from the socket to the door. I think she moves closer to him. "If there were no consequences," she says, nagging him, keeping up the pressure, "if no one gave a shit, you'd do it. You're afraid."

"Stop it!"

And I have to go in there. I don't even knock.

"Hello," I say, feeling quite perky, thinking about John's head popping into the kitchen—was that this evening? It seems only a moment ago. I wish I'd had a drink downstairs, though, a beer or something from the fridge; there's a dead spot in my stomach like cancer, I need a burn there, a buzz.

I grip the red handle—I can see it now, the light over Dad's bed is on. He's sitting on the far edge, the duvet pulled up round him, the side of his neck and shoulder closest to me uncovered except for various wads of gauze taped clumsily onto him over a battleground of bruised and battered flesh. He turns and my eyes move to Jessie. I was wrong, she's not naked. She's not wearing her shades. What she's got on is Mum's bathrobe and she looks strangely uncomfortable in it—it's wrapped too tight or something, as if she's suddenly turned frigid and decided to batten down the hatches. She is standing over Dad's side of the bed, sandwiched between it and Jack's cot, her body moving back and up as I enter as if she's been leaning her hands on the mattress or on him. Her face is odd when she looks at me—her mouth smudged with makeup, her eyes saddened with colors I'm sure weren't there earlier, in the kitchen. Just for a moment, until I focus on the bare legs and bare feet, she reminds me of two nights ago in the hotel, sitting at the window in her jacket and stockings, staring out at the storm lighting up the river and crying, though I couldn't be sure she was—only there's no sickly stink of amyl nitrate now, just the stale reek of our parents' bed, the Prick's spirity dressings, her pharmacist-blended oil.

"Tom, what's the matter? Are you all right?" Dad says this even as he registers the knife in my hands. His face is wearied by the sight of it rather than shocked or scared—as if this is another regrettable mistake, further evidence of my stupidity, my inability to behave like a sane human being.

My mind is blank, but I manage "Don't!" as he tries to slide his naked trunk off the bed and stand, the effort obviously stirring some temporarily banished pain in his back. He grimaces. Jessie stands, making no attempt to help him, her expression hardening in response to me, him, both. I push the door shut behind me and lean against it, holding the knife in my hand, blade up, in what seems to me a perfectly serious manner. "Stay there," I say, analyzing the relationship between their body sizes and mine. I need that superhuman strength now if I'm to do this. I should have pushed my hand in the socket outside.

"Tom, you never could handle a carving knife," Jessie says, trying that sister crap on me, although I think she is genuinely not frightened. But she knows my state of mind well enough to understand that this is more than a joke.

"I think I can do all right with this one."

And I hold out my left arm, the one that's not carrying the knife, turn my palm up and draw the tip of the metal down the underside, from elbow to wrist, avoiding the artery, not enough to weaken the arm, just enough to give me the extra degree of commitment I need. Even after the tram lines on the kitchen table, the blade is sharp. It doesn't need pressure. It doesn't drag at all, just slices neatly down, parting the skin like plastic, not even hurting for a second or two, then stinging as the blood comes.

My demonstration seems to impress everyone. "Tom, put the knife down," my father suggests, his brow cragging with the realization that I might just be unsettled enough to do something.

I try to smile but it doesn't quite work.

"Everything you think, you're right in." This is his serious voice, his man-to-man voice, the one he uses when he wants to bare his soul or whatever it is he has. It's warm in here. This is a warm room. "You have every right to—"

"SHUT UP!"

I didn't need to shout. I think my voice broke as I said it. My back presses against the door. It's been stripped, this one, and left unvarnished. It feels grainy and somehow satisfying to the touch. I let my left hand rest there, the arm aching a little from the cut. There aren't any pictures of me and Jessie in Mum and Dad's bedroom—not even of Jack. I hate that in other kids' parents' bedrooms, when there are smiling-faced family groups all over the furniture. Our smiling-faced pictures are downstairs in the hall where you can barely see them even in daylight.

"Who are you going to do first, Tom? Me or Dad?" Jessie tries to sound the way she does sometimes—like my sister. "You'll chicken out." But she touches her shoulder through the robe, where I burned her, and I see or think I see something like approval in her eyes.

"Watch me!" I say, staring at the belt tied round her waist, the soft rainbow colors of the toweling. Her tan underneath is like a Greek girl's skin or an Arab's. I feel momentarily confused—disoriented—as if I'm somewhere else. This cottage is somewhere else to me, it has no bearings, it floats on the sewage of my brain.

My father sees my state and seizes on it, trying to lever himself up off the bed with one arm. I point the knife and jerk it at him, kicking the door with my foot in a sort of reflex action. "If either of you gets too close," I warn them, no conscious thought involved in the words, "I'll use this on me. I don't care about you."

He eases himself back down on the edge of the mattress, watching me, better placed for movement than before—but I'm watching him. "I know you must find this hard to believe," he says, and I do, whatever is coming, "but I still love you all."

He is a slimy reptile. No! Reptiles aren't slimy. I think he means it, I think he has a place inside him for loving me—and Mum and Jack. Somewhere just above his bowels. He could almost be a human being if it wasn't for the fact that he was never one to start with.

I stare at him, trying to reach what it is that will make it happen. I speak slowly, thinking out loud: "I want to hear you say, 'Otherwise, you're fine.' " Time drags. My armpits are wet; I can smell them on my T-shirt.

"What?" He looks totally mystified.

"Say, 'Otherwise, you're fine.' "

"Tom, this is nonsense—"

"Say it!"

He is having a hard night. The dressing to the side of his right shoulder blade has darkened since he moved. There is sweat clogging his chest hair. He keeps the duvet balled protectively over his tool, but I've seen it—gray and shriveled, swinging like one of the poncey curtain tassels every time he tries to stand up. His voice is flat and resentful, as if I'm just trying to embarrass him and that in itself is enough. "Otherwise —" He searches my face for some sort of explanation. "Oh, this is ridiculous."

"SAY IT!"

He's like a robot: it means nothing to him. " . . . you're fine."

Nothing. I look at Jessie, try to imagine him banging into her but instead think of Sonny weeing all over my face. What does it take? My hand with the knife is steady, but it's going to shake soon. My other arm aches. I'm against the door and they are waiting there, on the bed, by the cot. I'm not as strong as they are—my dad is going to count on that in a moment—and still I'm pissing about.

Jessie speaks quietly. I think she wants to help. "Give me the knife. I'll do it. I'll kill him quite happily."

"Oh, Jesus Christ," Dad says and he laughs, his patience for sane argument exhausted, sick of both of us.

I believe her. I rock slightly, gripping the red handle tight, my other fist clenched, and look at her properly for the first time since I came into the room. She is in a fine state, wrapped in Mum's robe, her hair all tight and damp-looking the way it was that day in the bath, in the mirror, her smudged mouth set with a kind of manic determination that I think certain girls' schools—I've seen it on her friends, though never like this—must teach.

"I've been trying to find out at what point it changes," she says, and Dad leans back hard against the wall, banging his head in a sort of gesture of defeat and pressing one hand down onto the pillow for support. "At what point do you give it all up—your daring, the link between how you live and how you dream? Dad's got us"—she turns on him with the kind of contempt I thought she only reserved for me—"but we're not what he wanted, we're about two per cent of what he thought he was capable of."

"Right!" says Dad, looking for a fight now, straightening his back as if he doesn't fucking care how much it hurts anymore.

"Is it just fear?" Jessie's hand reaches behind her, searching for something—the cot, a reference point. "Are you just afraid that what's in you isn't so very special? Or do you just bury it? You work and you fuck and you load it with trinkets, property, children. You half remember it and something happens, you get extra daring one day, really charged with your own"—she searches for the word, watching him, watching him listen to this and try to deny it in his head—"essence, and you fuck me, but then you lose it again, you suffocate it, it's dead, it's worse than before."

All through this her other hand has been toying with the belt, twisting the half knot, untying and retying it, letting the robe slacken a little, then pulling it tight. "God, you're fucked up!" she says. "You'll do this—" And she turns and hitches the bathrobe up, sticking her bum out at us so we can see where she's smeared it with lipstick or something, right down the crack, a violent, raging red. "You'll stick your cock up my bum, but you won't give me what I want. You won't give me a baby!"

I feel winded; she's knocked all the fight out of me. I stare at them both with a strange kind of concentration, watching under water, watching him move as she turns back to us, opening the robe and shaking it down from her shoulders to show something quite obscene and wrinkled on her belly. He grabs for her but his movement is impeded by one hand sinking into the mattress so that he has to reach out twice. I start toward him with the knife, but Jessie is still talking, her eyes locked on mine, confusing me with my own guilt: this isn't something I should see: we've run into each other in the middle of a dream, in a school corridor or in Sonny's bathroom or on some weird sea wall with the water thrashing, and I've been watching her play with herself—I step outside myself even as I lunge forward and see how guilty I am; I'm at fault here; I keep having these dirty thoughts. "I want him to make me pregnant, Tom," she says, "but that's the one thing Daddy won't do."

"Jessie!" he screams, catching hold of the robe, which is hanging from her elbows now, and tugging her to him. But I slash with the knife, throwing myself on the bed and getting close but not close enough, burying it deep in the duvet, the mattress, and dragging it back. He lets go of Jessie and pushes me off, his hand ramming into my skull with a blinding pain, so that I stumble back off the bed but manage to stay on my feet with the knife still in my hand.

He comes for me now and I move for his arm, his right bicep, not certain how much I want to achieve but buggered anyway from anything more than a surface gash by his other hand swinging round to force my wrist up behind my neck, his strength—even though I've allowed for it—surprising me, it's so long since we've mucked about. The knife knocks against the door and he bellows, "Drop it!" and I could laugh because Jessie is yelling "Don't!"—and I don't know whether she means don't drop it or don't fight.

I try to floor him with a knee to his exposed groin, but he anticipates this and smashes my leg with his own, jarring me with the pain. "Stop this fucking nonsense!" he says, trying to push my hand with the knife back, but I grab the handle with my other hand, cutting the soft pulpy bits of my fingers in the process but bringing it down fast enough to stick him below the ribs with the blade.

And I feel sick. Suddenly everything looks different. I get the full belt of his breath in my face as he wheezes out and I realize that I don't want to hurt him like this. Some other way—but not like this. His stomach is wet with blood, though I didn't think I cut that deep, and Jessie looks stunned, bending to support him, Mum's robe still half off her, that thing on her stomach smudging up against him as she stares at me and says nothing more useful than "Fuck!"

I have an impulse to take my father and hug him but can't bring myself to do it. I feel freaky, more wired up and frightened than ever, not sure what I've done. I want to stay but I want to run more and I pull open the door and look back at Jessie, who has got Dad onto the bed—there's an awful lot of blood—and hear her say, "For Christ's sake, don't go now!" but I'm down the stairs and the front door opens with the third tug and outside the light is starting. I chuck the knife back behind me, taking in the wrecked barbecue and the smashed table on the lawn like a still life in some crisp, arty photograph, and race round the gate to where my bike is against the wall and run with it, hearing the chain spin and catch, feeling terrified and empty and realizing with a totally misplaced sense of shame that I've emptied my bladder in my jeans.

■

29

I keep moving but there's nothing behind me. Even before I am out of the village, the day seems disconnected from the night. The sun comes up and it's like something artificial—the sky on a dimmer switch. The rush of birdsong sounds electronic, an extension of the sea's interference noise, another track on the tape to create the total effect. A farm harvester (or whatever it is) crawls uphill in front of me, blocking the road, moving even slower than I can pedal, its heavy machinery like a sculpture: weird forms caked in a dried mud and dust that have nothing to do with the experience of my life.

I am back on the road to Exeter—three times in less than twenty-four hours, but the slog is druglike, I can deaden my mind through the sweat on my body, the ache in my injured arm and fingers as I grip the handlebars, pushing the pedals down-round-up, identifiable twisted bits of tree and broken bush approaching, then vanishing behind me. I pass the space where the oak was that caused us to crash the night Jack was born, but further on there's another space—another clearing in the hedgerow, another pit in the ground—and the fact that I don't really know which one it was seems to drag the shock of stabbing Dad back into some past and no longer reachable place in my brain.

I am not complete. I don't think I killed him, but if I did, it doesn't feel right, it doesn't feel like I wanted it to. I want more—but not more of the same. If I've killed him, he won't suffer. I don't want him to be dead, I want him to suffer. I think he will. But what I'm looking for now is personal satisfaction. The suffering is up to him.

There's a dead bird on the road and I run over it with my bike, little globs of it sticking to my front tire, then working their way off as I come into Exeter. My mother is here in the hospital and the bird gives me a mental picture of Jack's stomach, though I hope he's in better shape than that. It should be my father's guts I see but it's not and I'm here only because I've got to be somewhere. I head for the station, not the hospital, staggered by how long everything takes to do—the time it takes to cycle the length of a street, the dreamlike whir of a milk van moving in front of me, my almost stationary poise as I wait at lights, feet off the ground, swaying slowly as gravity enters my mind and pulls me sideways.

I abandon the bike and buy a ticket, puzzled by the money in my pocket—almost thirty pounds, although I don't remember putting it there or where it came from. Dad gives me money. Mum gives me money. I used to steal it from them too, but they never noticed so I stopped. I walk onto the platform, making a deliberate effort to move like everyone else. I am surrounded by faces I would not want to see at my trial, anyone's trial: they know they're right, this is the time for them, they've got their lives organized—even though they're fucked, they're making sure someone else is fucked worse than them.

The train journey has a reality of its own, woven in and out of my attempts to stay awake. If I could feel it, the speed would help. But only when another InterCity express flashes past in the opposite direction on a parallel track does any real sense of the danger penetrate the carriage. The possibility of swinging a door open as one approaches and diving out into its path occurs to me, but if I did that I'd want to take one or two of my turd-faced fellow passengers with me and it might get complicated. As it is, I want to remain anonymous, drinking a foul cup of coffee and dozing in my sweaty T-shirt and piss-stained jeans among these clean livers. If Dad is dead, I may face problems in London—that's why I bought a ticket, rather than risk a charge through the gate at Paddington. If Dad is dead (and if he is, I should be traveling under the train, my spine coupling the carriages), I don't see how Jessie could have avoided involving the law. If he isn't, he won't go out of his way to look for trouble.

■

I want darkness again and it's a long wait until then. Paddington seems vast and echoing when I arrive, a huge distortion of sound and movement. I pick my way through the crowd, the burger smells, stumbling into a knot of German tourists in Union Jack bowler hats, twisting my leg on a plastic bag as I move to get out of the way of an electric mail cart driving right at me and towing its own train of crap, watching as two uniformed guards manhandle a dosser through a door marked PRIVATE. I am clumsy and hungry but the burger I buy becomes a lump in my throat which even a flat, syrupy Coke can't dislodge and I wind up in the gents, my stomach feeling like a bag of wet sand that has to be dropped, my dead brain calculating that if I make it to tonight I will have been up for almost sixty hours without more than three or four of sleep.

I head off into the underground, aware that Docklands is a nonplace by tube, determined not to use the high-tech holocaust-shuttle my father's Texan thugs put money into—until rival high-level payoffs squeezed them out. I stare at the tube map, my eyes adding colors to it and failing to follow the same line for any distance. Finally I trace a route to Wapping, using my finger and moving my lips as I think, then lose myself in a blind circle of escalators and platforms until I smash my knee on a wall and sort myself out.

■

Twice I miss Whitechapel, where I'm supposed to change lines—once going there, then again when I switch trains and come back. A woman, a young mother not much older than Jessie, stands over me at one point in the empty carriage, a sick-faced leering toddler at her feet, and says in a really aggressive way—as if she's prepared to back up her words with a fight—"Have you got any money? I saw you counting your change just now. All my kid's had since yesterday break-fast is a bag of crisps and some orange squash." I must look abusable, beatable—at Earl's Court I had a man stick his clammy hand on the seat of my jeans.

The sun is out at Wapping and the river is so bright it just flashes on my brain, leaving shrinking purple images. I try to work out which way to walk by following it but have trouble remembering which side of my body to keep it on. There's a lot of new building going on here, like my father's wharf but not so poncey, less full of itself, its Covent Garden-reconstituted-Victoriana crappiness. In fact, it's ugly, that's what it is, it's fucking awful. It's hard to choose between the new functional ug-liness and the old functional ugliness, so why not nuke it all? The people round here wouldn't mind, I should think—not the ones who've been here a lifetime. They're used to being blitzed. Hitler's dead, Thatcher isn't—it doesn't make much difference to them. Because outside the electric gates and barbed-wire fences, not a lot's happening.

There's a whole stretch I walk through where the tenement houses are boarded up, windows broken, colored paint peeling off the doors. With a suddenness which really frightens me, I remember being high up on a roof with the Prick when I was little. We were standing on top of an office block that was waiting to be demolished, I think, and gazing at the view; he had his hands tight on my shoulders, probably convinced that I was going to go running off across the flat, unwalled roof. There was a high rise of grim flats some distance away, close enough to see the layers of weather-stained, wood-clad balconies where people kept their window boxes, the junk they couldn't fit inside their flats, maybe even a rabbit or pigeons. Out of the lot of them—I don't know, maybe fifty or sixty—one had had its creosoted brown wood painted orange and my father drew my attention to this. "Look at that," he said, and his voice was almost bitter or defeated or something. "One desperate attempt for individuality." It didn't mean anything to me—I was six, perhaps, or seven—but I think the extent of the silence that followed worried me. Now, stepping along, seeing the wreckage around me, thinking about what I'm going to do, I think I can understand what it was—the fact that nothing he could build could be anything those people would care about, anything less than his own huge wank, his own shot at imperialism. He should thank me.

■

I sleep on the grass in a tiny park by the water, but I'm troubled by the look on Dad's face as I stuck him, the sight of Jessie's stomach as she bent to help him. Then there's a terrible moment when I hear bird sounds and lorries moving and stir, thinking the crane driver who drowned off Dad's wharf has come out of the river and is standing over me, sludge dripping off him, his face horribly mutilated by the action of a ship's propeller—but there's no one here, only an old man on the path, talking to his dog and staring up at a grim statue against an orange sky.

I relent and find a working phone outside a petrol station, feeling worse for the sleep, surprised at how near to evening it is. I don't have a plan; I don't need one—just minimal preparation and luck. The sun is cooler now and I find my confidence draining with the warmth as the phone rings and rings. I begin to panic and try to calm down, forcing myself to put the receiver back and walk out onto the petrol station forecourt. If he's dead, what would have happened? Surely there'd be someone there? They could just be out, seeing Mum— telling her what, how would he explain this? Or of course he could be in hospital himself—was the wound deep? It felt like nothing, less resistance than sticking a knife in fruit.

I can't do this all in one go. I realize now it's not going to be easy. Two cans of petrol is the most I can manage, and I don't even have the cans. So I walk into the forecourt shop, in my jeans, running shoes and T-shirt, trying to look casual, trying not to look as young as I am, and I pick up two five-liter cans of oil, thrown by how expensive they are—I'm not going to be able to afford to fill them both with petrol, maybe I should just buy one? But like a sign that points forward, I see a stack of large plastic containers of purified water for sale, two for less than half the price of one can of oil, and I put the oil down and pick the water up and the woman behind the till doesn't give a shit what I do as long as I get out of her life now, so I push it—with a tired, shrill voice I tell her my dad's run out of petrol and I'm going to empty the water out and fill them both at the pump, is that all right?

She looks at me with a sort of bitten lip and small, hard eyes that she's probably got doing this job, and I gild the lily, I tell her it's a Bentley, a real old wreck, one of these plastic bottles isn't even going to get it sparking. And she knows I'm lying, and she knows I know it, but she doesn't want the aggravation so she says, "Give me the money for the petrol first," and stares with relief over my head as another customer comes in, a pompous little git in a suit impatient for a token for the car wash. She takes my money and gives me the change and I tell her it's wrong; then she gets nasty but we sort it out and I feel her small, hard eyes on me as I fill the containers at the pump, the rich stench of the petrol settling on my lungs, and I wonder if a match now would make her happy.

■

I don't hang around to try the phone again but walk on, carrying the petrol for a mile or so, getting lost and getting stuck in dead ends a couple of times. My head is sharper now, but in a disjointed way that makes it difficult to hold a thought for more than a moment. Part of me is looking for another phone; part of me is trying to keep moving toward the docks. I reach some traffic lights which seem familiar but have to duck out of sight of an approaching police car and try then to keep to the back streets, losing any real sense—without the river—of where I am.

In one narrow residential street there's a parade of three shops—two boarded up, one a Chinese off-license—and I realize I've hardly drunk all day, apart from the Coke and some water from an ancient, grimy drinking fountain in the park. I walk on and stash the petrol against the corrugated iron doorway of a blackened, burned-out house that someone's already done a job on, then double back to the shop and walk inside. It's as much a food shop as an off-license—there's even a stand of unidentifiable withered vegetables in front of the till—but I settle for just two small bags of peanuts, fix in my mind the location of the fastest-reached beer by the door, pay for the nuts and grab a four-pack on the way out, running like hell holding the awkward, hard-rimmed mass of cans to my stomach, one of them splaying out and dropping from its plastic loop to bounce on the pavement as I go. The old Chinese man who served me doesn't follow me onto the street, but seconds later as I look back a young kid, not much older than me—his son? grandson?—comes sprinting out, fast enough to worry me, and I leg it round a corner, down another dark, narrow street and through a brick passageway into a gloomy, forbidding courtyard at the back of a Victorian office building. I decide to fight, if that's what he wants; I've never fought anyone Chinese but he hardly looked like a killer, spindly arms caught inside a black, numbered baseball jacket, and I'd win because I've got to—I've got other business tonight.

But he doesn't appear and I open a beer waiting for him, keen to get out of the courtyard, which seems filled with death, and keener still to get my petrol back. The first gulp of beer does it for me instantly—I'm so tired and freaked out anyway, it's like a sane hand on my shoulder —and I drink the rest down, chuck the can into a basement well and walk out onto the street, clutching the other two cans and getting a weird sense of déjà vu as I try to connect last night with now and go back for the petrol.

■

I know where I am. I'm in a phone box, one of the old-style thick-paned red ones. It stinks of piss, they always do, but the phone works. My hand hurts. I cut it open again opening the second can of beer—let the ring-pull slice right into the dead flap of one of the fingers I cut last night switching hands with the knife in my tussle with Dad. I've kept the can as a souvenir, but not the ring-pull.

I am on the Isle of Dogs. I know exactly where I am. Not much of an island, is it? Enough to make a dog bark. How do you get one to? How do you get a dog to bark? Pour petrol over it, set it on fire and it goes woof. Well, I've got the petrol. The phone is ringing—the other end, not here. Nobody home again? Let it ring.

The entrance to the London Docklands Enterprise Zone is four streets from here. I've been there once already now it's got dark, walked right through within sight of the Texan hulk and back again. Nobody stopped me. But no phones in there, not ones I can use anyway. It's still ringing.

Click.

"Hello?" Jessie's voice.

Silence. London-to-Devon static. I wish I could touch her.

"Hello?"

"Jessie—"

"Tom, are you OK?" Cool; not entirely interested in my condition.

"I'm fucking brilliant. How's Dad? Is he hurt bad?"

"Where are you?"

"Just tell me, will you? Is he all right?"

"He's not dead. You really are a—"

But I've cut us off.

■

30

I'm alive for about two moments of it. The rest is like watching a video I've seen over and over; I've done this in my head so many times already tonight.

■

The first is out over the water, after I've tossed the beer cans (one empty, one full) and petrol over the fence ready for me and waited for the dogs to bark, the lights to blaze—but nothing. Stillness.

It's dark out here. The pyramid is lit up, maybe forty or fifty feet away, but softly from below, like a part-built aviary or a tomb or something, sheathed in scaffolding and plastic sheeting which ripples as it breathes the dank dockside air. Weird shapes inhabit the night here, the ghosts of huge Victorian cranes, old chimneys pointing up to nowhere, exposed bellies of warehouses thick with the sweat and greed and cheap pain that drove everything on.

I climb along a railing that carries the fence a few feet out over the water from the wharf. It's the only way in, short of walking up to the gate and blagging it with the guards—maybe Jason's on, with his cosh? The rust on the bars in the dark is like ground glass, savaging my cut hand and engraving itself on the other. There's virtually no toehold—the fence has been wired over the railing to block the gaps in between, where my feet might have wedged—but I drive my running shoes in against the wire anyway and use the crazy strength I've got now to drag myself along, inches above the black gaping mouth of the dock.

At the end of the railing, I cling on and swing out into the darkness, smelling the cold aura of the water, closer than I want to be to the poor bugger who's been festering down there for more than a week now—little bits of him breaking off like meat disintegrating in a fish tank. There's a sound water makes when it's still, or perhaps it's a nonsound, the suffocating of any other small sounds which might be in the neighborhood, and it's this I hear as I misjudge my reach round the railing's end and miss the bar I was trying for. My hand dives through space, taking me down with it, and I only just manage to stop myself in time by grabbing a rail further along. I freeze, my face that much closer to the water, my lungs heaving, one leg still swung out beyond the iron bars, counterbalancing my body. Slowly I bring it down and force my head and shoulders up, my foot slipping three or four times against the rails before I get a grip. The site side of the wharf is within reach now: all I have to do is get there. But I cling to where I am, my mind pulsing with a kind of empty, exhausted sickness, suddenly recognizing the fear that this could all be real—this exhaustion could be the last state I know. A part of me just wants to stay here and think about it. But that's the failure's way, that only guarantees more misery. If I'm going to do it, I've got to do it; spontaneous combustion requires a nudge. I'll nudge it.

■

The other is when it blows. When I've inched back onto the wharf, picked up my petrol and beer and made it safely across the trenches and unseen hazards of the site to the refuge of the pyramid. The scaffolding almost blocks off access to the main entrance—a huge as yet unfinished stone and steel hole complete with hieroglyphs and squared-off pricklike columns on either side—but I twist and duck round the poles and climb concreted steps littered with masonry slabs into the atrium.

The light from outside doesn't penetrate far in here, it just throws long shadows of the columns up across the vast space that extends the full height of the steel and glass of one side of the pyramid. It gives me a weird sense of my father now, as if he's here, I'm inside him, this is his brain and his bowels all in one, the wires and pipes all disconnected and poking out of ducts in the masonry, the jigsaw of service shafts and lift machinery and suspended floors overhead like the floating black pieces of his ego. I'm dwarfed, I have to say it, by what he can achieve, the size of his will when he wants to fuck the world. He's like Jessie: they can reach out and screw it, give it a good hiding; all I can do is piss about. Outside his shit piles, I can cope, they're no different to the monuments all the other grim bastards erect, carving their names on the planet's face with a razor. But inside—inside, they get to me, as if they're designed just to show me what I'm not, and I feel his boot crunching down hard on my skull.

What's hard, though, is to connect all this with the crumbling piss hole I left this morning. Something must have happened to drive him down there, to want to put that distance between him and this, not that I give a fuck. Was it Jessie? Were they already doing it—whatever she says—and he wanted to get her out of London to where he'd have her all to himself? That doesn't make sense. There's more risk of exposure in the village than anywhere. Maybe Jessie wanted it? I know what I saw on her belly last night: a baby, a little embryo in an egg curled up above her cunt, painted on in lurid colors like some sort of tribal thing, a taunt. Maybe she wanted him on hand for the summer—his prick on tap? He's smaller than her, he's afraid of something—I feel it here, this isn't a happy building, it's a vast empty vault. What's he got to be afraid of if it isn't her?

Me, for one thing. Now I know he's alive, I can go on hating him. I can do this. But this isn't for him, it's for me. He doesn't deserve this much attention. This is my entertainment, my madness.

I feel sharp. It's safer in here than it was outside—at least for the moment. I listen and hear nothing, so I test the silence by snapping open the last beer and shiver and drink some down. It's hard to see much in the darkness but I know what I'm looking for. Up above me, above what's going to be the huge pharaoh's arsehole of a lobby, is a skeleton of metal girders part cut away. I see or think I do the round noses, the dense bulks, of oxyacetylene tanks waiting to be used. They're a fair way up—maybe sixty feet away—but I'm good for the climb, so I drain the beer, stick the can back in its noose with the other, pick up the petrol and navigate round the crap and equipment on the floor in search of a way up.

The service stairs take me there. The climb is worse than I expect— I'm totally shattered now, running on chemicals I didn't know I had, losing the clarity that seemed to exist on the ground with each grinding step up, my legs limp and wet and leaden in the same moment. I'm almost there, moving off the stairs for a moment to check how far up I am, get my bearings, when outside the dogs start snarling and howling in a way that seems to lock right into every nerve end on my body and twist them viciously. But there's no suggestion of movement, no pack of slobbering monsters tearing up the stairs behind me to deprive me of what's mine, what's left to me. So I stumble on, my mind throwing itself against the walls of that stupid joke: How do you get a dog to woof? Pour petrol over it and it goes bark. How do you get petrol to bark? Light a match and it wags its tail.

It's not easy ripping my T-shirt—I must really be knackered, all my strength's gone—plus I'm cold. I unscrew the cap of one of the plastic containers and fill the two beer cans with petrol, pouring it in slowly with shaking hands through the tear-shaped holes left by the ring-pulls. The smell revives me, the fumes snaking up my nose into my brain to burn the outer layer, blow away the cobwebs. I soak the scraps of T-shirt I've torn and stuff them into the cans' holes, poking them in and cutting another finger in the process. Then I'm out over the steel grid—covered for the moment with planks of wood, their distance from the ground startlingly evident through the cracks—lugging the rest of the petrol to what is, as it promised to be, a store of welding tanks. I don't know if this will work for sure, the tanks may not puncture, their contents not ignite, but it seems my best bet. I try improving on their arrangement, hoping in the petrol-soaked brightness of my Boy Scout brain to pile them like the sticks of a fire, but I can't get them to budge, either I'm so weak or they're so heavy. So I just douse them where they are. I pour petrol over them and splash it all around—pissing in the dark with it, drinking in the smell. I plant the two plastic bottles on the sodden wood platform up against the tanks, leaving an inch or so of juice in each, then back off quickly, stumbling a little in the dark but immune to the drop on either side now, back to the cans.

There probably won't be everything I asked for in my Christmas stocking. I want at least nuclear fusion. I want the Prick's world and everybody else's to fall in on itself like a ton of shit, like those collapsing factory chimneys and high-rise blocks you see in slow motion on TV —but messier, more searing, like a blaze in Beirut, El Salvador, Johannesburg, where they've got a thousand better reasons than me for lighting the fuse.

But I light mine anyway. I toss the first can before it can blow up in my hand and watch it sail toward its target, a trail of flame from the burning plug of T-shirt. I reach for the second, but before I can touch it there's a flash the colors of old Catholic paintings—the colors of Jessie in Sonny's painting—and as I spin myself round a blast tears across my back and shunts me off the platform into the night.

■

31

The burn on my back hurts like hell. But I must want pain, I must feed on it, because this morning at the harbor in Kingstown I had my shirt off again and refused to put it back on even when an evil-eyed St. Vincent priestess refused to serve me in a cafe and shouted after me into the street as if my naked chest was some sort of personal affront. I think I'm trying for total skin cancer as a surprise gift for Jessie; she always liked to see me suffer. I reckon if one morning on the beach in Barbados can sear a blister right across my spine, a little lunchtime sun in St. Vincent ought to do the rest.

The Prick is paying for this trip, which is a joke in itself. For five years I've made him sweat over every penny he's tried to spend on me, refusing presents, then accepting them, then giving them back or, better, sending them back with sick reminders of what he's done glued together from newspaper and magazine print like anonymous, threatening letters. Now I've decided he's had enough. He's done his bit to undo the damage; he even persuaded my mother to see him last month for dinner, but she was like a one-woman assault force before it and came home afterward, shut herself in her bedroom and wept, so I think Jack might be seven, eight or older before he gets a chance to learn at first hand what a cunt he's got for a dad. But I think he's had enough, Dad. He's taken his punishment like a man. Now I'm going to start taking his presents graciously. His presents, his checks, his car, his self-respect, maybe even his girlfriends if I get the chance. Me and him can become good mates now. There are times when I'm with him when I almost start liking him again, but I won't let that stand in my way.

The boat to the island is typical Jessie: a fucked-up old sailing hulk peopled by an ugly mix of holiday-tanned tourists and yachting types and the quieter, funkier faces of locals who have learned to live with nutters like her making their homes here. There's even a scraggly goat tied up in the bow, together with a couple of pigs lying heaving in the sun between the crates of Coca-Cola and the baskets of green bananas. I could never quite work out if it was Jessie who influenced Sonny or the other way round but, whatever it was, Sonny seems to have left her mark.

Jessie told me in her letters about the skies here—sunsets rapid, green and sharp, as if the sun's on coke—but in the half hour since we left St. Vincent it's clouded over in readiness for giving me a hard time. The sea has quite a swell now and the boat is constantly tilted either one way or the other, but somehow the heat and voices and the sight of flying fish skipping over the water make it seem less vast and daunting than it used to in Devon—smaller, as if a few years or a few thousand miles have diminished its strength, its scope for impressing me. Maybe it's just the absence of cold—but perhaps it is cold down there, deep down there.

The world seems a small thing compared with my life these days. It took twelve days for Jessie's last letter to reach me, but the decision to come took no time at all and the trip itself was arranged in less than a week. Of course, Jessie and I never stopped seeing each other the way everyone else did. Even the month Mum had to spend with me in hospital, right after the blast (which was what saved me, me being thrown from the platform), when I was under psychiatric observation and the police were poking around and she was fighting like hell not to go to pieces in front of them—out of some weird, misplaced loyalty to Dad or to Jack or someone, or some middle-class resistance to outside interference, a determination that we could drive our own wedges between each other, pass sentence ourselves on the freaks and sinners in our midst—even then, Jessica managed to engineer a couple of meetings when Mum was gone and I was mobile enough to hobble down to the hospital chapel or the toilets to tell her what a hopeless bitch she was.

It's funny but this trip now—standing here, holding the side of this lurching, beat-up old ferryboat, halfway across the world from everything I know—seems to have the inevitability that drives some things in life, like a short circuit leapfrogging time, distance. She didn't so much invite me as order me to come ("You'll be a prick if you don't; this is the best time of the year. And, yes, I miss you—there's no one to pry into my personal life, and I've a friend I think you'd like"), but I know there's more to it than that. Dad has cut off her money because of the setup she's fallen into: a threesome built round an aging kraut architect and his fuck—or other fuck, I suppose. I don't think Dad's anger has anything to do with age, race or the risk of physical violence Jessie might run if passions get aroused on a remote island. It's more a question of professional rivalry—even if all this Nazi has achieved in the past three years is to rebuild some strange Wagnerian-style folly that was already there on the island. Dad has done sterling work himself in accepting that Jessie sleeps with other men (she claims, though I'm not sure if I believe her, that he now finds this a relief, he's lost the taste for his own flesh)—but another architect, as old or older than himself, is asking too much.

I think he was happy for me to come out here because I might bring her back. I'm happy to be here because, without Jessie, there's no pain. I am definitely addicted to her and, as this tub draws nearer to where she is, I can see her, only in my mind as yet; I can smell her breath, her skin; and I'm ready for her, for it to start again.

■

She picks me up in a clapped-out Jeep at Port Elizabeth, waiting on the quay with what looks like a markedly less aggressive assortment of the harbor life that hassled me and hustled me in Kingstown: porters ready to help unload the baskets and crates and trunks, townsfolk waiting to greet their relatives and friends from other islands, passersby just excited by the ferry's arrival, a Rasta selling fruit from a stand right in front of the tiny police station, children running everywhere in faded cockatoo colors, shouting and giggling and—unlike the St. Vincent waterfront brats—not demanding money from every foreigner.

"So what do you think?" Jessie asks after we've hugged a welcome that feels only slightly forced, false. She looks like she was born here: more tanned than ever, wearing a bikini top and a loose, flowery skirt which she hauls up round her brown thighs to drive the Jeep.

"You couldn't pick an island with an airport?"

She turns by the police station, shouts something in French at the Rasta, who laughs, and heads us up a road past scattered shacks and chalet-type buildings, the whole hill covered with huge palm trees and banana trees and God knows what else. "They're talking about building one," she says. "It will ruin this place. What's home like—cold?"

"Awful. I can take the winter but not the mood in the air. It's getting worse. It comes straight from the government. We're becoming a really corrupt, repressive country—more Third World than this is. We're a real banana republic!" I look at her. "But you never did care about those things."

"And you only said you did."

"Bullshit!" We've left behind us a Barclays Bank—little more than a concrete hut; presumably where Jessie would collect the money transfers from the Prick when they were still coming. "It's a tangible thing. You listen to those dodgy cunts in government speaking and you know they're too dangerous to ignore."

"How's Dad?"

"He should stand for Parlament. He'd fit right in."

"What's he working on?"

I look at her seriously for a moment. "Christ, Jessie, don't ask me. I don't care what he's doing, I don't want to talk about him. Doesn't he write to you?"

"An occasional lecture about the diseases carried by decaying German architects. I must have them all by now. He told me he'd seen Sonia—"

"Mum." Jessie won't call her that anymore, as if somehow Mum can be shafted with some of the blame. They don't communicate, not even at birthdays or during the drunken sentiment of Christmas and New Year.

"He wants to see Jack."

"Well, he can't."

"Ever? What's she telling the child?"

Child? He's her brother. It really is as if she's severed a biological cord. "I don't know. Mum can be every bit as ruthless as you, you know."

She keeps her eyes on the road as we reach the top of the hill and I get some idea of how small the island is—you could walk across it in a couple of hours. We drop down into a patchy forest of tall, feathery trees and I watch Jessie drive, grateful for the silence and shade.

She seems different. Her hair is longer, her face finer than when I last saw her—though the rest of her has gained weight and form. She looks healthy, but it's something else. She seems vulnerable, I decide, in a way she never has. Breakable. In place—in the sense that she really does seem at home here—but as if something's missing.

"Are you happy?" I ask.

She looks at me, driving the jeep fast over the bumps and ruts of what is now a dried-mud track. "Why?"

"I don't know. Somehow this doesn't seem enough."

She laughs. "It's more than enough! I was thinking—before you came—I can see myself here, a crazy old bint running a bar on the beach."

"They're all Seventh-Day Adventists, aren't they? Do they drink?"

"There are always yachts in Port Elizabeth—" Suddenly the jeep hits a rock and she slams against me, her head butting into my ear, dizzying me momentarily. She touches my cheek with her knuckles, driving with one hand. "But you're right, it's not enough."

■

They're not living in the Wagnerian thing yet, which apparently is cut right out of the hillside and which I notice Jessie doesn't take me to see straight away. They're in a house in Industry Bay, a clapboard box on the water's edge with a wooden jetty and a blue-painted veranda that looks as if the waves wash right under it.

There is no sign of Wolfgang, but Magda is there, who is Wolf's girlfriend and Jessie's too, I presume. Compared to Magda, Sonny was like a sister to me. Magda cuts me dead. She's sitting inside the house in virtual darkness when we arrive, on the floor, back against a vast, low armchair, white knees angled up out of a pair of long baggy shorts and a shirt that swamps her.

"This is Tom," Jessie says and Magda's eyes flicker up from the book she's reading, glance at me, then fix on Jessica as if the words mean nothing to her. My eyes adjust to the gloom and I see just how white she is—startlingly so for someone living here, with a ponytail of bleached blond hair which seems totally out of place, far too arch for the instant dismissal meted out to me. It's as if she's decided I'm an arsehole from the moment I walked in and doesn't give a fuck who knows it, though she's the type, I try and comfort myself, who doesn't give a fuck about anything. Maybe Jessie has fed her too much information about me? Or maybe I am just a prick—if Jessie tells me I'll like her, what else should I expect but a hard time? They've probably got some little humiliation lined up for me later.

"We'll eat early," Jessie says—for my benefit? Magda's? "Dinner is always early here. Life stops when the light goes, but we're up at dawn mostly. It's impossible to sleep past six o'clock."

She seems uncomfortable for a moment—more uncomfortable than I'm used to Jessie being, anyway—working overtime to make me feel like a welcome guest. But then Madame Cool puts her book down on the floor, pages open, and gets up, her legs unfolding with finishing school poise. She goes out, one hand brushing against Jessie's arm on the way in a gesture which may mean something and may not, I'm starting to feel so paranoid. We're alone.

"Fuck that," I mutter.

"Oh, Tom—" Jessie seems to think the whole thing's a huge joke; she's laughing. "It's so good to see you! You're here!" She hugs me again, tighter than on the dock, and I think maybe I'm overreacting, why should I care what Magda thinks? "What do you want to do? Rest awhile? Your room's ready."

Jessie is close, I can smell a deep flowery oil on her and her hand keeps snaking round my back, giving me a playful squeeze; through the open french windows leading onto the veranda, I can hear birdsong and the waves breaking and see a rectangle of stunning blue sky, but the room is dark and despite the bag at my feet and the colors and buzz of two days of traveling, I know where I am: I'm back in Devon, back in the cottage with the washing up in the kitchen and the shit-hole shelter up the hill and the presence of the Prick near at hand—only he isn't here and I've yet to meet his substitute, his island-life stand-in, the fat bearded Biermeister grinning inanely from the deck of a fishing boat in the framed photograph on the bleached-wood drinks trolley (it has to be Wolf, I know it, and the certainty numbs me in some strange way, that Jessie will let him fuck her). Magda is Sonny and this is Brixton, too, and I understand still further that the world is a small place, you take it with you, you can't escape it—your own particular heaven and hell is ground into the meat you drag behind you from your umbilical cord when you crawl out of the womb.

"I'd like to swim," I tell her. "I'll just dump my bag and then I'd like to swim."

■

A maid shows me my room—Jessie is cut off from all income, to my knowledge, yet she's living like this, with a maid. It must be Wolf's room, or a room he uses often, because there are old suits hanging in the wardrobe and a big, crumpled hat up on top and there's a shaving brush and a tube of soap on the chest of drawers and a thin, minty scent in the air, which I take to be his smell, his territory marked out like a dog's. There's another photograph of him on the wall, no fishing boat this time and he looks years younger, this must be how he remembers himself—unbearded, still all of his hair on top, a wide, mobile mouth pulled back in a joke grimace, but already a vaguely anguished look in his eyes, as if there's a guilt there or an anticipation of some horror to come. But there's no Wolf. He's not here and I feel puzzled by his absence, though why he should go out of his way to meet me as soon as I arrive, I don't know.

I stash my bag unopened at the bottom of the wardrobe and sit a moment on the bed, feeling weird, high on the heat and the unfamiliar birdcalls and insect hum through the window, but confused too: pissed off with Magda, despite my attempts to ignore her; somehow disappointed that this is all Jessie has managed, however exotic and nutty it may be; but, above all, thrilled to see her. I feel like I have a role here, there's a reason for me coming, she wants me here. I have a sort of knight-errant fantasy of myself, rescuing her from all this—but to what? And does she want to be rescued?

I go downstairs and out onto the veranda looking for her, but instead find Magda, kneeling on all fours on the wooden slats, still in her old baggy shorts and hanging shirt, working out. I'm behind her and she doesn't hear me—or doesn't want to—and I watch a moment as she raises one leg off the floor and extends it, pointing her toes in a white line against the brilliant Picasso blue of the painted wood. She does this several times, then switches to the other leg, aware by now that I'm watching, I'm sure, but buggered if she's going to acknowledge it in any way. I find myself tempted to kick her off balance, to hook my foot under her straightened leg and dump her down on the boards, but I resist, instead taking a nectarine from a bowl on a table and biting into it—the first food I've had since a lukewarm bowl of cereal on St. Vincent this morning.

One triangle of the veranda is in sunlight, fat bees hovering there at a large trough of violent red flowers. I cross toward it, scuffing my sandals on the wood deliberately to announce myself. "Do you know where Jessie went?" I ask, feeling like an intruder, feeling momentarily that what Magda clearly thinks is right—I shouldn't be here. She looks round, a little breathless, pouting in that Polish way I've seen my mother do (but not so much Jessica), her face lined with sweat but whiter than ever. The stare is a practiced one—everything about Magda is practiced—but the annoyance seems real enough, and I take it as a small personal triumph that I've got something out of her more than plain boredom.

I take another bite of the nectarine, which is disappointingly dry and grainy, and turn away, finding my way down some wooden steps to the sea.

∎

Then we're swimming, Jessie and me, just the two of us, bare-arsed in the water, out in the bay away from the house.

"Where's Adolf, then?" I ask, schoolboy-stupid again with Jessie, she still has this effect on me—I feel about nine and want to throw myself on her and fight. "When am I going to meet him?"

She rises up on a wave, a little above me, her eyes shining down, her tits refracted weirdly in the clear blue-green water. "You'll meet him," she says, poking at me with a toe. "He's working hard on his castle. He's so committed to it, it's an obsession with him, yet it's nothing much." She sounds almost sad for a moment, her voice small in the expanse of the bay. I watch her swaying up and down with the push of the tide, but I ought to remember this is when she's at her most dangerous. She fixes me with a smile and says: "I call it his pillbox, it's not much bigger than one of those wartime fortifications, really. You remember the shelter, don't you?" And I don't know what she expects—a prize for dragging my thoughts back to the shit hole between us?

There are several small boats moored in the bay and we swim across to them, acting like brother and sister almost—pulling on their mooring ropes and diving beneath their hulls. I catch my back on one, which sets it off again, stinging in the salt water and more sensitive to the late afternoon sun when I surface.

"These are all built here," Jessie shouts to me, swimming out in a wide arc round a tiny sailing vessel painted a soft white. "There are only two main livelihoods locally, other than tourism—boat building and whaling." I cut across to her, then float, slightly out of breath, on my back, half listening to the words and wondering what she's trying to convince me of.

"The kind of whaling they do here is pre-*Moby Dick*." She turns onto her back also and I glance at her, naked in the water, tanned and curved and beautiful. I shut my eyes on the image, trying to shut my mind, too. "They go out, eight or twelve men in a boat, and virtually throw spears at the creature—if they find one. Last time they caught one was nearly two years ago. But when they do, it's a feast, it's a major event, the whole island turns out. . . ."

"You weren't here two years ago." I keep my eyes shut, drifting, water knocking at my ears, feeling the orange light through my eyelids pulse inside my head. I've known moments like this; this is too perfect.

"You're right—" Jessie is inside there too, unscrewing my brain. "There are drawbacks. Some nights I go crazy, wanting just to get zonked and go out, go somewhere new. There is very little outside stimulus, all the drinking water has to be imported and, if you want to eat, you'd better like fish because meat is hard to get—it's fish for dinner tonight, OK?" I hear her kick her feet and splash or do something in the water. "But the rest of the time, it's brilliant."

That one word does it. I hear her voice, that Chelsea cool, drawn out even further by God knows what influences here, and I know she wants something.

I open my eyes and turn over, to find I'm facing the house, the blue-painted veranda like a matchstick model at the base of the dry, wooded hills behind it, seemingly alone in the water some considerable distance from the shore. Just for a moment I panic, then I spot Jessica's head as it breaks through a wave, further from me than I would have thought possible in the time, and I start swimming hard to follow her, follow her arse as it dips beneath the surface once more.

She's laughing when I finally catch up with her. I think I actually

resent the fact that she seems to be having a good time; I know I resent
that she always leads and I always follow. But she's broke, I tell myself,
and in many ways she's trapped on the island. "Why did you ask me
here?" I try, wondering if she expects me magically to unlock the Prick's
bank account.

But before she can answer—if she was going to answer—we're distracted by a foreign voice calling her name. Magda is standing on the
wooden jetty and, though it's hard to see her face, her cry (the only
word I have heard her speak, I realize) and her whole stance suggest
that her mood has not improved since I left.

"Come on," Jessie says, swimming for the shore, but I hold her back.

"How can you stay with these people?" I ask, not caring whether my
voice carries across the water to Magda. "They're morons."

And I stare at the whiteness of Magda's arms and legs against the
shoreline and instead see Wolf, grinning from the deck of his fishing
boat. My hand nudges Jessie's tit as I grasp her arm, the two of us
treading water, and I try to imagine Wolf's prick inside her, but I
can't—it just comes out as a fat, pulpy blob.

"They feed me well and fuck me well," she tells me, pulling away
with what might just be a desire for her girlfriend not to see us so close
together. "God, you're starting to sound so superior!"

I glance at the jetty; Magda has gone inside.

"You like Magda, do you? Does she know she's brain-dead?"

"Go to hell, Tom!"

And she puts her whole weight on me to push me under.

■

Dinner is on the veranda, with no sign of Wolf. To my astonishment,
Magda does everything, insisting that Jessie sit and relax. She still won't
address me directly but does at least plonk plates on the table in front
of me and then hovers, drinking iced rum and pineapple from a large
square glass and looking oddly flirtatious in a fine white eveningy mini-
dress while Jessie and I are in loose, cool clothes.

I start hitting the rum myself, partly because the burn on my back is
biting again, but also because this place is getting to me—Magda's
performance, Wolf's absence, the too perfect setting. The air is stoned
on this incredible sweet fragrance, which Jessie tells me is from the

frangipani trees round the house, and the sea as the sun starts to set seems to effervesce like soda water.

"Isn't the Caribbean where the Americans dump all their nuclear waste?" I inquire. "And toxic chemicals? They aim it at Cuba, but some of it must overshoot. Is this fish we're having?"

"No." It's the first word Magda has spoken to me.

"What?"

"It's not fish."

"Oh." I glance at Jessie, who seems surprised too. I can't believe that Magda would go to any great trouble for me, and yet she prepared the meal—apparently the maid only works in the afternoons.

Suddenly Magda is almost voluble. "David came while you were swimming." This to Jessie, not me. "He brought a delivery." She stares at the serving dish in front of her. "Pork."

Jessie knows I don't like pork, but this hardly seems the time to get fussy. She says nothing, just starts talking about the sunset, which is completely different from what she's led me to expect—like a weird memory of England. The sky is a shade of pale tropical orange I've never seen before, but the clouds are spread out in a familiar dappled fish-scale pattern—little hints of purple and blue here and there— stretching down to a horizon which only needs a railway track or a few Devon sheep superimposed over the palm trees to be somewhere else in my life entirely.

"We should have driven over to the other side of the island," she says, staring at me with those eyes which cut right through to my soul. "You could have watched the sunset better from there."

"Are you painting?" My voice sounds more aggressive than I'd intended, but I feel angry—she stole it from me once along with everything else, a sky like this, the world through my eyes.

"A little. Not enough, probably." She reads my anger; does she understand? "This island is hard on you. It's too easy to make pretty pictures."

She picks up her fork and digs it into one of the disturbingly neat slices of meat Magda has cut. She hesitates. Magda is still standing, drink in hand, some element in the thread of her hostess dress catching the fast-dying, greenish light and sparkling. My eyes keep returning to her, she's like an actress in a dream that's almost real. She sees me looking and stares straight through me.

Then Jessie wheels round to her, fork in hand. "For God's sake, stop this shit and sit down!"

The force of her outburst surprises all of us, I think. It relieves the tension, but only momentarily. Magda pointedly finishes her drink, turns the glass in her hand, rattling what's left of the ice against the side, then finally sits at the table with us.

Jessie starts to eat and I try to do the same, but the taste of pork has always made me gag and each mouthful requires an effort of will to swallow. I feel Magda somehow knows this, though, and I will not give her the satisfaction of asking for something else, hungry as I am. She picks at her food, not speaking, staring past me along the veranda most of the time, and for a while there is only the strained clink of forks and knives on the plates and the roll of the sea below the house. The sun dips and disappears quite abruptly and the electric light, when Jessie turns it on, flickers.

"Will Wolf be joining us?" I ask finally, sick of games-playing, this sense that I'm simply an unwelcome foil for Magda to play to.

"I thought he would." Jessie's voice, even when she pisses me off, is a ticket to some special, protected place. "But sometimes he sleeps on the job."

This sparks a snort from Magda, which I realize after a moment is intended as a show of humor on her part. It's clearly a private joke. She leans one cheek on the back of her hand and peers at me. "We have no telephone," she says. "He could be dead on the road and we wouldn't know it."

This is all I'm getting. She looks away. I push my plate back, tired suddenly, and sit watching the two of them. The light flickers again, but my eyes feel heavy and I think it's the rum. Then I'm plunged into darkness and Jessie says, "Shit!" and I know it's not me, the power has failed, but it's all right, it's more peaceful not having to watch Magda act and I just want to sleep.

"We have a backup generator—" Jessie bangs her chair on the floor of the veranda as she gets up. "But it's too much hassle to start."

I hear her go. I'm too smashed to move or do anything. The sound of the waves makes me think for a second that I'm back on the beat-up ferry that brought me here, but then I hear Magda put something down on the table (her glass? the darkness is total, I can barely make out where she is) and Jessie comes back carrying a candle and a thick wooden bowl.

She puts the candle on the table and sits with the bowl in her lap. It's grass and there's a flatly rolled spliff already prepared. When she offers it to me, I take it and light it with the candle flame, hoping it will bury the thought that's forming in my head. It doesn't; if anything, it makes it sharper and, as I smoke and pass it to Jessica and she passes it to Magda, I have the unsettling conviction that our roles have reversed, that she needs me, that I'm the stronger one—she may be older, but now I've a clearer idea of who I am, what I want. But do I? I want to be engaged, I know that, I want to be locked into something that's happening, somewhere, South Africa maybe or Nicaragua, and I don't care how I do it, I'll use the Prick's money happily, I'll take it from anywhere I can get it. I don't want this: a slow death on a tropical paradise, a nice, bourgeois fuck party, two dikes and an absent kraut. But I do want Jessie. There is no one I can find like her, that's the trouble—yet if our roles have reversed, it's no good, it's another one of those twisting, never ending, mind-fucking puzzles.

"What are you going to do?" The question is out before I even realize it.

Jessie looks at me, laughs. Her voice is stretched and a little twangy from the grass. "Tonight? Or for the rest of my life?"

Magda gets up and moves round to sit on the veranda railing across from me, her back to the night. Jessie watches her. It's a stupid question.

"Yeah," I say.

I stare at Magda, paler than ever by candlelight, as if she's trying for total anemia, the sight of her putting the mockers on anything I might think I've resolved. She sits on her perch, facing me, her straw-blond hair limp round her shoulders, the white dress taut across her legs, and I realize I have a fine view where her panties might be of her cunt, which has been shaved. The unsteady light makes it seem deeper and more shadowy than it might otherwise do, like a face in the dark. For a moment I'm riveted by it, I can't take my eyes off it, but then I start to recognize the hand of Jessie, consciously or otherwise arranging things, and I see now that Magda is watching me stare and I explode:

"Why don't you both just go off and fuck each other?" I get up, turning to Jessie. "This is another one of your parties, right?"

But Jessie takes hold of my arm and pulls me back. "Sit down, Tom. You're being foolish. You always get things out of proportion."

"Do I?" I sit down.

But my anger seems to have done the trick. Snow White gets down off the veranda railing and says good night. Not to me, of course, but to Jessie, bending to kiss her slowly on the mouth, her tongue pressing between Jessie's lips and teeth in what I take to be a Polish finger raised at me.

■

And we're alone.

"You love it, don't you?" I tell her. "Winding me up and watching me dance."

"You're just too easy to provoke." She smiles and her eyes have the deep, sharp light I miss when she's not there. "You know I love you."

She looks so beautiful—she always looks beautiful to me—that she makes me doubt myself again, doubt that I've come any distance from the cottage. I'm not stronger, I'm lost. She called and I came running. She has twisted the shape of my life—always—yet I give her more love, more commitment than I can ever find for any girl I've met or for Jack or for Mum. What she did to them was worse than the Prick's sick greed, yet I think of Jessie as a person and I tend more and more to think of them as victims.

"Yeah, I do," I say, just to say something.

"Come on, I'm not tired yet, are you? Let's go down by the water."

She picks up the candle and something else in the darkness and has me follow her along the veranda, down the steps and over a broken rock wall onto the wooden jetty. There's a constant hiss from the insects and the sea is lapping, getting on my nerves. There's no moon, only the stars and the light from the candle. Jessie turns from me and puts it down, dripping a little wax onto the deck of the jetty to stand it in.

She straightens up. She has a fruit knife in her hand.

"You weren't much good with one of these, were you?"

I feel sharp again suddenly, like I did with the grass. I want to laugh, but I feel seriously nervous.

"Is this what I've come for, then?" I say.

"You still don't know much, do you, Tom?" She points it at me.

Life is perfect. It has its own system of mirrors; it balances. I know

now what the Prick saw when I turned the knife on him. It's so close —your loved one with a knife. The line between holding it and using it is so fine. She'll do it if she wants to, I know that, and there's a part of me that wants to know what it would feel like, but it's not all of me. Not anymore.

Her voice cuts across the warm void between us. "Were you going to do it that night? Did you really think you could?"

"I thought I'd try." We haven't moved. I listen to the night: the nerves of the insects, the slap of water on wood. This is a magical place, but it's nowhere special, it's all the same. Devon could be back up the hill behind me. We need this.

"You know what really pissed me off?" She shakes her head. Should I try something, go for her arm? "You did it again—with that body paint or whatever it was. You took my moment from me."

She laughs. "That wasn't meant for you. You looked so—determined, coming in with the knife. I would have finished it."

"Would you?"

Silence. "I might. Move past me to the end of the jetty, will you?"

I stare at her. "Why did you ask me here?"

She twists the fruit knife slightly in her hand so that the blade catches the candlelight. It's small, smaller than the one I had that night. There's a tiny curve at the end, but the whole thing is so short I wonder how deep it would go in me.

"I miss you," she says. "I miss the thought of us."

"No, you don't." I watch that hand, the hand with the knife. "I was only ever your audience. What do you want? You want me to watch you and Magda knocking around? Or is she going to piss all over me?"

"I worry about you sometimes."

"That's crap! You've never felt guilt in your life."

"I have about you." She takes a step back. "Not guilt, maybe—I just wonder who we are." That's lost on me. "Move!"

I walk past her, carefully, then think, "Fuck it!" and turn my back on her, saying, "What are you going to do, push me in? It's only about eight feet deep."

I feel her move behind me. "Do you want to know how it started with Dad?" Her voice is just another part of the night. I stare at nothing—no, at the vague darkness of the water moving.

"The whole thing was the baby—the night Jack was born. It was the night we'd all been canoeing and swimming in the river—I'd tipped you in, remember?" She pauses, but I'm not hearing or only half hearing her. This is someone else's life we're talking about; I'm not interested in the past, any past. "We were alone in the cottage. You were asleep. I'd wanted him for a long time, Tom—I was just working up to it. And the birth, all that blood. I've thought about this and I've come to the conclusion that in a funny way Mum brought it on herself by having us there. I knew what I was doing—I wanted what she'd had! And yet somehow in my mind it became a kind of weird female solidarity, a sharing—everything was possible, the rules were suspended."

Somehow this hurts more than I thought it could. I turn my head and I'm surprised to find her standing over me—I've sat down on the jetty without even realizing it. The thin fabric of her skirt brushes once against my hair and I smell her smell, heavy like the frangipani and oddly threatening. I feel tense and want to move my head, but there's a dullness now in my mind that won't let me fight, won't let me move, as if my every reaction is on trial here when it should be hers.

I sense the knife behind me, like a cold element drawing the air toward it. My feet dangle over the dock. I hear my voice: another part of me, the part that can deal with this. I can't.

"And that's when he did it?" Him—the Prick—his cuntishness made it happen. I can't let go of that fact.

She touches me. Her knuckles brush the nape of my neck, chilling my spine. "It took half the night to get to it. We were drunk but he wasn't that drunk. He was sober enough to enjoy the fear. It had started in the river. Well, it had had a lifetime before that—my lifetime! But he was high on the idea of Jack—high and shit-scared at the same time. That was the only thing that gave him the balls with me: Death rattling off the numbers, reeling him in a little closer. But then I think he would have fucked anyone that night. I just made sure it was me."

It's nothing new. There is nothing in the world she could surprise me with. But still it hurts, when I remember how weirdly innocent that day felt—or feels now; perhaps the last time I really thought of us as a family. My head floats in the night with a knife at my neck, or perhaps it's still her knuckles?

I want to hit her. I feel a familiar pain—an opening onto a dangerous store of anger I don't want to touch because it's too long-established, it's like going back. I turn to look up at her.

"The baby—was that just more bullshit, or were you serious?"

She nods. "But he's terrified of fucking me now. Anyway, that's not what I want."

"What do you want?"

I think I know the answer, though I don't want to admit it—because admitting it means I've thought about it too. I stare at her legs. If I grabbed her now and pulled her down, I think I could get rid of the knife without too much trouble.

As always, she's ahead of me. "You'll see I do this better than you." And almost nonchalantly she swipes at me with the blade, cutting my cheek.

I go for her, but she's above me and she dodges to one side, bringing the knife down to trim a line through the shirt I'm wearing and across my back underneath, then tossing it into the water so fast and so decisively that I'm stunned.

"There," she says, like the schoolgirl she once was, proving her point. "I can't do it either. But I never wanted to."

I'm on my feet, the cut on my back feeling cool and fresh and dampening a little. Her tongue comes into my mouth and I jerk my head back, frightened by the taste of her, her breath, the hit of rum in her saliva. But I'm lying to myself, because I do want it, the click of our teeth knocking together, the replay of Magda's kiss running through my brain—as if we're in competition: I've got to go deeper, get beyond anything that mindless Polish zombie could.

I grip her, our mouths still locked, but hesitating, the part of me that wants to wrestling with a resistance to bending to her will, becoming her puppet once again. But that's a lie, too—there is nothing here but weakness and selfishness on my part. I want her, there's no excuse, no reason, and as I realize this and my mind enters a sort of limbo that's always been there, on the border, an element of doubt creeps in. She is struggling, she is fighting to push me away! But suddenly I am superpowerful and it's like traveling home: I span the sea, I'm in England one minute, here the next—what's to stop me? Anyway, I've been through too much, she owes me. She owes me this one fucking thing.

I force her down on the deck, keeping her away from the edge where we might both roll in. The skirt she's wearing is fine and loose and it bunches in folds when I shove it up to free her legs from her bikini string. I drag myself half out of my shorts and hoist myself onto her, but then I hesitate again, hearing the water and seeing the candle's suddenly blinding light. Like a shared thought, Jessie clamps her teeth down on the hand that's been covering her mouth and directs it—with a shaking, determined grip—toward the candle's tiny flame. I feel the bite and then the burn but stifle a cry, just as Jessie is silent, letting her hold my hand there a moment more.

She lets go and I crash onto my elbow, my hand crumpling with the pain. There is pain everywhere, across my back, across my face, driving me on with the realization that if I stop now I'll feel more appalled with myself than if I continue. She tries to slide out from under me, but I pull her back.

"Oh, God, Tom," she gasps, a hand clenching my Adam's apple tight, throttling me to hold me off. "Do it right. This isn't the first time."

And she stops me. I try to think of a connection, my mind flailing, a familiar sick hole boring its way through my stomach.

"It wasn't Sonny," she says. "You're not Sonny's style."

She is unbeatable. There is nothing other than her, though I've got to find something if I'm going to survive. She can live like this; I can't. I stay where I am, smelling the frangipani in the air, and I realize it's Jessie that I smell—it's a bit like I imagine death might smell. She is death for me. Whatever else I might do, finally I come back to this: the soft clasp of Jessie's thighs and the furry mouth in between.

"Do it right," she says, turning away. "I'll be a terrible mother, I'll let the kid just shit where it stands. But I want a baby. Do it right."

She crawls onto all fours, rolling her skirt up. She is facing the island, a soft, velvety black land mass in the starlight.

It's taken this long, but I love her.

■

I'd like to thank Charles Walker for his considerable contribution to this book; Brian Stone, for encouraging me to write it; also Lynda Myles, Dini and Jerry Gervais, Cherie Hoyt, Gus and Vi Hoyt, Spike, Nico, Bob and Anna Scott, Nikki Jolliffe, and David Gernert, my American editor, for his huge enthusiasm.

A.S.

ABOUT THE AUTHOR

ALEXANDER STUART has written film criticism and several screenplays. More recently, he was executive producer of Nicolas Roeg's film *Insignificance*. He now lives in England, where he is at work on a new novel, *Tribes*.